W9-CCQ-047

**Praise for the novels of
#1 *New York Times* bestselling author
Linda Lael Miller**

"Miller tugs at the heartstrings as few authors can."
—*Publishers Weekly*

"Miller's name is synonymous with the finest in Western romance."
—*RT Book Reviews*

"Linda Lael Miller creates vibrant characters and stories I defy you to forget."
—#1 *New York Times* bestselling author Debbie Macomber

"Miller's down-home, easy-to-read style keeps the plot moving, and she includes...likable characters, picturesque descriptions and some very sweet pets."
—*Publishers Weekly* on *Big Sky Country*

"Miller is one of the finest American writers in the genre."
—*RT Book Reviews*

"A passionate love too long denied drives the action in this multifaceted, emotionally rich reunion story that overflows with breathtaking sexual chemistry."
—*Library Journal* on *McKettricks of Texas: Tate*

"Miller's return to Parable is a charming story of love in its many forms.... [A] sweetly entertaining and alluring tale."
—*RT Book Reviews* on *Big Sky River*

Praise for the novels of Naima Simone

"Simone balances crackling, electric love scenes with exquisitely rendered characters." —*Entertainment Weekly*

"Passion, heat and deep emotion—Naima Simone is a gem!" —*New York Times* bestselling author Maisey Yates

"Simone never falters in mining the complexity of two people who grow and heal and eventually love together." —*New York Times* bestselling author Sarah MacLean

"Small-town charm, a colorful cast, and a hero to root for give this romance its legs as it moves toward a hard-earned happily ever after. [This] slow-burning romance is well worth the wait." —*Publishers Weekly* on *The Road to Rose Bend*

"I am a huge Naima Simone fan. With her stories, she has the ability to transport you to places you can only dream of, with characters who have a realness to them." —*Read Your Writes*

"[Naima Simone] excels at creating drama and emotional scenes as well as strong heroines who are resilient survivors." —*Harlequin Junkie*

LINDA LAEL MILLER

CHRISTMAS IN *Mustang* CREEK

HQN

If you purchased this book without a cover you should be aware
that this book is stolen property. It was reported as "unsold and
destroyed" to the publisher, and neither the author nor the
publisher has received any payment for this "stripped book."

Recycling programs
for this product may
not exist in your area.

ISBN-13: 978-1-335-45447-8

Christmas in Mustang Creek
First published in 2015. This edition published in 2021.
Copyright © 2021 by Hometown Girl Makes Good, Inc.

A Kiss to Remember
First published in 2021. This edition published in 2021.
Copyright © 2021 by Naima Simone

All rights reserved. No part of this book may be used or reproduced in
any manner whatsoever without written permission except in the case of
brief quotations embodied in critical articles and reviews.

This is a work of fiction. Names, characters, places and incidents
are either the product of the author's imagination or are used fictitiously.
Any resemblance to actual persons, living or dead, businesses, companies,
events or locales is entirely coincidental.

This edition published by arrangement with Harlequin Books S.A.

For questions and comments about the quality of this book,
please contact us at CustomerService@Harlequin.com.

HQN
22 Adelaide St. West, 40th Floor
Toronto, Ontario M5H 4E3, Canada
www.Harlequin.com

Printed in Lithuania

MIX
Paper from
responsible sources
FSC® C021394

Also by Linda Lael Miller and HQN

Painted Pony Creek

Country Proud
Country Strong

The Carsons of Mustang Creek

A Snow Country Christmas
Forever a Hero
Always a Cowboy
Once a Rancher

The Brides of Bliss County

Christmas in Mustang Creek
The Marriage Season
The Marriage Charm
The Marriage Pact

The Parable series

Big Sky Secrets
Big Sky Wedding
Big Sky Summer
Big Sky River
Big Sky Mountain
Big Sky Country

McKettricks of Texas

An Outlaw's Christmas
A Lawman's Christmas
McKettricks of Texas: Austin
McKettricks of Texas: Garrett
McKettricks of Texas: Tate

The Creed Cowboys

The Creed Legacy
Creed's Honor
A Creed in Stone Creek

Stone Creek

The Bridegroom
The Rustler
A Wanted Man
The Man from Stone Creek

The McKettricks

A McKettrick Christmas
McKettrick's Heart
McKettrick's Pride
McKettrick's Luck
McKettrick's Choice

Mojo Sheepshanks

Arizona Heat
(originally published as
Deadly Deceptions)
Arizona Wild
(originally published as
Deadly Gamble)

The Montana Creeds

A Creed Country Christmas
Montana Creeds: Tyler
Montana Creeds: Dylan
Montana Creeds: Logan

And look for the third book in Linda Lael Miller's
Painted Pony Creek series, *Country Born*,
coming soon from HQN!

Also by Naima Simone

Christmas in Rose Bend
The Road to Rose Bend

Trust Fund Fiancé
Ruthless Pride
Back in the Texan's Bed

Look for Naima Simone's next novel
With Love from Rose Bend
available soon from HQN.

CONTENTS

CHRISTMAS IN MUSTANG CREEK

Linda Lael Miller

* * *

For all those who believe in magic.

Dear Friends,

It's Christmas in Mustang Creek and you're invited to join the celebration! You'll catch glimpses of some of your favorite characters from *The Marriage Pact*, *The Marriage Charm* and *The Marriage Season*, *and* make some new book-friends, as well.

Charlotte Morgan, somewhat at loose ends after losing her high-paying, high-profile job in New York City, has come home to Mustang Creek to look after her aunt, Geneva, and the family home, a charming old Victorian in need of some TLC. Imagine her chagrin when the first person she runs into is Jaxon "Jax" Locke, the handsome veterinarian she *used* to love. When they wind up sharing a hotel room due to a raging blizzard—separate beds, please—the adventure begins.

Christmas in Mustang Creek is a magical story in many ways—for instance, what about the mysterious Millicent Klozz, the white-haired cooking genius of a housekeeper nobody remembers hiring?

And then there are the animals, always a favorite element in my stories.

The tree is decorated and sparkling with a thousand points of light. There's a fire crackling on the hearth, and snow is drifting past the windows. Sit right down, have one of Mrs. Klozz's delicious cookies and get ready to share in the joys of Christmas, Mustang Creek–style.

With love,

Linda Lael Miller

CHAPTER ONE

CHARLOTTE MORGAN SHOULDN'T have checked her bag for the flight from New York to Wyoming. Her layover in Denver had already been far longer than planned because of a storm that was coming in from the West Coast, and now she was—*finally*—waiting by a luggage carousel at the Cheyenne airport. And waiting… As her friend Karin always said, there were two kinds of luggage—carry-on and lost. And hers appeared to be of the lost variety.

December 21 meant it was almost the festive season, but her spirits were definitely on the low side.

This airport mess was typical of the dismal way her luck had been running lately.

Let's see. She'd had to arrange for her aunt Geneva to move into assisted living. Dealing with that, mostly by email and over the phone, hadn't been easy. Then there was the fact that a stranger was staying at Geneva's house, the house Charlotte had grown up in. Of course, she'd questioned her aunt about Mrs. Klozz, asking how she and the mysterious visitor had met, but Geneva's answers had been consistently vague, even evasive.

Worried, Charlotte had called Spencer Hogan, an old friend and Mustang Creek's chief of police, to request a background check. He'd chuckled and said that wouldn't be necessary; Mrs. Klozz was, as he'd put it, "all right."

Finally, Charlotte had decided to drop the subject. She'd meet the woman soon enough and form her own opinion.

Despite all this, she felt uneasy.

Then—just when she'd thought things couldn't get any worse—she'd been laid off.

Merry, merry Christmas.

Oh, the company, an advertising firm, had given her a generous enough severance package. Her boss had explained that budget cuts were taking a toll on everyone.

Not on him, apparently. *His* job seemed to be safe, unlike her own. It had taken some effort to not say something to that effect, but in truth, she just wanted to go home.

As she watched everyone retrieving luggage while hers was, predictably, nowhere in sight, she realized how ironic it was—as a teenager, she'd been convinced that all she wanted was to leave the small town of Mustang Creek, become successful, meet the right man and never look back. She'd done it. She'd left. She'd gotten a great job. She'd met the right man.

But she sure had looked back.

There was one other hopeful passenger waiting, and they exchanged a shrug of commiseration. The carousel was still moving, so maybe…

Yep, she'd left the small town. Got the dream job—and lost it. Met one Dr. Jaxon Locke, fell in love, and that hadn't worked, either.

The other passenger won the lottery and his case slid down.

"Happy holidays," he said in sympathy as he hurried away.

Then…a Christmas miracle! Her suitcase actually bumped out—no more than two seconds before she was going to head over to the airline counter to fill in the claim form—and began the journey toward her. Yay! Clean underwear for Christmas.

Aunt Geneva would tell her to count her blessings, and as she heaved her bag off the carousel and wheeled it toward the rental car area, Charlotte actually smiled. Things were already looking up. Oh, she still had to make the drive home with a giant storm roaring in, coasting a clipper from the Arctic, but at least she had her clothing. She'd need to make arrangements to have everything else sold or shipped home but would deal with that headache later. Her ridiculously expensive apartment had been sublet and all the rest of it was in storage.

The snow was coming in sideways when she finally reached her rental car. Nothing like driving an unfamiliar rig in bad weather, she thought, as she climbed into the midsize sedan and turned the key in the ignition.

She was on her way home.

After seven years in New York City.

Back in the day, she'd craved the city life, but now she simply wanted to get back to that big old drafty house, that *comfortable* house, where she'd grown up. Mustang Creek was the kind of small town where, if you sneezed, people were concerned you might be coming down with something and offered you their grandmother's favorite remedy. She wanted the fragrance of grass in the summer, the view of the Tetons, the old grape arbor in the backyard.

She wanted *home*.

Geneva needed her, Charlotte mused as she tried to figure out how to turn on the windshield wipers. But *she* might need this change even more. Losing her job wasn't a financial catastrophe since her aunt had taught her a lot about saving her money. She hated that the vibrant woman she remembered was slowly fading. Still, Charlotte viewed her own changed circumstances as a positive in some ways. They'd be able to spend time together. Quality time. Not just the fly-in, fly-out visits of the past few years. She could take care of the house, maybe use some of her savings to fix it up. The place had needed a new roof for at least ten years. She'd offered to pay for it more than once, but Aunt Geneva, her only living relative, had declined.

STUBBORN PRIDE WAS a family trait, no question about that. She came by hers honestly.

She should've looked more closely at the forecast, she decided when whirls of snow, like errant ghosts, circled her car. Almost no one else was traveling, which was just as well, since she could barely see enough to stay in her own lane. Other than the dim lights of one car some distance behind her, she had the road to herself.

She was happy that she'd grabbed coffee and a sandwich in the Denver airport, although—exhausted as she was—she could've used another coffee right now. She slowed her speed even more as she squinted at the increasing whiteout conditions. There was one other immediate problem she hadn't considered. She didn't have keys to the house. Aunt Geneva had been a seamstress, working at home; she was a wizard with her machine and had probably made most of the wedding dresses in Bliss County for the past half century. So Charlotte had never really needed one.

To be honest, she wasn't even sure there *were* keys. The doors with their beautiful faceted glass panels were original, and to her knowledge the locks had never been replaced. Maybe Aunt Geneva had given keys to the friend who was watching her house and taking care of her beloved cat and dog, but it was already after ten, and she wasn't going to get to Mustang Creek anytime soon at this speed.

It seemed wrong to go pounding on the door at midnight when she didn't even know this Millicent Klozz. She certainly didn't want to wake the poor woman from a sound sleep.

"Have Yourself a Merry Little Christmas" came on the radio, and Charlotte turned up the volume. She loved the song, which brought back memories of getting tucked into bed on Christmas Eve, Geneva reading her a story and forbidding her to go downstairs until daybreak.

She'd always heeded this admonition—except for the year she was seven. She'd gone downstairs in the middle of the night—not all the way down that creaky staircase because she'd known she'd get caught—and seen the packages under the tree. When she'd heard Aunt Geneva get up—for a drink of water, judging by the running tap—Charlotte had taken a small liberty and peeked at the gifts. Most of them had *her* name on them.

Then she'd climbed into her aunt's bed and nestled there, eyes wide. When Geneva had rolled over, she'd given a small scream, obviously not expecting a small face right next to hers, dimly visible in the glow of the hallway night-light.

"Santa was here," Charlotte had informed her excitedly.

"I hope he brought me a new heart," Geneva had replied, after gasping and pressing her hand to her chest. "Lord, child, you startled me."

"He came to our house!"

Charlotte still remembered Geneva hugging her, remembered the warmth of her arms, the loving smile on her face. "Of course he did."

Negotiating a slick turn, Charlotte wondered what her aunt had sacrificed to make sure Santa came to their house every year. As a child she hadn't comprehended the effort that went into raising a toddler. Especially if you'd inherited that responsibility in your late fifties, because your much younger sister and her husband had died tragically in a train accident. Geneva had been single and inexperienced with tantrums and packing lunches, and later on, cheerleading practice and track meets, sleepovers with giggling girls...

Her aunt had done it all unflinchingly, and when it had come time for college, given her guidance, but let her choose. Now it was Charlotte's turn to give back.

JAXON LOCKE HAD been chased all the way from Idaho by the storm and it was starting to catch up with him, mentally and physically.

He had no idea if he was being an idiot or not, going to Mustang Creek. After their breakup just over a year ago, he'd continued, though casually, to follow Charlotte Morgan on social media—they'd "friended" each other. A few days before, he'd checked in on her page and discovered that she'd left the firm. Even if she hadn't mentioned her plans to return to Wyoming, he would have known where she was headed.

No part of him believed it was a coincidence that both he and Charlotte had ties to Mustang Creek. She'd been raised there, and he'd been hired by his friend Nate Cameron to work as a veterinarian in Nate's practice.

He'd met Charlotte—Charlie, he called her—through an online dating service. Sort of.

Except he'd cheated. Sort of. He'd sat next to the girlfriend of one of his college roommates at a cocktail party. The event had taken place in midtown Manhattan. He had been working in a nearby Connecticut town at the time, and he'd come into the city for his friend Remy's wedding. This woman had studied him over the rim of her cosmopolitan glass, then asked, "Single?"

No doubt she'd made that assumption because while he'd taken the time to pick out what he considered a nice shirt, he'd still worn jeans and boots. His best boots, expensive, but he'd probably looked like a cowboy. "Not married, not dating," he'd answered wryly. "The invitation said casual dress. I took it to heart."

Her lips had twitched. "You could use a haircut, too, but the look you've got going suits your style. Put you in an Armani suit, give you a five-o'clock shadow and you could be on the cover of a magazine. You're from where?"

"Originally, Idaho."

She'd gotten right to the point. "I know just the girl for you."

He'd doubted that, not only because she was dressed in three-inch heels, wore too much perfume and spent most of the time talking on her cell phone, but also because they were strangers. "You don't know anything about me."

"Sure I do. Remy's mentioned you before. You're an animal doctor, right? You and Remy and a bunch of other guys all met at Ohio State."

He'd nodded. "We shared a house. And, yes, I'm a veterinarian."

She'd leaned in a little closer. "I work with this girl who's beautiful, smart and hates the city as much as you obviously do but won't admit it. Loves animals and is from a small town. Here's the catch. She refuses blind dates from friends. I do know that she's recently joined an online dating service. Let me write down her name for you, plus the site info. It won't hurt to check out her profile." Her smile was audacious. "Don't tell her I had anything to do with it."

"Since I don't know your name, that would be impossible."

"We'll do official introductions if the two of you actually get together, okay?"

"Okay with me," he'd said, figuring nothing would come of this odd conversation anyway.

"She's a Wyoming girl, Mr. Cowboy. I have a feeling you'll ride off for bluer skies and fresher air soon—and I think she will, too."

The deliberately mysterious woman's cell had rung again and while she'd answered it, she'd scribbled down *Charlotte Morgan* on a napkin, along with the name of a popular dating site.

Even though he'd basically just been playing along, passing the time, Jax had realized he was curious enough to take a look at Ms. Morgan's profile.

He'd never even considered online dating. Later, when he got home, he'd typed in the information and, eventually, been completely...well, the English would have called it *gobsmacked*.

Charlotte Morgan was beautiful, all right. More than beautiful.

They'd exchanged a few tentative, getting-to-know-you emails over the coming days, and one fine day they'd agreed to meet for coffee. He'd been doing a stint at a small animal practice just across the state line, so the trip had involved trains and various other methods of transportation.

When he'd finally met Charlie face-to-face, Jax had discovered that her pictures hadn't done her justice, and on top of her good looks, she was sexy, intelligent, charming...

A whirlwind romance later, Charlie still lived in New York and he'd had to go back to Idaho to help his dad, also a vet, after he'd had a heart attack.

Jax had missed Charlie, but he'd also learned something about himself. The West was still his home, the place where he belonged. He'd realized he wanted to stay—not necessarily in Idaho, since his father, once fully recovered, didn't really need his help, but somewhere out there, under that sweeping sky.

He'd asked—okay, practically *begged*—Charlie to join him, but for reasons he still didn't fully understand, she'd dug in her heels. Yes, she longed for the wide-open spaces sometimes, she'd said, but she liked her job, her neighborhood, her friends.

All of a sudden, she claimed to love the city, despite her colleague's assertion to the contrary, back at Remy's wedding reception.

They'd been at an impasse. He wanted to settle in a small town on the other side of the country. She wanted to stay in the city.

Jax recalled all too well the last time they'd tried to discuss the situation rationally, to arrive at some compromise. They'd just made love, she was still in his arms, but her averted face had made her feelings clear. It was true that she couldn't have a job making the same sort of salary anywhere except a place that was a major financial and cultural center. It was also true that in a small town she couldn't walk down the street and pick from a dozen different types of restaurants. No shopping, no theater, no symphony... The list went on.

A classic standoff. He might be Dr. Locke, but he didn't have a glamorous profession like most of the men she met. He helped cows give birth and he treated horses, driving to some remote places at some strange hours to do so. He vaccinated dogs and cats, spayed and neutered house pets. No, the work wasn't glamorous, but it was satisfying. Jax loved animals, loved his job and honestly couldn't see himself living in a big city for very long. He'd grown up bottle-feeding abandoned kittens and baby goats, ridden horses every day, dug fence posts with the best of them and rarely went to art galleries or museums, her favorite forms of recreation.

He liked the outdoors; she liked skyscrapers.

Let's call the whole thing off.

They had. Sadly, regretfully, unable to agree, they'd gone their separate ways.

The trouble was, Jax had never been able to get her off his mind.

So he was on his way to Mustang Creek, of all places.

What were the chances he'd know someone from her hometown, wind up practicing there?

Maybe this was more than a coincidence, a meant-to-be kind of thing. Like sitting beside the woman at Remy's shindig—her name turned out to be Kendra Nash—and just happening to hear about Charlie for the first time.

Was fate intervening again? Jax hadn't expected a job offer when he'd contacted Nate; he'd just wanted to know if there might be openings in the area.

Charlotte's last Facebook post had said: "Catching a flight back to Wyoming soon. Goodbye, NY. It's been nice but I'm heading home. Merry Christmas."

Jax punched the hands-free device when his phone rang, startling him a little. Beyond his windshield, the weather was getting worse by the second. "Hello."

"Jax, you're still driving, right? Making progress?"

Nate Cameron, the man he'd be sharing a practice with.

Jax answered a little grimly, "Sort of, if you call thirty miles an hour progress. I was hoping to outrun the storm, but obviously that didn't happen."

"I booked you a room at the motel on Main about two hours ago. Last room, in fact. I'd be happy to have you stay with me, but you'll never find my place in this mess. People miss the drive in broad daylight, never mind the middle of a blizzard. Besides, the way the snow's drifting, I don't care what kind of truck you have, you might get stuck. That's one wicked wind. In town at least they've got the snowplows out."

That sounded like a plan. He was starting to doubt he could even find the town; the road ahead was disappearing before his eyes. "Thanks. I'll call you tomorrow morning."

"Let's just meet up. This is supposed to blow through pretty fast. Betsey's Café is where I usually have break-fast, and it's next to the motel. Eight o'clock?"

"See you then."

When Jax finally saw the lights of Mustang Creek glowing in the distance, he felt a measure of relief. His shoulders ached from the tension, and what he really needed was a soft bed and a good night's sleep.

It wasn't hard to spot what he suspected was the town's only motel. The parking lot was full, and the one car that had been in front of him for miles pulled in, too. After searching for ten minutes or so, he found a parking spot then grabbed his suitcase and ran for it, flipping his collar up.

The dated lobby was empty except for the clerk and a very dismayed-looking young woman at the counter.

She said, "No rooms?"

"None. I'm sorry. The storm and all." The young man did seem apologetic.

Glossy dark hair swung as she turned around, obviously disappointed, and then she froze. "Jax?"

Charlie. She stared at him, incredulous recognition in those gorgeous green eyes.

"Yep. Hi." He was almost too stunned to speak.

Coincidence? No way. Fate or *something* was definitely messing with his head.

Yes, he'd expected to run into Charlie—Mustang Creek was a small community after all—but he'd never dreamed she'd be one of the first people he encountered, especially in the middle of a snowstorm.

"What are you doing here?" Charlie's eyes were wide and a little wary. Did she think he was stalking her?

"Job offer," he said lamely.

"Oh…well…" She seemed to be struggling for words, too. Small comfort. "What are the odds of that?"

Good, when a person actively pursues a goal, he thought wryly.

He cleared his throat. "*I* have a room if you need a place to stay."

The clerk hit a few keys on his computer. "You're Dr. Jaxon Locke? Last person to check in tonight. Room 215. Two queen beds. Maybe there's some holiday magic in the air, since you two seem to know each other. Let me get your key cards."

Just then, the sound system began to play "Have Yourself a Merry Little Christmas."

Maybe he would, Jax thought. Maybe he would.

CHAPTER TWO

No way was she sharing a room with Jaxon Locke.

Charlotte was incredulous, completely thrown off balance by seeing him there, the last person in the universe she would've expected to run into in *Mustang Creek*, of all places. This was *her* hometown, damn it, her safe place, her sanctuary. What was *he* doing here? She could almost believe she was dreaming, except that every part of her ached with travel fatigue and the rigors of driving for hours through that wicked snowstorm.

Nope, this was real. And just to make it worse, the man had the gall to look good, too, even with tousled hair that still had flecks of snow, rumpled clothes and the slope of weariness in his broad shoulders. His beard was coming in, an attractive stubble, and there was a hint of lively amusement in his eyes.

"I don't need a key card," she told the clerk in a more abrupt tone than she'd intended. She immediately felt bad because he'd been accommodating, this young, apologetic local. More graciously, she added, "Thanks for trying, though."

"I didn't help much. I'm afraid there's no place else to stay."

He was probably right about that. Despite its relatively close proximity to Yellowstone and Grand Teton National

Parks, not to mention the ski slopes that attracted winter-sport enthusiasts from all over the world, Mustang Creek was still a small town. Other than this hotel, there were a few modest motels and B and Bs, of course, but on a night like this one, and so close to the holidays, those places would fill up fast.

Jax stepped past Charlotte to slap his credit card down on the counter. Was that a smirk she saw, that faint twitch at one corner of his mouth?

"There are two beds, Charlie," he reminded her with a brief, sidelong glance. "Count 'em, two. Trust me, I drove here all the way from Idaho, and I'm so tired I might forget my own name. Your virtue is safe, for tonight, anyhow." He paused—he *was* smirking, damn it—and then brought the whole matter in for a landing. "Besides, what other option do you have? Sleeping in your car? Sounds chilly to me."

The clerk swiped the card with a cheerful flourish of resignation and said helpfully, "The temperature is supposed to drop like a rock falling off a mountain."

Great analogy. Maybe Mrs. Klozz was still awake...

She doubted it.

It was pushing midnight. Aunt Geneva would've been in bed hours ago. And what if Millicent Klozz was hard of hearing and Charlotte stood there knocking on the door, shivering?

Ending up here—with Jax—was an unexpected twist to a long, long day.

"Key card?"

Jax offered it.

After a moment she took it. "Don't look so smug."

"This isn't smug," he said, grabbing her suitcase and

his. "I feel confident that my normal expression of wry triumph would be considerably better than anything I can summon up at the moment. Let's go find our room so I can collapse. It might be the holiday season, but there's no cheer in *my* spirit right now. I'm damned tired."

And no room at the inn.

Ironic.

She followed him. This was definitely going to be awkward, and not just because she hadn't planned on having a roommate. Jax Locke might not be an ax murderer, but he wasn't precisely harmless, either, like a favorite cousin or an old friend or a trusted business colleague.

Oh, no.

She and Jax had a *history.* The last time she'd seen him was in New York, and suddenly, out of nowhere, he was in Mustang Creek?

What exactly was going on?

Something weird, that was what.

With a sense of the world being off its axis, Charlotte followed him down a hallway to the appropriate door and watched him open it. He waited for her. "After you," he said with the slightest bow.

This was *such* a bad idea. But so were her only other choices: waking up an elderly lady in the middle of the night, risking hypothermia by bedding down in her rental car or crashing in the lobby, which would be embarrassing.

The room was okay, she decided. It was generic, but what would anyone expect? There were the requisite furnishings—two beds facing a long, narrow dresser with a TV on top, a round table with a chair on either side and a hanging lamp suspended above it. The decor also included heavy draperies with plastic pull rods and color-ful but highly forgettable art on the walls.

The place looked and smelled clean, thank heaven.

And it was blessedly warm. No small consideration, with the wind howling outside the window.

"I hope they have a generator," Jax remarked, probably in an effort to make conversation. "This storm is amp-ing up into a full-scale blizzard." He sighed and added, "I'm going to take a hot shower and then sleep for about a hundred years. If you want the bathroom first, go ahead."

The window rattled under a fresh assault of ice-barbed wind.

Charlotte was just as tired as he was, and it was too much effort to argue, even though she had a question—or two—about what he was doing there. He'd had his rea-sons for leaving New York and settling in Idaho, but what could possibly have brought him to Mustang Creek? A job offer, he'd said. How…coincidental. Or was it? "Just give me a moment to brush my teeth."

"Help yourself." Jax sank down on the edge of the bed closest to the window and started hauling off his boots.

She hurried into the bathroom, clutching her cosmetic bag and the flannel pajamas from her suitcase. After clos-ing the door with a firm click, she brushed her teeth, changed and emerged to find Jax wearing only his jeans, brows raised as he took in her less-than-sexy garb.

What had he expected? A little number from Victo-ria's Secret, maybe?

Since his bare, muscular chest reminded her of other times, better times, she looked away.

"Pink kitty cats?" he teased.

Charlotte took a deep breath. "My aunt gave me these

pajamas," she said tersely, "so I wear them. They're comfortable. Not to mention warm."

"I believe that. Finished with the bathroom?"

She flounced toward her bed. No one ever *flounced* that she knew of—besides maybe a few select romance-novel heroines who did not do it in kitty-patterned flannel pajamas—but she tried anyway. She waved toward the bathroom door. "Yep. It's all yours." With that, she threw back the covers and scrambled beneath them.

"Thanks." He disappeared into the bathroom and shut the door, and she finally relaxed a little, settling in and staring up at the ceiling.

Then she heard the water running.

He was naked in there, she realized, with sudden, visceral clarity. She imagined water streaming in rivulets over the chiseled landscape of his body, a terrain she knew all too well...

You're hopeless, she told herself. Then, with tired resolution, she jerked the blankets up to her chin and once again came to terms with the baffling fact that *that* was then and *this* was now. And despite the bizarrely coincidental *It Happened One Night* situation she found herself in, things would return to normal in the morning. All she had to do now was close her eyes and let sleep take her under, enfold her in blissful oblivion.

Exhausted as she was, however, her brain remained busy, chewing and fretting, gnawing at a single thought.

Jaxon Locke was in Mustang Creek.

While she was in New York and he was in Idaho, she'd managed to ignore his existence. Mostly. She'd gotten on with her life, learned to live, even thrive, without him.

Mostly.

Now, all of a sudden, she was sharing a hotel room with him in a tiny Wyoming town.

Where was the logic?

And how was she supposed to survive this?

Simple question.

But no answers in sight, simple or otherwise.

She squeezed her eyes shut, determined to lose herself in sleep.

But she was still awake when Jax emerged from the bathroom long minutes later; through her lashes, she noted that he was naked, except for the towel wrapped around his lean waist. He seemed to know she was awake, although she was pretending she'd already drifted off.

"Listen to that wind," he said. "Sounds like a pack of hungry wolves. It's brutal out there."

She gave up on the sleeping-beauty act. He'd always been able to read her energy in some mysterious way, and fooling him was usually too much work. "Nice of you to share the room." There. She'd said something civil. Even cordial.

But distant, as well. She certainly didn't want to send the wrong message.

No way was she going to sleep with him.

Not that he seemed to expect it.

The problem was that a part of her *wanted* to leap from her bed to his—talk about sending messages—to open her arms to him, brazen as could be, and abandon herself to his lovemaking, to him. To the singular combination of *them*.

Even after all this time, and all the deliberate forgetting, her body remembered.

They'd certainly never had any problems in bed. Their

troubles had stemmed from other things, like his old-fashioned attitudes. He hadn't wanted a professional woman who could go toe-to-toe with some of the most intimidating people in the advertising world. Some of the bitterness flooded back, sobering and hurtful. No, as far as she could tell, Jax had wanted a carpooling, cookie-baking wife and mother for his children, someone who loved small-town life to the exclusion of all else. Or, at any rate, to the exclusion of any other kind of place. Someone who sewed gingham curtains for the kitchen windows and taught Sunday school and fussed over her flower beds.

All right, maybe he hadn't mentioned those things specifically, but they went with the territory, didn't they?

To Jax's credit, he'd never pretended to like New York City as much as she did. For him, it was a mere stopping place along the way to someplace else, third base in some metaphoric baseball game. Next stop, home plate.

Translation: wide-open spaces, pickup trucks, mixed-breed dogs.

The country.

Well, at least he'd been honest. That was more than she could say for a lot of the guys she'd dated, before and after him.

He'd been considerate, polite, intelligent...and sexy.

Very, very sexy.

Once again, Charlotte was stricken with quiet astonishment. One moment she'd been firmly planted in a reality she knew and understood. The next...

Well, the next moment Jax was *here*. She still didn't quite believe it.

"Of course I'd share the room," he said.

Charlotte was confused. Share the room?

Oh, yes. She'd thanked him earlier, and now he was responding.

Keep up, she chided herself silently.

It occurred to her then that Jax's voice had sounded a little too gruff. Maybe he'd picked up on her thoughts. Maybe he was going to drop that towel any second now.

She flipped over onto her side, facing away from him.

"Thanks," she murmured. For some reason, her throat seemed to swell, and her eyes burned.

"You're welcome." He hadn't moved. She would've known it, *felt* it, if he had. And his voice was still low, still hoarse. "I really want you, by the way."

There went that honesty of his, kicking in at exactly the wrong moment.

Charlotte tensed. "Not gonna happen." Was she warning him off—or reminding *herself* not to let yesterday's memories overwhelm today's good sense?

"Your choice, of course," Jax told her quietly.

She rolled back to face him again and said the worst thing possible. "It would be a bad idea, you know."

Great. She'd just admitted she'd been thinking about how good it would be to lie in Jax's arms, to let him awaken her body just one more time.

Jax grinned, and he had the single most appealing boyish smile of any man she'd ever met. "But not out of the realm of possibility?"

She might as well be honest with him, too. "Unless you happen to have a condom, yes, *way* out."

She was happy—and yet somewhat disappointed—that he seemed dismayed. "Yeah, good point. I don't."

"Then, go to sleep." Charlotte closed her eyes again.

She heard the whispery rustle as he pulled on whatever

he was going to wear to bed. He must've let the towel drop to the carpet... This whole thing was entirely too intimate, too familiar. If she could just fall asleep...

"Charlie..." Jax's voice was soft, and she wanted to scream, because she was trying so hard to distance herself. She was, wasn't she? Despite that dumb remark about the condom. But it wasn't working at all. "I really have missed you," he said.

Now he wasn't playing fair.

Charlotte wouldn't, couldn't, look at him. "Am I the reason you're here in Mustang Creek?" The question tumbled right out of her mouth, going straight from her subconscious mind to the tip of her tongue and neatly bypassing her normally competent brain. "I mean, I know you had a job offer, but..." She fumbled to extricate herself.

Must have been the exhaustion, she reflected, frantic to find an explanation for herself.

"Could be," he said.

Then he sighed, and she heard his mattress give way as he got into his own bed.

And that was it. Two seconds later he began to snore gently.

She, on the other hand, was wide-awake.

Momentarily, she considered homicide. A pillow over his face might do the trick.

It was certainly tempting.

JAX WOKE, BLINKING, confused at first, having slept like the proverbial rock, but then it all came back to him.

The long drive.

The blizzard.

And Charlotte, sharing his hotel room but not his bed. Right.

The storm must have eased up a little; the wind was no longer buffeting the window like a whole tribe of banshees trying to get inside. Intricate patterns of frost, stars and whorls covered the glass.

Water ran in the nearby bathroom, and he pictured billows of steam rolling out when the door opened.

Charlotte was in the shower. It felt good to lie there and imagine her gloriously naked, and so close by. He had an excellent memory, and she had the kind of body that did it for him: slender, nicely proportioned breasts, not big but not small, either, long legs that looked sexy when she wore a business skirt, but in his opinion would look even better bared by some cutoff shorts and tanned by the Wyoming sun.

He was definitely a leg man.

He enjoyed the fantasy he had going. A while later the shower was turned off and then, subsequently, the hair dryer. She appeared, wearing a pair of jeans and a light blue sweater, still barefoot, her dark hair shining and brushing her shoulders. She'd never worn much makeup; she didn't need it, in his opinion. Other than a touch of lip gloss and maybe some mascara to accentuate those green eyes, she personified the small-town girl she'd tried so hard to leave behind.

"Good morning." He said it cheerfully because he was feeling pretty cheerful, especially when her gaze dropped briefly to his bare chest before she realized it and looked him in the eyes.

"Uh, yeah, good morning."

"How much snow did we get?" He was just making

conversation, not actually expecting her to know, since she probably hadn't been up long enough to check the weather.

She surprised him, though. "About a foot, I think, but it's hard to tell with the window iced over." She rummaged through her suitcase, produced some socks and sat down on her rumpled bed to put them on. "My rental car is sporty—I'm not sure it has studded snow tires." A reflective pause. "I hope they have the streets cleared."

Jax felt the need to keep things on an even keel. "I have a breakfast meeting next door at eight. If you want to join us, I can take you anywhere you want to go afterward. My truck can handle it."

She hesitated, visibly preoccupied. There were tiny candy canes on her socks. Another gift from her aunt? He guessed that was the case, since the sophisticated woman he'd known in New York would not wear candy canes. He preferred the small-town candy-cane girl; he'd always known she was there.

Charlotte said, "I might call you if I have problems but I need to go home and make sure everything's fine so that when I see Aunt Geneva, I can tell her Can-Can and Mutley are okay. That's the first thing she'll want to know."

"Dog and cat?" It was an educated guess, based on previous conversations.

She nodded, and actually ripped loose with a tiny smile. "A friend of my aunt's is taking care of them. My aunt might be too…vague to have animals. Her doctors seem to think so anyway. The whole idea breaks my heart. She loves those critters so much. They're wonderful company, and she'd be lonely without them. I can't stand the thought."

He might have fallen more in love with her right then, if that was possible. "So you came back for Christmas," he said carefully.

She meant to stay in Mustang Creek for good, but he didn't want to let on that he knew, didn't want to confess that he'd been paying attention to her social media posts. He'd watched to see if she was dating anyone else while he was back in Idaho, and there'd been no hint of anything serious, not even one picture or perky post. There'd been images of her and friends here and there, but either she was just more private than most of *his* friends, or she hadn't really dated.

He figured it was the latter, and that gave him hope.

"I'm not going back to New York," she told him flatly, pulling on a pair of short boots. She stood and shook back her hair. "Aunt Geneva needs me, so this is where I'll be."

"What a coincidence," he said. That word again. "This is where I'll be, too."

"Coincidence, huh?" Charlotte seemed skeptical and a little intrigued. "I guess we'll just have to agree that this town *is* big enough for both of us." It was difficult to look innocent if you were wearing only a pair of boxers while the woman of your dreams stood in the same room. He adjusted the sheet. "I knew Nate in college. Now that he's gone into partnership with Tate Calder in the horse-breeding business, he needs an associate for the practice. So, yes, maybe it's a coincidence—that my friend from vet school happens to live in your hometown. I remembered how you'd described the place, and when he suggested I might want to join his practice, I jumped at the chance."

Her reply made Jax wonder if she'd heard his explanation at all. "We'll both be in Mustang Creek," she said. She sounded resigned, but he couldn't quite interpret her expression.

"We sure will. Maybe we can go out for dinner some-time. You can buy."

"Dream on, cowboy." Charlotte fished out a small knit-ted cap from her suitcase and slipped it on.

Her aunt had crocheted it, he figured. It looked home-made, and *she* looked delectable.

The woman he'd known in New York, always wearing designer outfits and pricey shoes, the woman he'd called Charlie, probably wouldn't have been caught dead in that hat, not in the city anyway.

Cute was the only word he could come up with, and it made him laugh. Charlie, the original uptown girl—cute? What a concept. "We spent the night together, so maybe you do owe me dinner. Just sayin'."

She pointed at her bed, but he could swear there was a gleam in her eye. "I slept here, and you slept *there*. Which means we didn't 'spend the night together,' not in the strictest sense of the term, anyhow."

"You're right," he said, with a twinkle.

"Jax, could you stop messing with my head for a sec-ond, please?"

He did his best cowboy imitation. "I'll try, but, darlin', you make it difficult."

Some nuance in his tone or manner must have gotten to her, because she blushed. Despite all the big-city polish, Charlotte was still a small-town girl. She said hurriedly, "I need to go. I haven't met this Mrs. Klozz who's been helping Aunt Geneva, but apparently, she doesn't have a cell phone, so I doubt she even knows I'm in town. I also need to check on the house and the animals, and then visit Aunt Geneva."

"Don't get stuck in the snow."

She muttered as she wheeled her suitcase toward the door, "I'll do my best."

CHAPTER THREE

THE OLD HOUSE was covered in snow, but it looked warm and inviting. A decorated Christmas tree stood framed in the big front window, and Charlotte could have described every single one of those beloved ornaments in detail.

She smiled at the blue one with the image of a small town that had "Silent Night" printed on it in lacy white letters. The twisty ones with frosted glass in various colors. The sparkly red reindeer she'd bought with babysitting money and hung on the tree when she was twelve, so delighted to contribute. It really didn't match the antique decorations, but Aunt Geneva had loved it, hugged her tightly, and the memory of her warm acceptance left Charlotte sitting in the car for a few minutes, teary eyed. This was hard.

Very hard.

Geneva should be coming out on the porch right now, wearing an apron like she always did and waving hello, her eyes alight.

Okay, put that aside. Life changed, Charlotte knew it did. Her aunt was in her eighties, and she'd seen a lot of Christmases over the years. The two of them had shared so many good memories; Charlotte refused to spoil them with regrets. She got out and shut the car door, noting that someone, no doubt Mr. Simpson next door, had plowed the driveway.

She didn't need a key after all.

The faceted glass front door opened easily. The smell of cinnamon and allspice immediately hit her, and Charlotte realized someone was inside, baking cookies.

It was very much like coming home—even without Aunt Geneva.

"Hello," she called out cautiously, not wanting to startle anyone.

Mutley came running, leaping all over her, barking with excitement. His breed certainly wasn't a known pedigree—more like a combination of half a dozen or so—hence his name. She appreciated being greeted with all that unbridled enthusiasm. Can-Can was curled up on the sofa on her special blanket, and she raised her head and gave a feline yawn, followed by her version of a smile before she settled back into her nap.

Both animals were fine. That was a relief anyway. Charlotte assured Mutley she loved him, too, fended off a few more dog kisses, then set down her suitcase and tried again. "Um, hello?"

"Hello, dear." The woman who bustled out of the kitchen was short and a little stout, white-haired, her eyes bright and her smile infectious. "I've been expecting you. That was quite a storm, wasn't it? I made coffee and there's a warm crumb cake, sweet rolls, too. It's a new recipe, and I need an opinion."

She tried for a semiformal introduction. "I'm Charlotte."

"Of course you are, child."

"Did Aunt Geneva tell you I was coming?" She hadn't

even told her aunt she was on her way, in case any of her flights were delayed or canceled. At least, she hadn't mentioned a specific day; it was a given that she'd be in Mustang Creek for Christmas.

"No, dear, she didn't. But there are pictures of you everywhere, so it was no trick to recognize you. You're just as pretty in person." The older woman smiled. "The cake is still warm. Are you hungry?"

Slightly bemused, Charlotte trailed her into the familiar kitchen. She *was* hungry, actually. She'd eaten her last meal, a prepackaged sandwich at the airport, yesterday afternoon. And the spice-scented air promised something special enough to make her salivate. "Yes, I am. It smells great in here."

The outdated kitchen was as immaculate as ever, with the same ruffled curtains at the window, the familiar wooden table and the ancient refrigerator humming away.

"I'm fairly sure the cake is fine, but I'm trying to perfect my cinnamon rolls." Millicent Klozz breezed over to the old oven, and the door creaked in its usual way as she opened it and took out a pan. "You'd think at my age I'd have the process down cold, but I believe life requires us to continually ask more of ourselves, wouldn't you agree?" She moved energetically between the oven and the table, setting out two plates. "I want an honest opinion. Too much vanilla in the icing? That's my biggest fear." She sat down. "Now, what's your young man doing today?"

Her *what*?

"I'm sorry?"

Mrs. Klozz handed her a plate with a roll and a fork as she tilted her head. "You know, the young man. The tall one. Good-looking."

Charlotte nearly choked on a bite of her pastry. Once she recovered, she managed to say, "I don't really have a *young man*."

"Oh, yes, you do. The one with the blue eyes." Millicent Klozz waved a hand. "He's a veterinarian, isn't he? Yes. That's right, I remember now. I don't want to seem old-fashioned, but you stayed with him last night, young lady. This *is* Mustang Creek."

There was the perfect amount of vanilla in the icing, Charlotte thought, although that was beside the point.

Yes, this *was* a very small town, but still… How many people had been out spreading gossip in a storm like that?

She shook off a twinge of—what?

"I shared a room with Jax because there wasn't any alternative. It was so late, I knew you'd be sleeping, and the weather was terrible. In any case, he isn't *my* young man." Wait, did she sound snarky? Defensive? She hoped not. "The roll is delicious, by the way. You definitely got the vanilla right. Thank you."

Mrs. Klozz's eyes fairly twinkled, and she waved off Charlotte's thanks with a good-natured smile and a motion of one hand. Then she rushed on, caught up in the story she was spinning. "He followed you here. It's quite romantic. What are you going to do now?"

Wow. The grapevine was in fine form, evidently.

Had Jax followed her to Mustang Creek? Charlotte had her suspicions, but he hadn't come right out and said so— had he? He'd come to town expressly to join his friend's veterinary practice; that was her understanding anyway.

Beside her, Mutley gave a very small begging whine. She ignored it. Aunt Geneva didn't approve of animals hovering during dinner, although Charlotte had been guilty of sneaking him a morsel or two if she was through eating, so his bad habits could be her fault.

Charlotte realized she'd been asked a question and offered a belated response. "I'm not going to do anything," she said. "Jax has his life, and I have mine. Mustang Creek might be small, but that doesn't mean we have to be in each other's pockets."

Brave words.

Mrs. Klozz didn't seem to be listening. She picked up a cinnamon roll, took a tiny bite and chewed thoughtfully. "Maybe some more brown sugar in the filling? Raisins? I always hesitate there. Not everyone loves raisins. An acquired taste." A pause. "What do you think?"

Charlotte wanted to laugh. She liked this woman already. "About brown sugar or raisins? It's delicious as it is."

"No, no, dearie, about Jaxon Locke. Keep up with the conversation." A second pause. "So…what do you have to say about that young man?"

Mrs. Klozz was pleasant, and quite eccentric, as well. Where *had* Aunt Geneva found her?

By then, Mrs. Klozz was beaming, offering up another cinnamon roll.

Charlotte helped herself. She was getting full, but the pastries were among the best things she'd ever tasted. "I… um, don't have a lot to say where Jax is concerned," she replied, picking up the thread of the discussion.

Millicent pointed a fork in her direction. "He's going to join that practice and take over the small-animal part of the business for now. Which reminds me, we need to take Mutley and Can-Can in to have their nails trimmed. I'm sorry to push the job of getting them there on you, but I hate the expressions on their furry faces when they realize where they're headed. Animals are so sensitive. Would you mind, dear?"

Mutley, sensitive guy that he was, scratched himself then, sort of ruining the moment. Mrs. Klozz ignored his less-than-charming behavior.

"I was unaware of his exact plans," Charlotte said, shoving about half a roll into her mouth. "Jax's, I mean," she mumbled.

They *were* talking about Jax now, right? With Millicent Klozz making one verbal hairpin turn after another, it was hard to know.

Apparently regarding the trip to the vet's office as a done deal, Millicent swung the conversation into yet another curve. "Geneva will be able to come home for Christmas, according to her doctor," she announced. "Oh, dear, I need to get more baking done. Then I can take cookies to the other patients. Just because dear G gets to come home doesn't mean everyone's that lucky. You're sure about the icing?"

She looked anxious, and Charlotte's mouth was still full, so she merely nodded.

"Well, good." Millicent settled back and sighed. "I love this old house. It's so comfortable, isn't it? That's the word for it. *Comfortable.* I'm very glad you're home, Charlotte. I was rattling around here all by myself except for Mut and Can, and I needed some company."

JAX SCRAPED THE snow off his windshield and tried to cheer himself up. Sure, Charlie had hightailed it out of there at warp speed this morning, declining to stick around for breakfast, but there was no point in reading something into it that wasn't there.

Maybe she hadn't wanted to sit through his meeting with Nate, and who could blame her?

They'd be seeing each other again soon. He was convinced of it.

He'd come to Mustang Creek to find Charlotte again. He'd succeeded. The job was a bonus, since it provided him with a legitimate reason to show up here, but he couldn't deny that she'd been his *real* reason.

Okay, last night hadn't been the evening of his dreams, although it came closer than any other evening of the past year.

So what if he hadn't gotten to hold her in his arms, let alone kiss her, let alone—

There was a downside to everything, he supposed.

At least he'd been with Charlotte. Just the two of them...

Anyway, the last thing he wanted to do was crowd her.

For now, he was content to be in the same part of the country. At one point during the night, he'd rolled over and lay there, listening to her soft breathing in the dark, and that had been enough. He wouldn't mind being a little closer the next time, but that was a start.

The meeting with Nate had gone well, too. His flourishing practice needed another pair of caring hands, Jax was experienced with both large animals like ranch stock and small ones, typically beloved pets, and the new arrangement seemed to be a good fit. If not for Charlotte, would he have stayed in Idaho and eventually taken over his father's practice? Probably. But it had been his father who'd encouraged him to pursue her, with that signature genial smile of his. *Son, seems to me you can't forget Charlotte, and I know you've tried,* he'd said. *I think maybe you need to take a trip to Wyoming.*

Well, he was in Mustang Creek, he had a job and now he needed to win the girl.

Mission not quite accomplished, but he was two-thirds of the way there.

The clinic was a low sprawling facility that had a simple sign and a parking lot big enough for trailers; inside, it was surprisingly modern, with computers at the reception desk and a full surgery suite. Nate was young and vibrant, just as Jax remembered him from vet school.

Nate showed him around enthusiastically. "Kennels here." He pointed. "And we have an excellent care staff. They love all the animals and make sure they feel as comfortable as possible in an unfamiliar environment. I have to warn you, we do an animal-rescue adoption on Christmas Eve, which is right around the corner. Free puppies and kittens, all shots included. That's one busy night. Hope you don't mind. Volunteer basis. If you have other plans, I understand."

He didn't have plans. Wouldn't be heading back to Idaho for the festivities. His dad would be all right; he was spending the holiday with his older brother, Jax's uncle Seth, which he did every year, so he wouldn't be alone. The two men usually celebrated Christmas Eve by swapping stories and reminiscing over spiked eggnog. Jax always enjoyed the informal get-together because *they* enjoyed it so much, but this year, he'd skip it. He had a new job, after all, and besides, he'd heard those same yarns time and time again.

All the same, he felt a little nostalgic, thinking about

his family. Christmas Day, the whole crew gathered at his aunt's house and utter mayhem ensued with excited grandchildren running amok, too many women in the kitchen, stray scraps of wrapping paper on the floor here and there...

He would miss that, but out of all the cousins, he was the only one still unmarried. No one tried to make him feel left out, but he couldn't help it, especially when everyone settled down to dinner next to his or her spouse, chatting comfortably. There was always the inevitable question—*So, Jax, you seeing anyone special?*

"The Christmas Eve pet-rescue deal is a great idea," Jax said, meaning it. Normally, he didn't encourage people to introduce pets to their households during the upheaval of a holiday, but he knew Nate would have some kind of screening process in place, and the need to find good homes for otherwise unwanted animals was year-round. "Count me in."

"Thanks." Nate glanced at his phone. "I'll see you at my place around four o'clock. I've got to go check on a husky that had surgery on his leg this morning and then run out to the Calder ranch because we have a mare who's about to drop. It's like an early Christmas present."

Jax walked back out to his truck.

Maybe Charlotte needed a kitten. Or a puppy. He had no idea what else to get her for Christmas. Someone had beaten him to candy-cane socks, and the pink kitten pajamas had already been done, too. He felt himself grin over that one.

A pet might not be a bad gift, but it was unfair to give an animal to someone who might not be ready to make that kind of commitment. Although he could take it if she decided to move back to New York…

He hoped she'd choose to stay.

Charlie was such a mix of country girl and city woman. He'd fallen for the city woman, and now he wanted to know the country girl. She'd looked right at home in the jeans and casual sweater that morning. It would've been even better if he could have taken them off and made love to her. He hoped that scenario was in his future.

Speaking of his future… He had a job, but he still needed a place to live. Sacking out on Cameron's couch, which he'd been invited to do tonight, was fine for the short term. It would get old fast, for both of them. The hotel was adequate, if impersonal, and he wasn't going to live there.

Time to look for a house or apartment.

So he got into his truck, started the engine and called Charlie. That took some fortitude. She didn't answer so he left a message. "This is Jax. I need a place and wondered if you could recommend somewhere."

Two minutes later, she called back. At least, that was her number on his call display.

Only it wasn't Charlotte's voice he heard on the other line. "Jaxon Locke?"

"Uh, yes."

"Oh, good. Charlotte accidentally left her phone behind. I think she was in a hurry. I can use these gadgets, but they aren't all the same, you know, so it's an iffy proposition. I guess I pressed the right button, though." A brief pause. "I'm so glad you're here."

Jax actually removed the phone from his ear, stared at it, then went back to the conversation. "I am, too. I'm not sure who I'm speaking to, but Charlie mentioned... Are you Mrs. Klozz, by any chance?"

"Call me Millicent, dear."

Call her Millicent. "So, Charlie—Charlotte—isn't home at the moment?"

"She's out" came the reply. "I'll tell her you called."

All well and good, but Jax still didn't understand why Mrs. Klozz—Millicent—had troubled herself to return someone else's phone call.

"O-kay," Jax said, drawing out the word. "Sorry to bother you."

"Now, don't you worry." Millicent went on with the disjoined conversation. "You aren't bothering me at all. Not one bit." She drew in an audible breath. "I did want to answer your question, though. You should just stay here. We have plenty of room."

Jax's mind went blank. "What?"

Millicent sounded sympathetic. "This is a big house, and we could use a man around here. I can't fix that stupid door on the upstairs bathroom—the one that won't close properly—although I swear I've tried. There are other small problems you could probably take care of much better than I can, so why don't you come and stay here with us? How ridiculous for you to pay rent somewhere."

He finally understood. And he could imagine how Charlotte would react to *that* idea. "Ma'am, that's very kind of you, but—"

"Call me Millicent," she reminded him. "I realize this might be construed as bribery, but I make some mean Christmas cookies."

He didn't doubt that, but...

"Here's the address. Even with Charlotte and me, there

are four empty bedrooms. Think about it that way, Jaxon. Two helpless women who could use a little protection and someone to fix the bathroom door would appreciate having you here. You need a roof over your head, and you and Charlotte already know each other. Perfect."

They needed protection? In Mustang Creek, Wyoming?

First of all, Charlotte Morgan could hardly be described as helpless. Plus, Jax might be new in town, but he was fairly sure that if he so much as dropped a quarter in the snow, some upstanding citizen would hunt him down and return it.

And how did Millicent know his name anyway?

Caller ID, maybe. But that didn't explain how she'd found out he was in the market for a place to live. Surely she hadn't gone so far as to listen to Charlotte's voice mail. And even if she'd been so inclined, how would she have gotten the password?

"See you soon," Millicent said breezily, ending the call.

Nate had emerged from the building at that moment and stopped by the truck, looking at him with amusement.

Jax rolled down the window. "The husky okay?"

"Husky is fine. Everything okay with you?"

"Not sure," Jax said, scratching his jaw. "I think a little old lady just railroaded me. I might not need your couch, but don't lend it to anyone else yet. Not all the parties involved have weighed in."

"Okay. If it doesn't work out, just walk in, shove off the dog if you can manage it because he weighs about a hundred and fifty and settle down with a pillow."

Jax had to laugh. "Rufus sounds like quite the watch-dog."

"He's conscientious in his own way. He barks if he can

see the bottom of his food bowl. You could steal my car and he'd sleep through it, but try to take his bowl. And if you end up with no place to stay, remember that Rufus can sleep on the floor." He went to his SUV, got in and waved cheerfully as he drove out of the parking lot.

Jax planned on getting a dog of his own someday. A midsize animal, maybe a beagle mix. Beagles barked a lot, even bayed now and then, but they were sweet tempered, good around kids and well mannered in general, although you had to keep an eye on them where low-lying food was concerned, because they were unabashed thieves.

Family friendly, though.

Jax chuckled, shook his head. Must be the season—he seemed to be thinking about settling down a lot.

Family friendly.

Really?

He needed to talk to Charlie.

CHAPTER FOUR

CHARLOTTE WALKED UP the front steps of the extended-care facility with a heavy heart.

It was an attractive place, cheerfully decorated for the upcoming holidays, with wide, ice-free sidewalks, a gazebo and a small pond with a fountain, out of service for the winter, of course. A seven-foot snowman stood near the main entrance, with one chunky arm raised in welcome. His eyes and mouth consisted of colorful buttons, and his nose was the customary carrot. To complete the look, Frosty sported a plaid neck scarf and a spiffy top hat.

For all that, it hurt to think of Aunt Geneva as a permanent resident, to acknowledge that when she came home, it would only be for a visit.

She'd always been a homebody.

On a brighter note, Charlotte came bearing gifts. She carried a quantity of baked goods that would lighten anybody's mood, Scrooge and the Grinch included.

Mrs. Klozz had definitely outdone herself, loading Charlotte down with spritz, oatmeal chocolate chip, molasses and peanut butter cookies, and that was just for starters.

She'd gain ten pounds a week if Millicent kept baking like this.

She stepped inside, juggling her purse and the big box of goodies she'd come to deliver.

There was a reception desk with a smiling middle-aged woman behind it, and Christmas music played in the background. A large fragrant tree in the corner glittered with lights and ornaments, and there was a display of opened Christmas cards on the desk next to a guest registry.

"Good afternoon and happy holidays," the receptionist chirped. "May I help you?"

"I'm here to see Geneva Roberts," Charlotte explained, setting down the brightly colored box festooned with ribbons. She could swear it weighed about twenty pounds. "My aunt's friend baked a few things for the staff and tenants."

"Oh, that Mrs. Klozz!" the other woman cried joyously. "Isn't she lovely? Everyone will be delighted when we serve afternoon coffee." Her smile flashed as bright as the Christmas tree in the corner. She wore dangling earrings shaped like tiny elves in green suits, and her cotton scrubs were printed with lavish red poinsettias. "You must be Charlotte. Geneva talks about you all the time. Please sign in and I'll give you a map of the facility and direct you to your aunt's room."

Although she'd chosen the place and made all the arrangements for Aunt Geneva's admittance, Charlotte hadn't actually seen the building in person until today. Despite the shiny brochures and high recommendations from the family doctor, she'd had moments of doubt. Along with a few disturbing dreams, in which she'd glimpsed dingy halls smelling of antiseptic and glum residents clad in gray, like characters in a Dickens novel.

The reality was more than reassuring.

Just the same, it was hard to imagine her aunt being truly happy anywhere but that big old house on Maple Street, where she tended her garden every summer. In the winter she'd sit and watch her "programs," as she called them, knitting or crocheting, while Can-Can slept next to her on the sofa and Mutley lay curled up on the rug at her feet. Charlotte could barely recall the days when her aunt had worked as a bookkeeper for a local supermarket because she'd immediately cut back her hours to make sure she was there to see Charlotte off to school in the mornings and greet her when she came home every afternoon. That was when she'd started taking in sewing, specializing in wedding gowns and outfits for the bride's attendants. Eventually, she'd worked from home full-time; as a seamstress, she was constantly in demand. Suddenly finding herself with a small child to raise couldn't have been easy, but Geneva had certainly made it seem that way.

And there'd always been that big old house. Geneva and her sister, Charlotte's mother, had been born and raised there, and she'd inherited the place while she was still fairly young. There'd never been a mortgage.

Now, through an arrangement Geneva had made long ago, ownership of the house would be transferred to Charlotte.

She had mixed feelings about that.

On the one hand, she knew she'd cherish the place, couldn't have stood to see it sold, torn down or occupied by strangers. On the other, having the deed put in her name meant Aunt Geneva couldn't manage the place anymore.

And that was sobering.

Furthermore, owning a house, especially an old one, was a responsibility. While she was fine for now, financially speaking, Charlotte would have to get another job sooner or later, and Mustang Creek wasn't exactly a hotbed of opportunity. Another advertising job seemed unlikely.

But she'd worry about things like that once Christmas was past and the New Year's glitter had been swept up. Not that she and Mrs. Klozz would be having a party with champagne and confetti. More like white-chocolate biscotti and maybe a splash of something decadent in their coffee.

Yeah, she could see the spritely Millicent Klozz going for that. Just once a year, but the gleam in her eyes said she was up for a little innocent mischief now and then.

Someday she'd have to pursue the question of how Mrs. K. and her aunt even knew each other.

"Down that hallway." The receptionist pointed to the map. "Take the first turn to the right. Her room is D-25. We have staff popping in, just in case anyone needs anything, so you'll have to pardon us if there's an interruption to your visit. It's why we're here—to be of service."

"I'm glad to know Aunt Geneva's being looked after," Charlotte responded in a genuinely grateful tone.

The room was easy enough to find, and Charlotte's throat tightened when she saw the wreath on the door was the paper one she'd made in the fifth grade, battered after all these years but carefully preserved, with pieces of tape keeping it together. She had to stand there for a moment and compose herself before she knocked.

"Aunt Geneva?" she called tentatively.

When the door opened, the familiar face lit up in a smile of joyful recognition. "Charlotte Jean," Geneva said, opening her arms. "You come here."

Charlotte reciprocated her aunt's warm hug 100 percent. To her relief, Geneva looked much the same, healthy, with a hint of pink in her cheeks, wearing a patterned pink top and white slacks, slippers instead of shoes. Her space was furnished with pieces brought from the house. The parlor table with the old lamp, that green chair, the faded rug under the coffee table...

"Let's go sit down. I've made tea."

The routine was familiar and therefore comforting. Smiling, she glanced over at Aunt Geneva's treasured antique teacups, lined up on a shelf next to the mantel.

"Everything here is so nice," Charlotte said honestly, noticing framed pictures of her at various ages on the walls. The sight made her throat constrict again. "Do you like it?"

Her aunt looked thoughtful as she went straight to the green chair, a book propped on one cushioned arm. "Well, let me put it this way. It's restful. I don't think I realized how anxious I was until I moved here. Before that, I used to wake up in the middle of the night, more often than I like to remember, and wonder if I turned off the stove or locked the doors or made sure the cat was inside." She stopped speaking, just long enough to bite her lower lip. "I forgot my medication now and then, nothing drastic, but still not good. I probably fed Mutley ten times a day because I lost track of whether I'd done it or not and I didn't want him going hungry. One night I let him out and forgot to let him back in. It was cold. The next morning there he was, shivering on the porch." Moisture glistened in her eyes for a moment. "I'd like to think I'm smart enough to know when I need help. The doctor says I'm suffering from a mild case of dementia, and I don't disagree. Let's face it, honey, I'm no spring chicken. Let me put it this way. I no longer want to live alone."

It was a practical attitude, but one that Charlotte found hard to accept. Geneva seemed so entirely normal.

And she clearly missed Mutley and Can-Can.

Pets were allowed at the retirement center, Charlotte knew, but that didn't mean Geneva was up to taking care of them.

She perched on the edge of the couch, folding her hands, choosing her words carefully. "I'm back now," she began. "We could—"

"No, we can't," her aunt interrupted kindly, but with conviction. "I won't have you putting your own life on hold, Charlotte. I do pretty well most days, although I need extra care. Besides, you'll have your hands full with that big old house. It needs a new roof, by the way."

Charlotte nodded, smiling. "Yeah," she said. "I've known about that for a while."

"I think the furnace is from the Roosevelt era," Aunt Geneva remarked, pouring tea for both of them and picking up her cup. "It was installed some time during his third term, if I remember correctly. If it quits, go down to the cellar and give it a good kick. So far, it's holding up, but that's not going to last indefinitely."

Charlotte laughed. "I love you," she said.

"Not as much as I love you," Aunt Geneva retorted on cue. It was an old game. "Now, tell me what's been going on with you. How's what's-his-name? The veterinarian."

"You know perfectly well that we broke up a long time ago. And you also know his name is Jaxon."

"I was so sure he was the one," she mused sadly.

Charlotte sighed. "He's actually here in Mustang Creek."

Aunt Geneva looked delighted. "I *knew* it! Oh, I am so going to win that bet with Millicent Klozz."

What?

"You two bet on my love life?" Charlotte was laughing again, but still chagrined. "Or lack thereof? No wonder Millicent knew his name."

Aunt Geneva waved a frail hand. "So *he's* in town. What happens next?"

There was only one answer. "I have no idea."

IF THE CHOICE was either to share a couch with a blood-hound or move into a Christmas-card house like this one, well, no contest. Unfortunately, things weren't that simple.

The complication? Charlie.

Despite the cold, Jax paused on the snowy sidewalk to take it all in.

He'd seen pictures of the old place, of course, and Charlie had told him dozens of stories, but this was his first actual, real-time visit.

So he savored the moment, admired the wraparound porch, the ornate front door, the shutters, the gables and arches. A picket fence surrounded the spacious—make that huge—front yard, and Jax knew there was even more room around back. He knew about the big garden plot and the clotheslines and a couple of gnarled old apple trees, still producing fruit every summer.

Jax sighed, suddenly wistful, opened the gate and started up the recently shoveled walk.

Getting closer, he could see that the paint was peeling in a few places and the roof over the porch sagged.

His knock was answered by an elderly woman who flung the door open wide and beamed at him.

"Jaxon?"

"Yes."

She wiped both hands on her apron and offered one that seemed to hold a slight dusting of flour. "I'm Millicent Klozz," she said.

"Yes," he answered. "Hello." *Of course you are.*

Her smile was welcoming, and she stepped back, making a sweeping gesture with one arm. "Don't stand out there in the cold," she said cheerfully, raising her voice to be heard over the happy barking of the dog at her feet. "Come on in. You can choose your room."

He was being steamrollered, and he was letting it happen. *Enjoying* it, even. But he also knew he was playing along, although he wasn't entirely sure why. He couldn't just move in; Charlie, who couldn't possibly know what was happening on the home front at the moment, would freak when she found out.

And he wouldn't blame her.

Come on in. You can choose your room.

Indeed.

If he'd known Millicent better, and if she'd been about a hundred years younger, he would've quipped, "That's easy. I'll take Charlotte's room."

He didn't say that, of course.

But he might as well have, because the sweet old lady answered as if he had. "Behave yourself, you rascal," she mock-scolded, with a twinkle and a little ringing laugh. Then she bustled up the stairs, which looked like solid walnut and, with some refinishing, would amount to a showpiece.

Jax recovered quickly, deciding he must've imagined at least part of the exchange. "Maybe we ought to wait," he called after her, hesitating at the foot of the stairs. "Talk this over with Charlotte."

"Oh, she'll be fine with the idea," Mrs. Klozz said merrily, standing on the landing and gazing back at him with an expression of mild and totally benevolent impatience.

Well, that confirmed his suspicions anyway. Charlotte had no clue what was going on. The situation was downright odd—and kind of funny, too. Like something that might happen in a Christmas movie.

"She doesn't know," he said. It wasn't a question.

"Not yet," Mrs. Klozz told him, still blithe. "I'll handle it. Now, if I were you, I'd take the larger one on the east side of the house, but then, I'm an early riser and I like a good dose of sunlight first thing." She paused, regarded him with a smile. "Come along, dear. I don't have all day."

Despite his reservations, Jax climbed the stairs.

When he reached the top, Mrs. Klozz led him down a long, well-lit hallway. There was more fine woodwork, all of it intricately carved, and a huge stained-glass skylight cast beams of dancing color everywhere.

The place was almost magical, and Jax knew Charlotte loved every plank and pane and peg of it.

Then, why had she left? Meanwhile, Millicent launched into the tour. "Wouldn't this house make an excellent B and B?" she said with an expansive gesture and a contented sigh. "That's the bathroom door," she informed him, pointing. "It doesn't latch properly, so you might find Mutley in there once in a while. He likes to sleep next to the register. He's a darling, but he sheds. You don't mind pets, do you?"

Considering his vocation, he should hope not. "Um, no, ma'am."

Her smile was back on high beam. "Of course you wouldn't, you're a veterinarian. I swear, sometimes I don't think my memory is any better than Geneva's, bless her heart. You'll want to watch out for Can-Can—the cat—because she finds men irresistible and likes to lounge on the window seat in your room in the morning. It's the eastern exposure, you know."

His room. Right.

Until Charlotte came home.

"Naturally, Mutley will adore you," the lady prattled on. "He's a sweet soul, like most dogs. Still, enough can be enough, and if you forget to close your door at night, you might find him in bed with you. Can-Can, too." Before Jax could wedge in a comment—he was still playing along, humoring the old woman—she continued. The merriment was gone, and she looked just plain sad. "They miss Geneva. And so do I."

Jax opened his mouth to say something kind—he hadn't decided what—but he missed his chance.

Millicent had brightened again. "Come to think of it," she said, "Mutley could use a walk. Would you mind once you've got a minute? I worry about icy sidewalks at my age."

Jax replied that he'd be glad to walk the dog. He looked down at their furry escort and smiled.

Mrs. Klozz stopped in front of a door and opened it, gesturing for Jax to step inside. The early riser's bedroom, he assumed.

He went in. The room was big, the floor hardwood, and instead of the flowery wallpaper he might have expected in a house inhabited by women, there was just paint. No frilly curtains at the bay window, either, and the cushions on the built-in seat underneath were plain, too. The bed was antique, a brass four-poster, covered with a colorful homemade quilt. An old hope chest sat at the foot, and he saw a sturdy desk and chair on the far side of the room.

Jax could imagine living here, sleeping in this room, working at the desk, surveying the snowy landscape from the window seat.

This game, he thought, was getting out of hand. Charlotte would never agree to Millicent Klozz's plan.

But he found himself wishing she would.

Once again Millicent seemed to be reading his mind. "Don't you worry about a thing, young man," she said quietly. "Charlotte is a sensible woman, and she will see reason." A confident sigh followed. "She'll be gone a while longer, though, handing out cookies and catching up with Geneva. In the meantime, would you mind taking Mutley out for that walk?"

Jax, still bewitched and bewildered, was grateful for the distraction. "No," he said. "Not at all."

They went downstairs, closely followed by Mutley. He was aging—at least ten, Jax figured—and obviously going deaf. The name suited him, since he was of no discernible breed. Millicent produced a leash, attaching it deftly to the dog's collar.

"When you get back," Millicent said, "you can have a look at that bathroom door."

"Er—right."

"Wonderful!" Millicent trilled. "Now, I have something in the oven, so please excuse me. I don't want it to burn. It's for the church bake sale."

Mutley was waiting eagerly, tail sweeping back and forth.

Jax smiled and bent to ruffle the dog's ears. "I guess we're out of here," he said.

Mutley all but dragged Jax to the front door. There was some terrier in the little guy, he decided. Maybe some spaniel. Could be some border collie in there, too. He was probably too small to be part Airedale...

Jax was like that. He analyzed.

By then, Mutley was definitely ready to roll; he was high-jumping at the door.

"Whoa, slow down," Jax said with a grin. Good thing he'd never gotten around to taking off his coat. "The great out of doors isn't going anywhere, buddy."

It was snowing again, not blizzard-style like last night, but in fat, showy flakes, drifting lazily from a heavy sky.

It all looked perfect. *Too* perfect.

For a short while, though, he could pretend that walking Mutley was his job. Ditto, fixing the latch on the upstairs bathroom door.

Yep. He could do that.

That and a whole lot more, if Charlotte gave him half a chance.

What he had to do now was relax, trust, let things unfold.

Easier said than done. After all, he'd made a huge emotional investment, moving to Mustang Creek, pretty much staking the rest of his life on a relationship that might be one-sided.

Still, he thought, watching Mutley trot through the snow at the end of his leash, it hadn't *seemed* one-sided last night. He was hardly a player, but he knew when a woman was thinking about sex, especially when that woman was Charlie. She'd been…well, *thinking*.

There was a chance, a good one. If he'd believed there wasn't, he wouldn't be here, walking Charlotte's aunt's dog through mountains of snow. Wouldn't be looking forward to starting the new job, finding a place to live, any of that.

There he went, analyzing again.

Time to shake it off. "So what do you think, Mut? Am I wrong? Stupid? A stalker?"

The dog didn't even look at him, just pitched his ears forward, sniffed the sidewalk and wagged his tail.

No help there.

He was on a conversational roll, though, so he went right on talking. "Let me ask you something else. What should I get her as a gift? Charlotte, I mean."

Mutley turned, spotted a dog across the street and tried to make a break for it, barking excitedly.

Jax had to laugh. The other dog looked like a beagle mix to him.

A sign?

Okay, part of his shopping list was done.

Charlotte was getting a puppy for Christmas.

CHAPTER FIVE

THE FIRST THING Charlotte saw when she got back to the house was Jax's truck parked at the curb.

Now, that was interesting.

Charlotte pulled into the driveway and marched up the steps. She'd forgotten her phone, unheard of for a businesswoman, especially one who worked in advertising. Or used to. She acknowledged grudgingly that if he'd called, she wouldn't have been able to answer. Usually that phone was her constant companion; she'd carried it everywhere for the past seven years.

Strange how she'd left the thing behind and never missed it. At least, not until she'd decided to call and ask Millicent if she needed anything from the store.

There was a certain freedom in her new circumstances and she knew that, but she mustn't lose perspective. She'd just arrived, and there was a lot of important stuff on her personal agenda.

Now was probably not the best time to embark on a relationship with an all-too-attractive veterinarian. She needed to get the house in order; she needed to get her *life* in order, look after her aunt and Mutley and Can-Can, too.

She got out of her rental car—which needed to be returned and replaced with a vehicle of her own. As she did, she heard that familiar woof and turned around to look. What was Millicent thinking, going out with the dog when the sidewalks were still icy in some places and totally impassible in others? She could break a hip, for heaven's sake!

Only it wasn't Mrs. Klozz.

No, it was Jax, coming her way.

Mutley was with him, straining at his leash, wagging his tail in welcome, eyes luminous with joy at the sight of Charlotte, as if she'd been gone for years, not an hour and a half. Jax's boots crunched the snow, and the hint of a smile curved his lips. He drawled in what he must imagine was a cowboy accent, "Howdy, Miz Morgan. Shore is a fine day, ain't it?"

It was, actually, now that the blizzard had passed, replaced by a gentle snowfall.

The mountains were gorgeous in their glistening blanket of white against the softened sky—a sky that would be the same piercing shade of blue as Jax's eyes, once the clouds parted.

She wished she hadn't thought of that but, when it came to Dr. Locke, her mind, normally so well organized and reasonable, tended to run wild.

"Um, yes, it is." She frowned. Why was he here? "Did I leave something at the hotel?"

"No." He leaned down and caught the dog by the collar just in time to keep Mutley from flinging himself at Charlotte in his exuberance and covering her in slushy paw prints. When he straightened, Jax asked seriously, "How was your aunt?"

"Fine." Charlotte eyed him suspiciously. "It's nice of you to walk Mutley, but what are you doing here?"

"Can we discuss this inside?" he asked. "The storm

of the century might be over, but it's still pretty chilly out here."

The expression on Jax's handsome face was a touch too innocent, Charlotte felt as she opened the door moments later, but he had a point. As festive as that feathery snowfall was, the temperature was probably in the single digits.

Besides, he'd been a total gentleman the night before, hadn't he? And now he'd taken Mutley for a much-needed walk. It wasn't his fault, after all, that she was overly susceptible to his smile.

The least she could do was be courteous.

As they stepped inside, into the warmth and the enticing aromas of whatever was baking in the oven or cooling on the kitchen counter, or both, Charlotte's thoughts jumped the curb again.

What would've happened if he'd had a condom?

Nothing, she told herself firmly.

Liar. You were tempted. You would've given in and you know it.

Mrs. Klozz was belting out a rendition of "Jingle Bells" from the kitchen, and the cheery sound was comforting. Charlotte couldn't imagine walking into the house and finding it empty and quiet, like her former apartment back in the city.

Jax bent and unhooked Mutley's collar and then hung the leash in exactly the right spot before unzipping his jacket. "Can I take your coat?"

Considering it was her house, Charlotte reflected, she should probably be the one offering to take *his* coat, but he'd already hung it on the antique coat tree. He seemed awfully...well, at home.

Not surprising, really. It was almost Christmas, and

there was magic in the air. The house was cozy, despite its size; it seemed to enfold visitors, make them feel welcome.

Naturally, Jax was comfortable here. Everyone was.

He collected her coat as she unwound her knitted scarf, and he automatically took that from her, draping it over the hook that held her coat. "Thanks," she said, a little awkwardly. "Can I get you something to drink before you explain why you're here?"

There. She could be polite, too, and still get her point across.

He smiled, very much at ease. "Mrs. Klozz was making a fresh pot of coffee before Mutley and I took our walk. Let's go sit in the kitchen. That's the most beautiful tres-tle-style table I've ever seen, by the way."

Charlotte blinked. Was she having an out-of-body experience or something?

Mutley might be deaf when it suited him, but he heard the word *kitchen* and trotted off in that direction to check on his bowl. Jax looked at her expectantly. She muttered, "I agree about the table." She raised one eyebrow. "How long have you been here?"

"Long enough for the grand tour. This is a great old house. Please tell me it always smells this good in here."

That seemed an odd thing to say. The smell was fabulous, yes, but Jax was merely passing through. Why should he care about *always*? "I… Well… She likes to bake, apparently."

He gestured, then bowed slightly. "After you."

Gracious of him. Charlotte walked into the kitchen and not surprisingly, there was a plate of sugar cookies on the table, decorated with red and green icing, and what looked like banana muffins. Also a plate of chicken-salad sandwiches on homemade bread. Plus a carafe, two coffee cups, two plates, a small creamer and a sugar bowl...

Mrs. Klozz had switched her personal playlist from "Jingle Bells" to "Silent Night," but stopped in midrefrain when they entered the room. "Oh, you're back, I see, both of you. How was my dear Geneva?"

"Good. Much better than I expected her to be." Charlotte wondered if this woman was more wizard than sweet little old lady. "They all said thank-you for the cookies."

"Oh, my pleasure. Now sit down and help yourselves. I have the shameful habit of tasting everything as I cook, so you'll rarely find me sitting down to a meal."

Jax was invited to lunch. She wasn't surprised, since Millicent seemed that sort of person, but there was an undertone she didn't understand. Something was afoot.

Earlier, Mrs. Klozz had referred to Jax as Charlotte's *young man*. How did she even *know* that?

Through Geneva, she assumed. Charlotte hadn't given her aunt the details about their relationship; all she'd mentioned was that she'd met someone and they'd clicked immediately, but their lives were headed in different directions.

That didn't explain how Mrs. Klozz had known Jax was in Mustang Creek.

Millicent had the good grace to blush slightly. "I invited him over," she confessed. "You see, he called your cell phone, and I was worried it might be important, so I tried to answer, but I wasn't fast enough. Then I started punching buttons, and lo and behold, that cunning little device just called him right back. He picked up and, well, here he is."

Charlotte tilted her head to one side, wondering exactly where she'd lost track of the conversation.

"Okay," she said.

"Such a modern world," Mrs. Klozz went on, still talking about the phone. "I don't mind technology, you understand, but change is always a challenge, especially for an older person. By some miracle, I managed."

Charlotte was finding out for herself that change was a challenge, and she had the distinct impression that this sweet old lady could manage anything she wanted to. At least it explained why Jax was there.

Sort of.

Jax was focused on the food. "This looks fantastic."

He was right; it did.

"The way to a man's heart." Mrs. Klozz glowed, either heedless of the timeworn cliché she'd uttered or not caring. Before meeting Millicent, Charlotte hadn't been aware that people could actually glow, but here was proof.

Not standing on ceremony, Jax picked up the plate of sandwiches and offered it to her. "Ladies first."

JAX KNEW HE'D have to come clean, and quickly, because Charlotte was intuitive; she'd guess that something was up. If she didn't want him there—and he was sure she wouldn't—he'd go dislodge Rufus and sleep on Nate's old couch. The thought overwhelmed him with loneliness. And the old house really was homey.

He had to wonder what Charlotte was going to do with a place like this. She was used to sleek apartments, cabs and limos and subways. While the small-town girl with the crocheted hat might thrive living within these walls, he wasn't so sure about Charlotte's alter ego, the no-nonsense city woman. And right now he hadn't figured out which Charlotte he was dealing with.

At Millicent's urging, they took their places at the table.

In the next moment, Mrs. Klozz bustled off to some other part of the house, presumably to give them some time alone.

Charlotte immediately tucked into a sandwich. Well, that answered one question anyway. "I can't believe how good this is." Between bites, she dropped her voice and whispered to Jax, "She can't stay. I'll gain a thousand pounds."

Jax smiled at the picture that arose in his mind. "I doubt that," he said. "A hundred pounds, maybe. But a thousand?"

Charlotte was still fretful. "This is just too delicious."

Jax agreed. "Best I've ever had."

City Charlotte was back, as quickly as that. "You never answered my question. Why are you here?"

"I...well... I've been invited to live here."

For a few seconds, he really thought Charlotte was choking. He was *this* close to performing the Heimlich maneuver.

Then she recovered. "Oh, you mean in Mustang Creek. You're joining Doc Cameron's practice." She hesitated and reached for a second sandwich.

"Well, it's more than that," he said solemnly. Might as well get this over with. "I called earlier, as Mrs. Klozz mentioned, to ask you where I should look for a place since you're familiar with Mustang Creek. One thing led to another, and before I knew it, the woman was showing me the east bedroom, apparently convinced I'd be moving in right away. She even came up with a few odd jobs for me to do, starting with walking Mutley."

"Here?" Charlotte paused midbite, her green eyes wide. "You mean, *here* here? In *this* house?"

This was how he'd pictured the conversation going, but it was little comfort. Against all reason, he'd already started thinking of the place as home. When had *that* happened?

"I wouldn't be around much," he heard himself say. "I'm good at fixing things. And I do need a place to stay, as I said before." He studied Charlotte's face; she seemed astonished, though not affronted. "But it wasn't my idea, Charlie. I swear."

"You can't sleep down the hall from me." She wasn't looking at him; she seemed to be lost in thought.

He should have shut up, he knew that, but he couldn't refrain from trying to make his case. "Charlie, I'm not going to ravish you, all right? Remember last night? We were in the same room and I didn't so much as touch you, did I?"

Her response couldn't have surprised him—or delighted him—more. "I'm not worried that you'll *ravish* me, Jax. I'm worried *I'll* ravish *you*."

The instant the words were out of Charlotte's mouth, she regretted them. She reddened, obviously horrified. She glared at him, but he could tell she was bluffing. "Forget I said that," she ordered.

Never.

Things were already improving.

"I'll lock my door," he promised, taking a banana muffin. He was very careful not to smile, although he wanted to. God, how he wanted to. He cleared his throat and tried to look earnest. "Seriously, I don't want to make you uncomfortable. I'll find a room or apartment somewhere, and in the meantime... I've slept in worse places than Nate's couch."

Right on cue, Mutley came over and laid his head on Charlie's leg, gazing up at her. She said curtly, "Mut, don't take his side. Hasn't anybody told you that dogs are supposed to be loyal?"

Jax sensed victory. "He loves you, that's all," he said in the animal's defense.

And so do I.

"It's a male conspiracy to make me say yes."

Just before Jax took a bite out of a muffin, he asked hopefully, "Is it working?"

"Maybe. I'm fond of Mutley. He's a hard guy to refuse."

"Well, then, there you go."

"Plus, it wouldn't hurt to have some money coming in."

Jax allowed himself a grin. "I'll pay double the going rate," he said.

"Don't push it," Charlie warned. Then she sighed again. "If Mrs. Klozz is behind this, and of course she is, I might as well go with the flow. I'm powerless to resist."

He felt the same way.

Jax took his time, using his napkin to wipe his mouth as an excuse not to respond immediately. "Let's take this slowly. I'd appreciate the hospitality, at least for tonight, because the alternative is either the hotel—if they have a room available—or bedding down on Nate's couch. With his bloodhound, Rufus by name. I'm as fond of bloodhounds as the next guy, but they're heavy and they drool a lot. A bed here would certainly be preferable."

Charlotte rubbed her forehead, looking beleaguered—and amused. "Go ahead and stay until you find something else. You should know, however, that I haven't got the slightest idea what I'm doing with my life. That's about as honest as I can be. I lost my job, for one thing."

"I gathered that from your online post." *Oops*. He blamed his slip on the muffin; it was delicious. Beyond delicious. "I'm sorry about the job, but not sorry you left New York. Want a bite?"

She plucked off a morsel and ate it. Her shoulders slumped. "I'm not sorry, either. I just want it understood that I have no idea where my plans are right now. Let me get through the holidays first."

He might argue with the assumption that he was there in pursuit of her, except that it was true. It made sense. If you lived in Idaho, met a woman in New York City and then showed up in someplace like Mustang Creek, Wyoming, your intentions were pretty unmistakable.

Subtle, he wasn't.

"I'm planning to spend Christmas Eve at the clinic," he threw out, in case she thought he'd need hand-holding over the holidays.

"You're in charge of the pet adoption thing this year? Aunt Geneva was telling me about it today. She still reads the weekly paper from cover to cover. Luckily, she'll be home for Christmas. I'd find it hard to feel merry without her."

Mrs. Klozz came back in then, followed by the cat, his tail swishing. "I've been informed that cats need to eat, too." Her comment was punctuated by a demanding feline yowl. "You see? Jaxon, would you mind getting Mutley out of here? If only they made dog food that tasted like cat food, then everyone would be happy. He shamelessly eats it in one gobble, and poor Can-Can is left in the lurch."

Another chance to be useful. At this rate, he'd be indispensable in a matter of days.

"Thank you, Mrs. Kl—Millicent. For lunch, I mean. Mut and I will go up and check the bathroom door. Come on, boy."

He had to grin at the pensive way Mutley looked over his shoulder, as if he suspected somebody was about to break out a can of cat food, but he followed Jax out of the room.

"We men have to stick together," Jax told the dog as they climbed the steps to the landing.

The dog barked. Jax took it as a sign of agreement.

On closer examination, Jax discovered that the latch on the bathroom door was stuck because the handle mechanism no longer fit into the frame. With Mutley supervising, he took it apart, using the screwdriver on the pocketknife he carried all the time unless he was dressed up for some reason, which wasn't often in his line of work. He tightened all the screws, then put the lock back together. It worked like a charm.

Walk the dog. Fix the door. He put a mental check beside both items.

He was getting a lot done; he'd checked out of the hotel and he was ready to move in.

With Mutley at his side, he went out to his extended-cab truck to fetch his suitcase, shaving kit and laptop from the backseat. He'd checked out of the hotel, assuming he'd be staying at Nate's. There were still a few boxes, but Jax decided to leave those where they were for the time being. The balance between him and Charlotte was delicate; he didn't want to come across as pushy.

Upstairs in his new bedroom, Mutley lay down, panting, to watch as Jax unpacked his clothes, hung up his shirts, stowed away his other belongings in the antique dresser. He set his laptop on the desk and plugged it in to charge.

That done, he sat down on the edge of the quilted bed and dispatched a brief text to his dad. Just your basic update, a "hello, I'm fine, how are you?" kind of thing. This time of day "Doc Locke," as the locals called him, would still be with his furry patients. Jax would call him later with his new—temporary—address and the phone number at the veterinary clinic.

In the meantime, since he had the afternoon free, maybe he'd go out and do some Christmas shopping. Get a look at the town in the process.

Now that he was acquainted with Mutley, who seemed a perfectly adequate canine, he was having second thoughts about presenting Charlotte with a dog. So he was back at square one when it came to buying her a Christmas gift. He'd bought gifts for his dad and various other family members online, so that was done, but he wanted to pick up a little something for Mrs. Klozz, for the vet techs and receptionist over at Nate's clinic and for Charlotte's aunt, too.

There was one problem, though.

"Hey, Mut, what do old ladies like?"

The dog unhelpfully gave a small snore, sound asleep in a stray patch of sunlight coming through the window. He opened one eye when Jax went to the door, then closed it again. Evidently, old Mutley had had all the fun he could stand for one day.

CHAPTER SIX

HADLEIGH GALLOWAY CERTAINLY hadn't changed much, Charlotte thought as she entered the quilt shop, and the bell on the door jingled. They'd seen each other last summer when their friend Bex Stuart had gotten married, but hadn't had a chance to really talk amid all the bustle of the wedding. Not to mention that Hadleigh had a newborn then, so she'd been more than a little preoccupied.

The shop looked festive with garlands along the ceilings and a wreath on the wall behind the desk. All the gorgeous quilts on display had a winter theme of pine trees or reindeer, most of them patterned in the traditional red and green, but there was a particularly lovely one in pale blue and ivory, picturing a church covered in snow.

Festive music played softly in the background.

"Charlie!" Hadleigh left her perch on the stool behind the counter and came around to hug her. "You're home for Christmas. I was hoping to see you."

Charlotte hugged her in return. "I'm home for longer than just Christmas this time. I've moved back here. Guess I'm more of a small-town girl than I thought and, anyway, Aunt Geneva needs me. Other than that, I'm not sure what I'll do next."

"We'll have a girls' night out with Melody and Bex and

catch up soon. Make the men watch the babies and kids instead of football."

"Sounds perfect." While she'd certainly made friends away from Mustang Creek, her roots were deepest here. They'd all gone to school together—she, Bex, Melody and Hadleigh.

Hadleigh's eyes sparkled. "So the new vet... What's *that* story?"

"How could you possibly—"

"Mrs. Klozz sometimes brings me suggestions for new quilt designs. Like that one." She pointed to a child-size quilt featuring a reindeer wearing a Santa hat. "She breezes in, usually with a treat, like those yummy tea cakes with white chocolate drizzle, and chats for a minute or two. She's mentioned Dr. Locke more than once. And keep in mind this is Mustang Creek, where everyone knows everything." Hadleigh stopped to take a breath. "Let's see, Bex is married to Tate Calder, and Doc Cameron is Tate's partner in the horse-breeding business. He acquired a new vet for his practice, so it was just a matter of connecting the dots. He followed you here, correct? Did I miss anything?"

Seven years away from Mustang Creek was apparently too long. "I have so much to handle right now, I can't even begin to figure out how I feel about Jax."

"Want some coffee? You can bounce your ideas off me."

"That would be great, if I *had* any ideas. I'd love a coffee, though." Charlotte chose a wing chair by a small gas fireplace that gave the shop some of its cozy ambiance. Hadleigh vanished into the back room and returned a few minutes later with two steaming mugs and a huge smile.

"I love that fancy machine Tripp bought me. Pop in one of those little pods, push a button and presto, instant anything-you-want." She sank down in the opposite chair. "So how have you been? Bring me up-to-date."

That was where they were five minutes later when Jax strolled through the door.

He was a lot of things, but deceitful wasn't one of them. Charlotte knew the look of surprise on his face was genuine. He stopped abruptly about two feet into the shop. "Oh."

"How many times in one day do I have to ask why you're somewhere I don't expect?" Charlotte teased, enjoying his discomfort just a little.

Hadleigh was hardly slow. She glanced at him, then over at Charlotte, and said with evident amusement, "Hey, call me Sherlock. By the process of elimination, I've deduced that you must be Dr. Jaxon Locke." She stood up, stretching out her hand. "Hi. I'm Hadleigh Galloway."

"Hi." He took off his cowboy hat—it looked perfectly natural on him—and stepped forward to shake Hadleigh's hand. Then he said to Charlotte, "I swear I didn't know you were here. I asked my grandmother what your aunt might want for Christmas, and she suggested a quilt. Mrs. Klozz agreed and recommended this shop."

Mrs. Klozz. Of course she'd be involved.

Charlotte sighed and pointed. "That blue one. It's beautiful and she'll love it. I was going to buy it for her, but go ahead." She was joking, actually. The quilt was one of a kind, and it was bound to be expensive. Why hadn't his grandmother suggested something more manageable, like talcum powder or fancy soap?

Hadleigh was definitely laughing. Oh, she was trying to hide it, but without success.

Jax bought the quilt, which *was* expensive, without a second's hesitation and beat it out the door pretty fast, and Charlotte had to laugh then, too. "I can't win. I walked in and took one look at that quilt and thought of Aunt Geneva. He's moved here to my hometown, into my *house* and won over the dog. By tonight, tomorrow at the latest, the cat will be all his, and you can bet he'll charm my aunt."

"He's really cute, Charlie."

No argument there. He was. And that, of course, was part of the problem.

"We don't want the same things, Hadleigh. I don't know if you remember, but we were a couple for a while when I lived in New York." At that, Hadleigh nodded vigorously. "He always seemed impressed by my job, but deep down, I have this fear that he has visions of a sweet little housewife. A woman who'll have his babies and make sure supper's ready when he gets home from work every night. And I'm nothing like that. I'm a go-to-the-office and pick-up-takeout kind of gal. He seems to have his life all sorted out, and I'm as confused as ever."

"Don't despair. It only took Tripp and me about ten years or so to come up with a plan."

"Oh, that's comforting."

It was true, though; the road to true love had been a rocky one. Tripp had barged into Hadleigh's first wedding, slung her over his shoulder and carried her out of the church to prevent her from marrying the wrong man. He'd done the right thing. But a pending divorce—his; a sense of outrage—hers; and a job out of state—his again, had all conspired to keep them apart. Until recently…

Hadleigh said, "I couldn't be happier, but both Tripp and I had to make adjustments. So Jax knows what he wants, and that's you. Now it's your turn. What do *you* want, Charlie?"

Charlotte felt philosophical. "Before this, I probably would've said I wanted Jax—but the big-city version, if you know what I mean. I think I knew all along that that wasn't going to happen. He had a great job. He made enough to pay all his student loans—and he liked New York well enough. He just didn't *love* it. Not the way I did. It was hard to imagine him living in the East indefinitely. He missed tending horses and cattle, I could tell, but he missed the West even more. He's the kind of man who needs a broad sky to look up at, and miles of space in every direction." She paused, gazing into her empty mug. "Mustang Creek will suit him."

"Does he suit you? If not, you're very picky, Charlie Morgan. He's handsome as all get-out, and he's obviously nice. Hmm, maybe if he cured cancer or wrote a best-selling novel, you'd be impressed. Come on, Charlie."

The truth was, she sometimes thought Jax suited her a little *too* well. She could lose herself in a man like that, become somebody she no longer recognized. She'd seen it happen, had watched, appalled, as smart, capable women gave up parts of themselves, one by one—shedding jobs, opinions, religions, even friends.

Especially friends.

"It isn't his problem," she admitted at last, "it's mine."

"Now we're in agreement." Hadleigh sipped her coffee. "You're scared, Charlie. Plain old *scared*. Well, here's a newsflash—love is risky. *For everybody.* It's also worth taking a chance on." She reached over, patted Charlotte's hand. "Let's sum up here. He's in love with you and you're in love with him. You're living in the same house, but Mrs. Klozz is living there, too, so what can possibly happen?" Maybe the next statement made sense to Hadleigh, but it sailed right over Charlotte's head. "It's still two days before Christmas. I think you should go skiing."

"What? Skiing?"

Hadleigh pointed toward the mountains. "See those? That's where you go skiing. You strap those wooden things to your feet—"

"I know what skiing is." Charlotte had to laugh. "Do me a favor. Explain *why* we should go skiing."

Hadleigh got up and came back with a set of keys. "It's too late to go today, but tomorrow would be good. There's all this romantic snow, and Tripp and I have a condo up in the Tetons. Don't ask, it's some sort of corporate thing left over from when he owned the charter jet service. Anyway, I refuse to lurch down the slopes with a baby strapped to my chest, and we haven't even used the place this season. Maybe the two of you could go there and talk."

Talk. Right. Charlotte was fairly sure they'd just fall into each other's arms and not leave that condo, never even set foot—or ski—on the slopes.

She took the keys. Slowly, but she took them. "Thanks. I don't know how much talking we'll do. Jax doesn't officially start his new job until Christmas Eve, and I'm currently unemployed. And while this may well be the worst idea on earth, I might eat my weight in pastries hanging out with Mrs. Klozz. A little exercise couldn't hurt."

"There's no better exercise." Hadleigh twinkled.

Charlotte said drily, "Are we still talking about skiing?"

"Uh-huh." Hadleigh took another sip of coffee, did her level best to look innocent and failed completely.

AT SUPPER TIME, Mrs. Klozz—*Millicent*—served a pot roast that would make his grandmother's famous recipe fade into the recesses of culinary history, which meant he was never going to mention it to her, and he had three helpings of the mashed potatoes.

Forget Charlie. He might just go ahead and propose to Mrs. Klozz. She was a bit old for him, but still...

"That was better than good," he told her, when he was finally full. "I think I'm on a food high." Both Charlotte and Millicent scooted back their chairs to rise, but he stopped them. "No, no, stay where you are. I'll clean up. Least I can do."

"You're a very sweet young man." Mrs. Klozz relinquished the plate she'd picked up.

Sweet? Not so much. This was an act of self-preservation; he needed to move around before he fell over. He was used to grabbing a sandwich and calling that dinner.

Charlotte ignored his offer, took the plates from his hands and walked to the sink. "Way to suck up, you *sweet young man*, you."

He couldn't help watching the sway of her hips. Those feminine curves really did it for him. "I meant what I said. Let me do the dishes."

"We'll do them together. Anyway, you don't know where everything goes. I'll dry."

He relented, but only because he liked the idea of standing next to Charlie. "That's fair."

As he washed the dishes, she asked unexpectedly, "Do you ski?"

"I'm from Idaho." He rinsed a glass and handed it over. "Yes, I ski. Can't remember when I didn't. My dad taught me, probably as soon as I could walk. He still loves the slopes, but he's been told to lay off since his heart attack. Why?"

She hesitated.

Jax waited with slightly lifted brows.

"Oh, hell, here goes," Charlie said, her eyes reflecting uncertainty. Then the words tumbled from her lips in a breathless rush. "I have friends who offered to lend me their condo near a resort. You met Hadleigh this afternoon. She and her husband, Tripp, have a new baby and haven't had a chance to use the place this season. I wondered if you wanted to go up there with me tomorrow. I've checked the forecast on my phone. It's supposed to be just like today, cold with intermittent snow flurries. If you have other plans—"

"I'd love to," he interrupted swiftly, unable to stifle a smile, but trying not to look too elated.

A secluded night with her after a day on the slopes? *Early Christmas present for sure. Thanks, Saint Nick.*

"I'm a little rusty," Charlie continued with uncharacteristic shyness. "I went skiing a few times in upstate New York with friends, but it's been several years." She put away another dish, keeping her face averted. Was she blushing? God, he hoped so, because that would mean she knew what he was thinking, might even be thinking the same thing herself. "And I'll have to dig out my skis from the basement. You can rent equipment at the lodge."

"Are you kidding? Do you suppose I'd come to a place

like this, right by the mountains, and not bring mine? They're in the back of my truck. My poles and boots, too."

"There's a nice restaurant at the lodge. Maybe we can have dinner there unless it's completely booked, which is possible, with the holiday rush. I'll call and check. The food won't be as good as it is here... What did she put in those potatoes?"

"I have no idea," Jax replied, wiping off the gravy boat carefully; it was obviously antique—Spode, he saw, turning it over—and probably irreplaceable. "She must've waved a magic wand over them or something. How long has she known your aunt?"

"I asked, and Aunt Geneva was pretty vague about it."

He wasn't quite sure what to say, so he thought about it before asking neutrally, "Was she vague in general?"

"No." Charlotte's voice was firm but held a hint of sorrow. "Smart as a whip, to use an expression of hers. But she's aware that she's having some issues in the memory department, and she can't manage this big house. That I understand. I think she's happy to be in a community of people like her, and it's a comfortable place. She'd love to have Mutley and Can-Can there with her, but she's afraid she won't be able to take proper care of them. I guess it makes her feel better to know that someone else—Mrs. Klozz, and now me—is on it, and that eases her mind."

Now me. Jax hoped that offhand phrase meant Charlotte intended to stay in Mustang Creek, that she hadn't changed her mind. However, it could just as easily be interpreted as *for now me.*

Well, they'd see, wouldn't they?

Maybe this ski excursion would be a turning point. Back in New York she'd been confident and settled in the electric life of that city. Now he sensed a new vulnerability in her, one he understood well. When he'd gotten the call that his father was in the hospital, recovering from a near-fatal heart attack, *his* world had certainly changed.

His first priority had been to go home.

He understood her current dilemma, too; it wasn't easy, juggling your own responsibilities and the needs of an ailing loved one. Plus, it was tough to admit that someone who'd cared for you all your life was no longer the same strong person you'd come to depend on.

"I'm anxious to meet your aunt." He touched Charlie's shoulder, then dropped his hand. His sudden reappearance in her life probably wasn't helping the situation, but in his own defense, he would've been an idiot not to take the job with Nate, not to accept Mrs. Klozz's unauthorized invitation.

And what about the ski trip? He certainly hadn't orchestrated that.

"She's going to love that gorgeous quilt," Charlotte said. "As I mentioned earlier, I sort of had my eye on that as a gift for her myself. Luckily, she's not hard to shop for. I bought her a sweater and a new pair of slippers in a boutique down the street from Hadleigh's." She looked away for a moment, then added quietly, "It was nice of you to think of her. She'll be so pleased. She'll also give you a lecture for spending too much money."

He let the money reference pass. He wasn't rich, didn't even aspire to be, but he'd always had enough. "I'd like to think I'm a nice guy," he said immodestly. "Besides, I have a thing for her niece." Now, *there* was an understatement. "Um, any thoughts about a gift for Mrs. Klozz? I'm stumped there. I'd buy her a new cake pan, but that seems a little self-serving."

Charlotte laughed. "Maybe a little. My friend Melody makes the most gorgeous jewelry, and she'll have some pieces with a Christmas theme. I'll call her to see if we can stop by the ranch and look at what she's got."

"No man in his right mind would turn down that kind of help." He took the last glass from her and put it away, closing the cupboard. "If you want a power tool or a chisel or something like that, I can help out. Otherwise I need major assistance."

"I doubt that Mrs. Klozz would appreciate a chisel."

"There you go. I'm hopeless."

Not quite true. A skiing trip with Charlotte? He was hope*ful*.

CHAPTER SEVEN

CHARLOTTE HAD JUST packed a small suitcase for the trip. She was latching it shut when Melody Nolan—no, it was Melody Hogan now—returned her call. "Mel, thanks for getting back to me so quickly. And happy holidays, by the way. How are Spence and little Delilah?"

She loved that name.

"We're all fine—and I'm so glad you're home, Charlie. According to Hadleigh, the four of us are getting together after Christmas. I can't wait to see you again."

"Me neither, but I was wondering if you could help us out—I mean, help me out—with a gift suggestion or two. Do you have anything on hand for a sweet older lady, probably in her seventies?"

"Uh, let's see. I do have some ornaments that are hand painted. Christmas village, North Pole and all that. I was going to do brooches, but the design got away from me, which happens sometimes, so I decided to make them bigger. How about one of those?"

An ornament on their tree for Mrs. Klozz. Perfect. "That's a huge help. Can Jax and I come over?"

"Absolutely. Jax? I've heard about him."

Of course she had. Hadleigh kept no secrets from Mel as far as she knew. Their friendship was as strong now as it'd been when they were six years old. "We're going skiing."

"Knew that, too."

Charlotte laughed. "We'll be by in a few."

"Delilah's sleeping, but at this point, I can still vacuum under her bed and she doesn't wake up. I'm told that'll change soon, and then start again when she hits puberty."

"My aunt never allowed sleeping in, even on Saturday mornings," Charlotte said. "So I wouldn't know. It used to kill me if there was a football game the night before or I'd been out on a date. Of course, I had a strict curfew, too. Served me well in college. I got up early to study when it was quiet and skipped the frat parties because by the time they got started, I was ready to sleep. Kept me out of trouble."

"Good parenting advice. Keep it coming. Maybe I should go visit your aunt and see what other tidbits she can toss my way. Dee's still an infant, and Spence is already talking about what kind of car we should buy her when she gets her license. Can you say spoiled rotten?"

"Aunt Geneva would love to see you. Me, too. It's been a while."

"Too long," Melody said warmly. "Word of warning, Harley will run up barking his head off when you pull in, but your only danger is he might love you to death."

Harley, needless to say, was the Hogan family dog.

When the call ended, Charlotte took mental inventory of what she'd packed. Toothbrush, small cosmetic bag, change of clothes for after the slopes, several pairs of wooly socks, cozy robe, gloves, hat, boots...

Pajamas? Almost an oops there. Would she need them? And if so, what kind? Casual or more feminine? Maybe she'd been subconsciously putting that decision off. She had no illusions about the outcome Jax was hoping for after a romantic evening in a ski condo. She didn't want to inflate his ego by confessing there'd been no one since him, and darned few before him, even if she was thirty. She'd never viewed sex as a casual thing, and she wasn't looking at it that way now.

So her kitty pajama pants and a T-shirt, or...something slinky and feminine? In the end, she packed both. The final decision could be made later.

She met Jax on the stairs, her suitcase in tow, and he took it from her. "Dog's been walked—again—and sidewalk cleared," he informed her, his smile surfacing. He hefted the bag. "I think I packed about a third of what you did, but that seems to be how it goes—a male vs. female thing. You got thirteen pairs of shoes in here?"

She sent him a scathing look. "No, I do not. I talked to Mel and we might be in luck, in terms of our gift dilemma. On the downside, I emailed the restaurant and they're booked solid. We'll have to improvise on that one."

He let her go past him on the stairs. "I can whip something up. Just give me a loaf of white bread, peanut butter and a jar of jelly, and I'll take it from there."

"I can do better than that," Charlotte said archly.

Truthfully, though, after seven years in a place that had every sort of fabulous restaurant on earth, and living alone for so long, she'd lost interest in cooking ages ago. Besides, it was lonely making one meal, setting a single place at the table.

But maybe cooking was like riding a bike—once you knew how, you never really forgot.

She was still thinking that lavishly optimistic thought

when Mrs. Klozz hurried out of the kitchen, lugging an elaborate cooler.

Jax put down Charlotte's suitcase—his own must be in the truck—and took the cooler from her.

Ignoring his concern, Millicent announced, "Here you go. I was up early, and since you couldn't get restaurant reservations, I threw together a few things for your trip. Just put the casserole in the oven, 350 degrees, for thirty minutes. The bread is fresh, and that vegetable salad is a secret family recipe, so don't ask me to list the ingredients, because every female ancestor of mine would roll over in her grave if I breathed a word."

Charlotte was speechless. More than that, dazed.

Exactly how had Mrs. Klozz known that the lodge restaurant was completely booked?

Despite the cooler in his arms, Jax managed to plant an appreciative kiss on the older woman's cheek. "That was very thoughtful of you," he said. "Thanks."

Millicent winked at Charlotte. "My pleasure. Have a good time."

When everything was loaded in the truck, Charlotte slid into the passenger seat. "She's matchmaking."

Jax, looking incredible in a dark blue ski jacket, smiled at her. "Ya think?" He closed her door and went around to climb in and start the vehicle. "Directions to the Hogans' ranch, please."

"I can do that." She fastened her seat belt. "Take a left on Main."

As they traveled out of town, Charlotte asked, "How did she know that?"

"Know what?"

"That there were no reservations at the restaurant."

"I assumed you told her."

"No."

He sent her a quick glance. "You do realize that our Millicent reads minds? Either that or she simply made an educated guess that, with the holidays practically on top of us, the restaurant might be booked up."

No doubt he was right about the educated guess. And she definitely agreed that Millicent Klozz was a mind reader. "Still—"

Jax shrugged. "Look on the bright side. We can ski all day, and you don't have to cook."

That was a valid point. The weather was excellent, too, cold and crisp. Charlotte nodded. "Works for me. I'm sure everything she made will be delicious."

"Me, too. But whatever you had in mind for dinner would probably be—"

"Not half as good." She knew it and he knew it, too.

"I never said that."

Charlotte made a face at him. "Turn at the next light and follow the highway."

He grinned. "Yes, ma'am."

She gave up on the cooking and let herself feel relieved that she wouldn't have to do it. She was decent, but she wasn't in Mrs. Klozz's league.

And that was okay.

CHARLOTTE'S FRIEND MELODY HOGAN turned out to be a beautiful, slender blonde with a baby in her arms. She greeted Jax and Charlie at the door, smiling, and, after introductions and a breathless mutual fuss over the infant, Melody led her guests toward her studio.

The rooms they passed through were simple and they

were decorated, not surprisingly, with artistic flair. The place could only be described as impressive, and the view from several large windows was magnificent.

So were the Christmas ornaments they'd come to see.

Made from porcelain, they were hand painted and exquisite, tied with silk ribbons for hanging, and if he was any judge, Mrs. Klozz would love any or all of them, but the one Charlotte selected was a cottage in the woods with drifts of snow up to the windows and an elf walking up the path, bright lights in the windows.

"That's the one I'd choose," he assured her.

"It's almost magical," Charlotte mused. "Oh, Melody, this is so beautiful. You are *so* talented!"

Melody looked pleased, even a little shy. "It was inspired by an old Swedish print I ran across somewhere."

Jax selected a second ornament, this one an oval picture of a decorated tree with snow falling and two deer walking past—truly a work of art.

The baby, meanwhile, began to gurgle and squirm a little in Melody's arms. "Maybe I could hold her," Jax offered, having already extracted a credit card from his wallet. "While you finish up the transaction?"

Melody smiled and immediately handed over the wiggle worm. "Thanks."

He cradled the child carefully, looking up to see Charlotte watching him.

"You're a natural," she observed, her tone pensive.

Jax felt his heart swell slightly. "I've had lots of practice," he explained. "All my cousins have kids. Fact is, I'm not sure how I'll recognize a Christmas with no kids knocking over their milk, having meltdown tantrums about something or eating mashed potatoes with their hands."

Charlotte's eyes held a soft light, lingering on him and the baby. She had a crocheted cap on again, this time in red, and her dark, gleaming hair spilled out of it, curly and thick. "If it helps," she said with a grin, "I've been known to knock over my wineglass. Probably can't do anything about the tantrum or mashed potatoes part of it, though." Another grin. "Well, maybe the tantrum."

He laughed, wishing that particular moment could last.

He noticed that Melody, who'd been busy tallying and wrapping, was smiling to herself. She'd missed nothing and obviously drawn some conclusions of her own. Receipts were signed, the cards returned to their respective owners and then Melody took the baby from Jax. The small, decorative shopping bag had been placed in Charlie's custody.

"Enjoy," Melody said, with a nod toward the bag.

Charlotte hugged her. "Mrs. Klozz is going to love these. Thank you."

Melody arched one eyebrow. "Mrs. Claus?"

"'Tis the season," Charlie said, amused. "But no, it's Klozz with a *K* and two *Z*s."

The child was straining toward Jax by then, both arms out. Melody kissed her curly head and chuckled. "She likes you," she told Jax. "I'm not going to be the one to tell Spence his baby girl has a new favorite man." Melody made a shooing motion with one hand. "Go forth and conquer the slopes, and have a wonderful evening, too."

Jax saw the knowing look Melody sent Charlie's way. As they walked back to his truck, he asked in amusement, "Is there such a thing as a secret in this town?"

"Nope. It's probably just like the town you grew up in over in Idaho. Get used to it, Dr. Locke."

"Our ski trip is a matter for local gossip, then?" He opened her door.

"Count on it." She climbed in.

"Then, I hope to make our excursion gossip-worthy."

Maybe if he hadn't shut the door, she would've had some comeback for him. Moments later they were headed toward the mountains.

The drive was picturesque, the roads lined with stately pines and Douglas fir, their branches laden with snow. The aspen trees were barren this time of year, but still graceful. They spotted two elk that stopped and gazed at them as they passed, and Charlotte sighed. "I can't believe I ever left this place."

Jax wanted to say he couldn't, either, but instead decided to be tactful. "There's a lot to be said for the city. Convenience. Excitement, that special energy, bright lights—all the shopping and food. A lot of people obviously prefer those things to country roads and wildlife."

"But not you." Was that sadness he heard in her voice?

"No," he answered. "Not me." The roads were slick and he slowed down to negotiate a curve. "It's part of me."

He wasn't inflexible, he thought, but he only had this one life to live, and he didn't want to be miserable. He visited big cities, enjoyed them in small doses.

But he *lived* in places like this.

Charlotte had grown wistful. It was as though, for once, she'd lowered her defenses. "I have no idea what I'm going to do next. I know my time with Aunt Geneva is limited, but my choices here in Mustang Creek are, too." She rubbed her forehead. She was wearing red mittens to match her hat. The way she wore whatever her aunt cro-cheted for her was pretty cute.

Maybe her options weren't as limited as she seemed to think.

Tread lightly, buddy, warned a voice in his mind. *This is delicate ground.*

He was so sure of what he wanted—Charlie and the life they'd make together—but convincing a very inde-pendent, successful woman to let herself be taken care of, even a little, would be tricky.

He knew she wanted a career, and he had no problem with that—her quick mind and inborn ambition were part of who she was, after all, the way country life was part of him. But when it came to job opportunities in her line of work, she was right.

Mustang Creek wasn't exactly the advertising hub of the Western Hemisphere.

No, that was New York.

"Ever thought of opening a bed-and-breakfast?" he blurted, as surprised by the outburst as Charlie probably was. "You've got a big house. You'd have the summer season, that's popular with tourists, and then the winter crowd, for skiing and snowboarding and all that." *Where* was this coming from? Oh, yes, Mrs. K. had made some comment about how the place could be turned into a B and B; she must've planted the idea. Intentionally? Who knew? "If you could hire Mrs. Klozz to do the cooking," he added, "you'd have a shot at a four-star rating."

Charlie stared at him as if he'd lost his mind—and he wasn't entirely sure he hadn't. "Jax, the place needs to be remodeled," she pointed out. "*Extensively*, from top to bottom. Besides, inn keeping isn't part of my skill-set. I created advertising campaigns, handled brand management, stuff like that, remember? I wouldn't know how to decorate or—"

"Melody would. Know how to decorate, I mean. Besides, your skills would help you promote the business, wouldn't they?"

He'd scored a point there, he could see that. Two points. She even nodded.

But then she slouched down in her seat and shook her head. "I can't."

He'd never learned when to shut up. "This town doesn't have enough decent hotels. Didn't you tell me your friend Bex's husband arranges trail rides because he raises horses? You could set up a summer package that includes riding."

"Tate? Yes, he does, *sometimes*. Now, would you cut that out? I hereby order you to stop putting impossible ideas in my head."

"Impossible?" Jax retorted. "As long as I've known you, Charlie, I don't think I've ever heard you use that word."

Wow. Good one, Locke.

And he was just getting started. If he wanted to spend the rest of his natural life with Charlie, he had to get things moving.

But carefully.

She folded her arms, and her head was set at a stubborn angle. "Well," she said, "now you've heard me say it. Impossible. Impossible, impossible, *impossible...*"

"You can stop that anytime now," Jax said.

"I'll stop when *you* stop."

He could barely keep a straight face. "Stop what?"

She punched him in the shoulder, hard, and then

laughed. "This isn't exactly an adult conversation, is it?" she asked.

He grinned. "Have we had one of those recently?"

"Not that I can recall."

"Hmm."

"The fact remains that I know nothing about running a small business."

"No, your expertise is running *big* ones."

"It's not the same."

"It *is* the same, Charlie. It's just a matter of scale." He watched out of the corner of his eye while she digested that. "You could pick Hadleigh's brain—she's been pretty successful, right? And what about Bex? Doesn't she qualify as an expert with all those fitness centers? And then there's Melody—"

Charlotte groaned. "You should've been a lawyer. Or, better yet, a politician."

"God forbid," Jax said with conviction.

It lightened the moment. She gave a sputtering little giggle.

Jax picked up the proverbial ball and ran with it. "You could put brochures in all the rooms, advertise Hadleigh's quilt shop, Bex's gyms, Melody's jewelry and other artwork. Quadruple win."

"Stop."

"I can't."

"Obviously."

"You could offer dinner on the weekends, too. Mrs. Klozz suggested that."

Charlie sat up very straight, as if she'd backed into the business end of a cattle prod. "You've been discussing this with Millicent?"

"It would be more accurate to say she's been discussing it with me. She's a fast talker, that woman."

"I'm surprised she managed to get a word in edgewise."

"Very funny, Charlie."

"I thought so," she replied. "And the subject is closed." With that pronouncement, she turned her head to stare out her window.

Jax smiled. She was thinking it over.

And that was good.

CHAPTER EIGHT

PREDICTABLY, TRIPP AND HADLEIGH'S condo was a charming second-story unit with a view of the chairlift and lodge, and its own balcony. The enormous kitchen boasted granite countertops and stainless-steel appliances, and spiffy travertine tile on the floor. The furniture throughout was modern with sleek lines. The bed was king-size, graced with one of Hadleigh's artistic quilts, a museum-quality piece with an appliquéd mountain scene, and there were his-and-hers closets. Not to mention his-and-hers bathrooms.

Charlotte found herself thinking about quilts. Patchwork. Log Cabin. Wedding Ring.

Well, maybe not Wedding Ring.

They'd strike just the right note, colorful and cozy, in a bed-and-breakfast.

Not that she was seriously considering Jax's idea about turning Aunt Geneva's lovely old house into anything of the kind.

That would be downright reckless, from a financial standpoint. A new roof, already in the forecast, was merely the beginning. Each of the bedrooms would need its own bath, and it would be only sensible to put in an elevator, in order to accommodate elderly guests or people with disabilities.

"Nice place." Jax set Charlotte's bag by one of the closets, snapping her out of the B and B fantasy. It was something of a jolt.

As fancy as the condo was, there was just one bedroom.

Well, they'd managed all right at the hotel the other night.

Except they'd had two beds.

Might as well go straight to the heart of the matter.

"I haven't decided yet if I'm going to sleep with you," Charlotte informed him.

"You mean you haven't decided if we're going to *make love*," he said. "That's up to you. However, you're definitely going to sleep with me, because this appears to be the only available bed."

Charlotte felt a rush of heat, but tried not to let on. "There's a couch."

"Yes, I noticed. It's big, it's cushy and it's as white as the powder on the ski slope. I don't think it's meant for sitting on, never mind sleeping on."

He was right, of course. When Hadleigh and Tripp visited the condo, they probably didn't spend a lot of time sitting around in the living room, admiring the view, as beautiful as it was.

They'd be skiing.

Or making use of the bed.

Charlotte felt an unmistakable tingle. That bed was the size of a farm field, but it didn't mean she and Jax wouldn't collide.

Hadleigh hadn't mentioned the limited sleeping arrangements.

Imagine that.

Jax chuckled, apparently reading her mind. Or maybe

it was her body language. "Must be fate, the way we keep winding up in this situation."

"Fate?" Charlotte fussed. "Or plain bad luck?"

He rested his hands on her shoulders, drew her a little closer. "Relax," he said. Where had she heard *that* before? "Do I want to make love to you?" His voice dropped. "Yes, I do. I don't think that's any big secret. I moved to Wyoming from Idaho, which isn't like crossing the street. And I did it because of you. I want you as much as I ever did, maybe more, but the fact remains, Charlie—it's your call. Unless you say the word, nothing's going to happen between us, whether we're sharing a bed or not."

Jax wasn't the only painfully honest person in this equation. Charlotte sank to the edge of the three-acre bed and sent him a reproachful look. "You must know I've been thinking of practically nothing *but* sex ever since the other night."

His grin was quick and easy. "I had my suspicions," he said.

She flopped backward on the bed to stare up at the ceiling. The mattress was unbelievably comfortable. Naturally. "The timing for us, for getting involved again, is terrible, Jax. The house, my aunt, no job, the fact that I'm going to have to start my life over. I don't trust myself, either. I thought I wanted a high-profile job in a big city. I liked that life while I had it, and yet…it wasn't enough. I can see that now. I almost killed myself in college getting that MBA so I'd graduate at the top of my class. It isn't going to do me a whole lot of good in Mustang Creek. Neither will my experience organizing major advertising campaigns for national brands. Here, it all seems… irrelevant."

Based on what he'd said earlier, she knew he didn't agree, but at least he had the grace not to argue. "Let's change clothes, get out there and do some skiing. This condo is fabulous, the powder is wonderful according to the news and you don't have to make every decision right this minute."

She'd already made a radical one—by inviting him on this little trip in the first place.

So who was she trying to kid here?

Herself, obviously.

"You're right," she said. Then she stood up, pulled off her sweater, tossed it on the floor and started to unfasten her jeans. "Can we put off skiing for a little while?"

The look on Jax's face was priceless.

For a moment he seemed paralyzed.

It really was funny.

But then her practical side kicked in. Sort of.

She froze. "Oh, no," she said.

Jax's eyes widened. "What do you mean, *oh, no*?" he demanded, his voice husky.

She managed not to laugh. "Please say you brought condoms."

His relief was billboard obvious. "Yes." His voice was more of a rasp. His blue eyes were intent. "I wasn't going to make that mistake again." He was quiet for a moment. "Charlie, are we talking about *now*?"

She unfastened her bra, baring her breasts as it slipped off. "Is this a bad time for you?"

"Hell, no." Jax's gaze was riveted south of her face. He pulled his shirt off over his head after unfastening only a few buttons. His boots went next, then his jeans, then—

When he joined her on the bed she was naked and ready, and so was he.

He held her, nuzzled the sensitive skin beneath her ear, his breath warm on her neck. "Charlie," he murmured.

She put a finger to his lips. "Shh," she said. "We always get into trouble when we talk. Let's just *do*, okay?"

His reply was a rumbled, "Okay."

So they did.

Charlotte watched him rip open a foil packet, then allowed her eyes to drift shut, giving herself up to sensation, to the moment, to him.

He gave her the pleasure she not only wanted but also needed, in long, smooth strokes, in tender touches and soft words, until she trembled in his arms and wished for one insane second that she hadn't insisted on a condom.

The thought was soon lost in a torrent of mounting passion, each shared breath, each motion of their joined bodies more exquisite than the last.

When Charlotte climaxed, she cried out, the sound guttural and exultant, and Jax's surrender was simultaneous.

After what seemed like a very long time, they finished, and lay still, breathing audibly and in perfect sequence, their bodies entwined so closely that she could feel his heart racing. Or was it hers?

Once they'd recovered a little, Jax was the first to speak, lifting his head, his eyes alight with humor and the sultry aftermath of release. "Charlie, I've missed you."

In reply, she put her hands on either side of his face and kissed him, hard and deep. It would be easy to suggest they skip the skiing altogether and spend the afternoon in bed, but she was well aware that she was sifting through some complicated emotions, and she held back the words. Instead, she ran a fingertip down his nose in a playful caress. "I'm so glad. Because, in case you haven't noticed, I've missed you, too."

He considered that for so long, she thought he was about to tell her he loved her.

Instead, he said, "We need to make a pact." He was braced on his elbows, gazing down at her.

"Okay." She spoke cautiously.

"I've been pushing you, Charlie, and I'm sorry." He kissed her shoulder. "The truth is, we both need a chance to relax, to learn about each other again, so let's keep it simple and not talk about the future—or worry about it, either. That'll be our Christmas gift to each other."

It was the reprieve she needed, although a part of her wanted a declaration of love, a proposal, a lifelong promise. And *now*, damn it.

But she knew he was right. "Good idea," she said.

He nibbled at her lower lip, arousing her all over again.

How, she wondered, had she ever managed to resist him?

She brushed a lock of his hair behind his ear. "You need a haircut."

"Do I?"

He drew her down, pulled her against him. And then they made love again, slowly this time, sweetly.

"I have to be honest," he told her, much later, when they were getting ready for the slopes. Starving, they'd raided the cooler they'd brought from home. "I might be in love with Mrs. Klozz," he teased. "That casserole could be the deciding factor in who I choose. Do you have any clue what's in it?"

"None," she said.

"And that bread."

"Yeah," Charlotte agreed. "The bread."

He lowered his voice. "You have some tough competition."

"I happen to have a few advantages of my own," she reminded him.

They were sitting at the kitchen table, and Jax reached over, tugged Charlotte out of her chair and onto his lap.

It was immediately apparent that he wanted her.

Again.

Which was fine, because she wanted *him*, too.

The perfect powder out there on the ski trails would just have to wait.

OH, YEAH, HE was going to sleep tonight.

First a long afternoon of making love to the woman of his dreams, then a few hours of downhill under floodlights, on some challenging trails—now, at least, they could say they'd actually skied—followed by a spiked hot chocolate at the lodge bar to take the edge off the winter chill.

Here he was, showered and dressed and standing in the condo's spectacular kitchen, pouring wine into two glasses as the most fantastic aroma wafted from the oven.

It had been one of the best days of his life—so far.

"What's in that?" He pointed at the casserole as he handed Charlotte a glass of merlot. Since Mrs. Klozz had packed enough food to last for two weeks, they hadn't broken into the casserole yet. "I don't think I'll even need to eat it—I'm getting full on the smell alone."

Charlotte's eyes sparkled and she looked delectable in the kitty pajama pants and a pink T-shirt. "I know.

It seems to be some sort of chicken stew, and Millicent tucked in written instructions. We're supposed to drop biscuits on top at a certain point in the baking process. I almost hate to tell you this, because I'm not positive I want to share, but there are brownies, too, and they did not come out of a box."

"Brownies?" he repeated with a mock groan. "I'm going to have to go to the gym about fourteen times next week."

Charlotte sipped her wine and leaned against the counter. "I'm afraid Millicent might grab the lead in the romance race once you taste that casserole," she joked.

He was glad Charlotte seemed easier, less tense, maybe even comfortable, with her decision to give in to the attraction between them. He understood about crossroads; he'd recently been there himself. Once you made the decision to take a certain path, forward was the only way you could go, because life was too short for much backpedaling. Everyone had regrets now and then; it was inevitable. But he didn't intend to be one of hers.

"I have a big heart," he said magnanimously. "I think I can love you both."

"Glad to hear it," she responded with a laugh. "The casserole does smell good, doesn't it? We have another twenty minutes according to her instructions. Sit by the fire?"

There was a gas fireplace in the living room, and through the glass doors the Christmas lights of the lodge were visible, twinkling in the distance, reflecting on the snow. He was pleasantly mellow from physical exercise and the glass of wine in his hand.

It was only by the grace of whatever powers controlled the universe that Charlotte's cell phone rang, or he might have yielded to the impulse and proposed marriage on the spot, never mind all that talk about giving themselves the gift of time and space.

She answered the call.

Apparently, the caller was Charlie's aunt. He tried not to listen while they discussed their plans for Christmas Eve, but it was hard without leaving the room.

When he tried, Charlie reached out, pinching his shirt-sleeve, and shaking her head. Mouthed the word *stay*.

So he stayed. His name didn't come up, but he was going to be busy tomorrow night anyway. He understood, and yet it stung.

After Charlotte ended the call, he asked as casually as possible, "Big plans?"

Charlotte threw him a look. "You know you're invited. I believe you live at our house now."

"Does your aunt even realize I exist?"

"My aunt? Sure. I've mentioned you."

"I'm glad I'm worthy of a mention, at least." He didn't know why he was being snarky; it wasn't like him. And it didn't feel good.

"Interesting to see a grown man sulk." Charlotte leaned back in her chair, her expression amused. "She's bound to love you as much as Mrs. Klozz does, so you don't need to worry. Charming young men always impress sweet old ladies."

"First of all, I wasn't aware I was charming."

"Not all the time, certainly." She gave him a saucy little smile. "But mostly."

He chose to ignore that. "Second, I wasn't sure whether you'd told her about our previous relationship."

The fire, visible through the wide archway between the

kitchen and the living room, was romantic, and the place was redolent with the aroma of the casserole warming in the oven. Jax was surprised all the neighbors weren't pounding on the door demanding a taste of it.

Charlotte didn't comment immediately, but after a few minutes, she said quietly, "I told her I'd met the right man at the wrong time. She understood. Aunt Geneva never got married, but she said she'd once met the right man, too. I get the impression he might've been married to someone else. There's a story there, although she hasn't told it to me. I'll probably never know. I figured if she'd wanted to explain, she would have, so I didn't ask."

The right man. He liked the sound of that.

Once more, he was tempted just to go ahead and ask her to marry him. Looking past her shoulder, Jax considered the flames. *Whoa*, he told himself. He only planned to propose marriage once in his life, and he wasn't going to jump the gun, risk spoiling everything. Especially after suggesting they take things slow.

"More wine?" he asked instead.

"I'll have some with dinner."

On cue, the buzzer on the oven dinged. He practically jumped to his feet. "You get the food and I'll set the table. Deal?"

"The way to a man's heart. Oh, the wisdom of the ages—and Mrs. K."

His smile was deliberate. "You don't need to find your way into my heart," he said. "You're already there."

Easy now.

Clearly, Charlie had no idea how to respond, but she didn't seem put off.

Rummaging around, Jax found quilted place mats—

Hadleigh's touch, of course—in one of the drawers. Then, with a little searching, he located plates and cutlery, too.

Place mats, no less.

His father, a widower since Jax was barely two, had been casual about things like place settings. Their meals, while ample and certainly healthy, were catch-as-catch-can affairs. That was the life of a country vet; often his dad had to leave the house at a moment's notice, climb into his battered truck, drive off and tend to some emergency.

Over the years, Jax had a girlfriend or two who'd been picky about what side of the plate the fork went on, but by and large, he'd always figured that having everything there, all the necessary plates and utensils, was good enough.

The dish Charlotte took from the oven turned out to be even more delicious than its aroma had promised, which hardly seemed possible.

As a man who was holding back a proposal, Jax did his best to not eat too fast, a clear indication of poor table manners, but Charlie seemed to be keeping pace. The creamy sauce and tender chicken were balanced by the flaky biscuits, but the brownies eclipsed all expectations.

And things just kept getting better from there.

CHAPTER NINE

CHRISTMAS EVE STARTED with light snow and a gentle wind tossing up white swirls. Charlotte woke to the solid weight of a male body next to hers, Jax's breathing gentle in her ear, one of his strong arms curved around her waist. The fairy-tale evening was over, she thought as she watched the flakes float down outside the balcony doors, the breeze building small drifts against the glass.

She was grateful for that one special evening, although Hadleigh and Mrs. Klozz had been the elves who'd delivered at least part of the magic.

Beautiful surroundings, wonderful food, great conversation...*and* fantastic sex, she added wryly. She was probably an idiot, because unless she sorted out what she was going to do next, this Christmas gift to herself could end up being a huge mistake. Until she saw the lawyer, she'd have no clue about the state of her aunt's finances, and paying the taxes and utilities on the house, plus the assisted-living place, might require moving to someplace like Los Angeles, Denver or Chicago. Someplace she could get a job...

It might be possible to work from home, perhaps as a consultant, but it wouldn't be nearly as lucrative and she'd have to build a client base on her own. That would likely involve small businesses, and it would take a while.

And then there was Mrs. Klozz. Had Aunt Geneva been paying the woman a salary? Or was the woman simply an old friend, someone Charlie had never met or even heard of? Or—another possibility—was Aunt Geneva the one doing a favor for a friend?

What if Mrs. Klozz was helping out because she needed a place to stay?

If that was the case, Charlotte might find herself with *two* elderly dependents instead of one. After all, she couldn't just toss poor Millicent out into the street, especially after the way she'd helped Aunt Geneva and taken care of Can-Can and Mutley.

"Hmm, good morning." Jax stirred and stretched, looking boyishly sleepy. "Sleep well?"

She was sore, thanks both to him and to skiing for the first time in a very long while, but yes, she'd slept very well. "I did."

"There's nothing like waking up next to a beautiful woman." He touched her shoulder, trailing his finger along her collarbone. "Even better when that beautiful woman's naked."

"Happen to you often?"

"The last time was in New York. I think her initials were C.M."

"Smooth, Dr. Locke."

"I try. What a pretty morning. Appropriate to the holiday."

Good pillow talk, but Jax had never failed in that department. His major flaw—and she conceded *she* had her share of flaws, too—was that he was too much of a romantic. He wanted a simple life, a big family, and she suspected she might come around to his way of thinking sooner or later.

He was living in the same house, and now they were sleeping together again, although she couldn't let that continue once they were home, not with Mrs. Klozz in residence. And it went without saying that Aunt Geneva wouldn't approve.

Charlotte sighed. To Jax, life was straightforward, and decisions were clear-cut.

Her life was a lot more complicated. An elderly aunt who'd selflessly cared for her, given her a childhood, an education and all the unconditional love anyone could ask for. An elderly aunt who was slowly slipping away.

Her life was losing a job she'd been proud of and inheriting an old house she probably wouldn't be able to keep but couldn't bear to part with. It was moving back home because every plan she'd made for herself had fallen through all at once.

Life was falling in love with a handsome veterinarian but not being certain that they wouldn't end up going their separate ways—just like last time.

How would she stand that?

Jax propped himself up on the pillows. "It isn't?"

Charlotte was momentarily at a loss. Then she remembered. He'd been saying how pretty the morning was.

"It's beautiful," she agreed, wondering if her hair looked halfway decent and guessing it was a disaster. "I'll find my robe and make us some coffee."

Hadleigh's kitchen had one of those instant-gratification machines, like the one at her shop. They took less than a minute, and a person could choose almost any conceivable flavor from a variety of single servings. Charlotte's was still packed away in storage, with her books, furniture and many of her other belongings.

That was another issue, she thought as she put on her robe and padded barefoot into the kitchen. If she stayed in Mustang Creek, having miraculously discovered a way to make a living, she'd have to get rid of most of her furniture, and she needed to buy a car, too. She couldn't keep paying the exorbitant rates to rent the one she'd been driving.

She hadn't owned a vehicle in New York, because parking made it a nuisance and public transportation was frequent and reliable. Without a job, a loan was out of the question, so there would go a chunk of her savings.

Not that she didn't have money; she did.

And she wanted to keep it that way.

She might have driven Aunt Geneva's old sedan, but Geneva had sold that once she realized she was having problems remembering where things were, although she'd lived in Mustang Creek her whole life. She'd told Charlotte on the phone that she'd needed to pick up her prescriptions and had gone to the post office instead of the drugstore.

"At first I just thought, silly me, so absentminded," Geneva had gone on to explain, "but one day I couldn't remember how to get to the grocery store. Can you imagine? Well, to be truthful, honey, that scared me. What if I accidentally drove out of town and got completely lost? There are some remote roads out here. Besides, I might be a danger to others if I can't pay better attention. So I sold the car. It was getting to be kind of a rattletrap anyway."

As the recipient of that call months ago, Charlotte had felt her first true misgivings about letting her aunt live alone. So she'd arranged for her groceries and medications to be delivered and for someone to come in and help clean that big house, and she'd asked Mr. Simpson, a kindly neighbor, to walk Mutley. He'd agreed immediately, and begun taking the dog out twice a day instead of once. He was retired, he'd said, and a little bored. He needed something to do.

"I can get my own coffee, Charlie. You don't need to wait on me."

Jax had followed her into the kitchen. His hair was tousled and he was shirtless, wearing only his jeans. He had an athletic body, not too heavily muscled but well defined, and he could certainly outski her. He hadn't lied about knowing what he was doing when it came to downhill, and he said he also enjoyed cross-country on silent snowy mornings. Great exercise, he promised, and if she'd never done it, he'd love to teach her.

She handed him a cup. "Here you go, already made. I hope you still like breakfast blend."

"I like the cup of coffee I'm holding. Thank you." He took a grateful sip.

It was unsettling that she remembered how he liked his coffee—basic, black, no sugar. She looked at the clock. "When do you have to be at the clinic?"

"Midafternoon. Should be an interesting experience. I'm a great fan of these rescue programs. I hope a lot of people show up." He rested his elbows on the counter. "Free shots and discounted spay and neuter coupons for when the animals are old enough. Smart. That way, people are more likely to do the responsible thing and vaccinate and neuter their pets. It costs the clinic in vaccines, but if the doctors volunteer their time, it's a nice gift to the community. Great idea of Nate's."

He was definitely a good guy and a whiz with animals. Mutley loved him. Can-Can wasn't fond of vet visits and went into hiding at the mere suggestion, so Nate had come to the house more than once to handle various concerns and had good-naturedly searched under beds and in dark corners to locate Geneva's beloved cat. "You know he's a partner of my friend Bex's husband, Tate. She really likes him. I'd volunteer to fill out paperwork tonight at the clinic, but I'm picking up my aunt around four. That's why I kept my rental car."

Jax frowned. "I guess I hadn't thought about that—you not having wheels of your own, I mean. Once you return the rental, feel free to borrow my truck anytime. In fact, you can drop me off at the clinic and use it all day if you want." His quicksilver grin appeared. "Just don't forget about me after the adoption event so I have to sleep in a kennel or on the floor."

Charlotte was touched by the offer, perhaps a little too deeply, so she spoke in a light voice. "If I could forget about you, last night wouldn't have ever happened." She'd chosen caramel drizzle as her flavor of the day, and the coffee was delicious. Charlotte wrapped both hands around her mug. "Like I said, I have some decisions to make and a car is one of them, but I might take you up on your offer once in a while, after the holidays are over. I rented the car for two weeks."

"No problem, then."

"You can be maddeningly likable at times, you know that?"

He replied with a crisp nod. "I'm a *very sweet young man*," he said. "Just ask Mrs. Klozz if you don't believe me." Laughter lurked in his eyes.

"Would she still think so if she knew what we did last night?"

Jax shrugged, his expression comically rueful. "Probably. If you suppose she expected us to politely sleep in separate rooms after a chaste good-night kiss, you're incredibly naive. That woman knows *everything*."

Even that I'm in love with you? Does Millicent know that, too?

Mentally, Charlotte answered her own question. Of course Mrs. Klozz knew.

The brownies had heart-shaped chocolate pieces in them. Where you'd find heart-shaped chocolate chips in a place like Mustang Creek was a mystery, but the message was clear enough.

Charlotte moved to the sink to rinse her cup and put it in the dishwasher. "I won't make you sleep in any kennels, I promise, but I don't think it'll be an issue. I'm going to start looking for a car."

JAX COULD TELL that Charlie was uncomfortable being dependent on anyone else, even in a small way, but that wasn't news.

She was stubborn, intelligent and determined; she was also sensitive and more sentimental than she cared to admit. Her personality was a wall a man could slam up against, and yet Jax wouldn't have changed that, or anything else, about her. He'd never been drawn to the needy, indecisive type anyway.

No, he wanted *her*.

He sighed. It had been a memorable night. At least *he'd* never forget it.

But that party was over.

Briskly she said, "I'm going to hop in the shower and then we should head home. But first, would you mind stripping the bed?" She looked appealingly disheveled, her usual smooth fall of dark hair tangled—probably his fault—and she wore only a soft blue robe with a sash knotted around her waist. Jax would like nothing better than to suggest they go *back* to bed, but didn't want to push his luck.

"Sure."

"Hadleigh said the maid service will wash them and make the bed. I guess they come in once a week to dust and check on the place."

They'd cleaned up the kitchen together the night before. Jax had felt a sense of domestic accord that reinforced his conviction that once they were married—and he was more committed than ever to making it happen—they'd get along fine. Not just in bed, but in everyday life.

They were perfect for each other.

Now all he had to do was convince Charlie.

The main problem, as he saw it, was that Charlotte was never going to be content without a career. She was used to high heels and business meetings and classy restaurants. Still, he thought philosophically as he took a pillow from its slip, she'd been born and raised in Mustang Creek.

Roots, his father often said, were roots. You could put down new ones, but where you were born was where you were from.

He would always be from Idaho, even though he was willing to put down new roots. He'd done that, in essence, by accepting the job with Cameron and moving closer to Charlotte. Now he wanted it to be worth the effort. Not that it was a hardship to move to a town that reminded him of his own. He wouldn't mind raising his children here, but he and Charlie had to be in agreement where life choices were concerned.

After Jax had stripped the bed, he brewed a second cup of coffee and gazed out the window. It was a classic Christmas scene with the snow drifting lazily down and the chalet-style lodge sporting pine garlands and colored lights. A huge lit tree filled one of the lobby's massive windows, and there were two smaller decorated trees on either side of the ornate front door. The view really inspired a holiday mood.

Skiers were already out, winding down the slopes, some graceful, some taking a tumble now and then, their bright coats and hats vivid against the white background. Jax couldn't sing as well as Mrs. Klozz did, but he found himself humming "The First Noel" and was still standing by the window when Charlotte emerged from the bathroom. Her hair was damp, and the scent of her shampoo wafted along with her as she went to her suitcase and rummaged through it for clean clothes. To his disappointment she didn't drop the towel but hurried back into the bathroom.

He heard the sound of a hair dryer, and when she came out again she was dressed in a midthigh soft gray tunic over black leggings with short boots that matched the sweater. A black belt emphasized her slender waist.

Jax was, as his dad might have said, "bowled over" by the sight of her.

"You look great," he said softly. "I tend to think that all the time, though, so feel free to take it for granted. In other words, I'm a not-so-secret admirer."

A tinge of color came into her cheeks. "Thanks. Sorry I was in the bathroom for so long. Your turn."

"I'll take about five minutes. That's the advantage of being a guy sometimes, but there's a trade-off. I won't look half as good as you."

Charlotte raised her brows. "Oh, don't sell yourself short, Doc."

He shaved carefully, so it was more like seven minutes, but since his real introduction to Mustang Creek was happening this afternoon, and he was going to meet Charlotte's aunt—if she was still awake by the time he left the clinic—he wanted to look decent.

When he went to get dressed, he saw that Charlotte had set her suitcase by the door and washed the coffee cups and put them away. She even had her coat on. Back to real life, he thought in resignation as he pulled on a pair of clean jeans, a denim shirt and his socks and boots. Two minutes later they were out the door, but he hoped for another visit soon.

He owed Hadleigh Galloway big-time.

However, when they reached the parking lot, there was a problem.

His truck wouldn't start.

He was handy with cars, due to an uncle's enthusiasm for working on them when Jax was young and hanging around, absorbing tips along with some colorful language. He'd already had a few issues with the engine turning over too slowly—he'd blamed it on the weather—but when a couple leaving the resort offered to jump-start the vehicle and it still wouldn't turn over, he decided he knew what the problem was.

"It needs a new battery." He dropped the hood into

place, sending up a poof of snow. "At least I suspect that's what's going on. Not the best timing, but it happens. Let me go into the lodge and see who we can call. Sorry."

Fortunately, Charlotte wasn't someone who went to pieces over every inconvenience. "It does happen and always at the worst time. We both need to get back." She sighed. "If I know Aunt Geneva, who's early for everything, her bags are packed and she's sitting there watching the clock." She sighed again. "Oh, well. Can't be helped."

They dodged a snowy group of skiers as they went in the front doors and approached the desk. The young woman working it looked harried but smiled brightly. "Merry Christmas. What can I do for you?"

"Merry Christmas to you, as well," Jax said. "We aren't actual guests. We stayed in one of the condos last night, the one owned by the Galloways, and now my truck won't start. I think it needs a new battery. Is there a local auto service?"

She typed something into her computer. "There is. They close at noon, in about a half an hour, because it's Christmas Eve. I can call, but getting them out here could be a problem. You could go there yourself—if you can arrange for transportation. I'm afraid we can't help, since staffing is minimal due to the holiday."

He swore mentally until someone behind him said, "*I* can help."

Jax turned and saw a young man with a stocking cap and engaging grin, clad in a green jacket and dark ski pants. "I think you're dressed for it, and Sheba could use a warm-up before we get started. I was going to take her out anyway."

The guy's car was named Sheba? Okay. At least he seemed willing to lend a hand, and Jax was grateful.

"Thanks..."

"My ride is outside. Half an hour is cutting it close, so let's go."

They didn't have a lot of options, so they followed him and saw—of all things—a horse-drawn sleigh out front. The real deal, with large runners and a chestnut Morgan in harness.

"I'm Vince." They exchanged a quick handshake. "Climb in. Blankets in the back. We do sleigh rides on Christmas Eve and she's a great horse, but like I said, a warm-up would be good. We can have you there before it closes."

Charlotte whispered as they got in, "Seriously? A sleigh ride? Did you plan this?"

"I wish I'd thought of it." He sat next to her and grabbed the blanket as they took off, draping it over both of them. "Apparently, fate's been smiling on me this holiday season. Generally speaking, there's nothing romantic about buying a battery for your truck on Christmas Eve, but I suppose doing it by sleigh might qualify."

Charlotte laughed at his disgruntled tone. She said, "It does."

And then she leaned over to kiss him.

He'd never considered car problems romantic, but there was a first for everything.

CHAPTER TEN

LATER, BACK IN Mustang Creek, as she and Jax pulled up in front of the house, Charlotte could still hear those sleigh bells ringing, *jing-jing-jingling*. And she was still smiling at the memory.

They were running a little late, but everything had gone pretty well, considering. They'd reached the auto parts place just minutes before closing time, purchased a new battery for Jax's truck and, after sledding it back to the lodge, Jax and their bearded rescuer had swapped the old for the new in a matter of minutes.

Now, as they reached the house, Charlotte was definitely in the Christmas spirit.

Aunt Geneva was going to get a major kick out of the whole sleigh-ride story. Millicent would enjoy it, too.

Charlotte hummed a carol under her breath as she climbed out of the truck.

Of course, relating the tale would mean explaining that she'd been stranded at a ski resort with a man. Aunt Geneva wasn't a prude, but she had certain ideas about how relationships should be conducted.

First, a sweet romance.

Then the altar.

Then, and *only* then, overnight visits to places like ski resorts.

At least, it was *supposed* to work that way, according to her aunt's generation.

Charlotte's heart remained light as she hurried up the front walk. She'd fallen in love and was fairly sure Jax had as well, but love by itself wasn't enough.

On the porch, Jax reached past Charlotte, opened the door and held it for her with a sheepish look on his face. "I almost knocked. I don't want to make Mrs. Klozz drop everything and answer the door, but it's going to take time getting used to walking right in."

"It's going to take time getting used to having you live down the hall." She walked past him, bracing herself for Mutley's usual enthusiasm. She needn't have worried as he dashed past her to jump all over Jax, instead. Charlotte sent the dog a mock glare. "Traitor."

Jax scratched behind the dog's ears. "Hey, it'll pass once I start coming in smelling like the clinic every night. No doubt the cat will shun me completely, at least until after I've showered. Speaking of which, I'd better get cleaned up, grab my lab coat and get out of here. I'd rather not be late, especially on my first day."

Charlotte nodded, feeling a little distracted. She'd called her aunt from the lodge to warn her she might be late, and she'd been told not to worry about it. Still, Geneva was eager to come home, even if it was only for a day or two.

She told Jax, "I'll wrap the gifts when I get back here with my aunt. She can visit with Mrs. Klozz. What is that fabulous smell, by the way? It involves chocolate. I have a keen inner sense of chocolate radar, and the screen is beeping."

"Don't know, but if you bottle it, there's a million bucks

in your future. Go find out and I'll bring your suitcase to your room."

Charlotte watched Jax as he headed toward the stairs, flecks of snow still in his hair, his strides long and athletic. Mutley had decided he still loved her and stayed behind, transferring his affection. She leaned down to pat his head. "He's a good guy, right, Mut?"

Mutley wagged his tail in vigorous agreement.

She laughed. "Well, for a vet anyway, huh? Okay, let's say hi to Mrs. Klozz and then go pick up Aunt Geneva. Want to ride along?"

Clearly, he did. From her blanket on the couch Can-Can gave him a look of disdain and yawned, but she'd lifted her head at the mention of Geneva's name.

Animals were just so darned smart, she thought as she went into the kitchen to find Mrs. Klozz there, wearing one of Geneva's aprons and peering into a pot on the stove while she stirred its contents. Her white hair was coiled in its usual bun, and she was pleasantly flushed.

Without turning around, Millicent said, "Hello, dear. I'm so glad you had a nice time with your young man."

Charlotte wasn't sure how the woman could know if she'd had a good time or not, but she was getting used to living with the mysteries of Mrs. Klozz. "It was lovely, and dinner was wonderful. Thank you so much."

"Oh, just something I threw together." She raised one hand in a dismissive wave. "However, I'm quite concerned about this soup. Would you mind taking a small taste?"

Charlotte was willing to taste anything made by Mrs. Klozz. "My pleasure."

The older lady spooned some of the concoction into a small bowl and handed it over, endearingly anxious as

Charlotte sampled it. Closing her eyes, Charlotte identified the flavors of cheese, various vegetables and shrimp.

Not the source of that chocolate aroma, then.

"Delicious," Charlotte said, with perfect honesty. "Please tell me we're having that with supper."

Millicent actually seemed relieved. Had she really thought any dish she made could turn out badly? "Yes. It's the first course."

There were going to be courses? Charlotte vowed to get a membership to Bex's gym. Jax would faint in gratitude when he tasted that soup. "I think I also smell dessert."

Mrs. Klozz's eyes twinkled. "A special surprise. I know how you love chocolate."

She did? Charlotte wondered again, for just a moment, but then it came to her: almost everybody loves chocolate. "I confess I have a weakness for the stuff."

"Well, we shall see if this is up to par. I suppose you're off to pick up Geneva?"

"I am. And I'm taking Mutley with me. I invited him and he accepted."

A flicker of sadness crossed Millicent's gentle face. "That poor dog misses her something terrible," she said. "I try to take up the slack, but—"

Charlotte gave the other woman a quick, reassuring hug. "You're a godsend," she said. Meanwhile, the dog in question, sitting nearby, perked up his ears as if listening to the conversation. Most likely, he understood every word. "You're working too hard," she told Mrs. Klozz. "When we get back, please let me know what I can do to help."

Mrs. Klozz smiled widely, and it was as if the clouds had parted. "You *have* helped, my dear, just by coming home. Geneva is happy, and your friends are happy, and so, of course, is Jaxon. You've given us all a very special gift, one that can't be wrapped and put under a tree."

Charlotte was moved. "You're giving me way too much credit," she said. "You're the one who's made all the difference!"

Mrs. Klozz had assumed a modest expression, but her wink was mischievous. "As folks tend to say hereabouts," she confided, "you ain't seen nothin' yet."

JAX WAS IMPRESSED by the turnout for the rescue pet adoption. The waiting room was jammed with people, most of them with excited children in tow, so the noise level was high enough to virtually drown out the seasonal music wafting from the sound system.

One older lady informed him she'd driven a hundred miles one way, as he finished examining the tiny black-and-white kitten she'd selected.

"My friend told me about this, and my old cat Peterson recently passed." She teared up at the mention of her departed pet. "He was eighteen years old, though, and that's a good long life for a feline. Millie said I should come straight here and get myself a new companion."

Millie?

As in Millicent Klozz?

Couldn't be.

Could it?

Jax asked, as casually as possible, as he handed over his tiny charge, "Does she have white hair?"

The older lady laughed and patted his arm as he signed the paperwork. "A lot of us do," she said. "My friend Millie included." She looked years younger than she probably was, holding the small adoptee close to one cheek and closing her eyes for a moment. "Thank you so much for this little sweetheart. You're a fine young man."

A fine young man. It was unsettling, that phrase. He'd rarely heard it—until he met Mrs. Klozz.

On the other hand, he supposed, it could well be in common use, especially among elderly women.

The important thing was that this cat would be cherished and probably spoiled. It was purring in an audible hum as the woman carried it away, draped like a tiny furry boa over her shoulder.

Good start to the evening.

Two boxer-husky mix puppies went next, both to the same family, and Jax felt duty bound to warn, "They'll make wonderful pets, but they dig. They also have loads of energy and will grow to a fair size. I hope you have a big backyard."

"Ranch," the youthful father said, watching fondly as his twin boys played with the puppies. "Those dogs can dig all they like out at our place. They were all the kids seemed to want for Christmas—our old shepherd, Barney, died last spring—so I thought, why not? I doubt it'll be a peaceful Christmas Eve, but then again, it hasn't been for the past six years." He held out a work-worn hand. "Thanks, Doc."

Jax shook the man's hand, smiling. Then he gave him the coupons for the neutering. "Cute dogs and even cuter kids. You can count your blessings this Christmas."

"I always do." The rancher tipped his hat and headed out, followed by his beaming wife, a pair of happy dogs and two delighted young boys.

Naturally, Mrs. Klozz had donated cookies, presenting Jax with a huge box just before he left the house, and they disappeared fast. Jax grinned as he heard the murmurs of appreciation, especially for some sort of fudgy mint bar that one woman, who picked out an older calico cat with a sedate disposition, claimed was a little bit of heaven on earth.

He sincerely thanked her on behalf of Mrs. K. and also because she'd adopted a mature animal and they tended to be harder to place. "She's already been spayed," he said, handing over the coupon, "but if you know someone with a pet that hasn't been, feel free to pass this along."

"Thank you, Dr. Locke." She squeezed his hand. "Merry Christmas. And don't forget to track down that recipe for me. Remember, it's the one for chocolate-mint bars."

"Merry Christmas to you, too," Jax said. "I'll get the recipe, provided it's not a family secret. Call the office next week."

Nate gave him a cheeky grin from the next exam table, during the brief gap in the stream of adopters and adoptees that followed. "The older ladies seem to like you a lot," he observed.

Jax thought about Charlotte's aunt. He'd be meeting her soon, and he wanted to make a good impression. "Here's hoping that trend continues." The evening seemed to be flying by. "How many people are still waiting to adopt?"

"Twelve," Nate answered. "This is a bigger turnout than usual. Obviously, people are feeling generous."

Jax cleared several more kittens and a German shepherd pup before he realized that the next young woman in line appeared to be bringing in a puppy instead of taking one home with her. He didn't recognize the animal.

Her expression was apologetic. She was probably in her early twenties, dressed in a coat with a hood, her face pink from the cold. "I didn't come here to adopt," she said, in a small, regretful voice. "But I'm hoping you could—well—help me?"

Something inside Jax softened. He focused on the energetic little guy in her arms. "I'll do my best," he said quietly, feeling sorry for the girl.

"My roommate moved out of town and left her dog behind. I work long hours, and I can't let him loose in the apartment while I'm away, so he has to stay in one of those cages." She paused, bit her lower lip. "I hate that," she went on miserably. "And so does he. But all the neighbors are complaining because he howls all the time and I—" Tears welled in her eyes. "He's a *really* nice dog, though." Another hesitation. She set the pup on Jax's exam table. "I heard about the adoption on the radio and wondered if anyone here might want him."

Jax could hardly believe what he was seeing. The dog was a beagle mix.

And he'd been hand delivered.

"I think so," he said in a voice that was slightly hoarse. All afternoon, he'd been weighing the pros and cons of giving Charlie a puppy for Christmas, and getting no closer to a decision in the process. This little guy, maybe three months old, was lively, all right, and he looked healthy. When he reached his full growth, he'd be about the same size as Mutley. "Shots?" Jax asked.

The girl shrugged, her expression uncertain. "I don't know," she said. "Probably. I'm pretty sure she brought him here—my ex-roommate, I mean—once or twice. I remember her complaining about how much it cost. You could check your records, couldn't you? His name is Felix. The address would be 83 Aspen Place, apartment 14."

Felix was busy licking his hand by then, and Jax picked him up. "I can check, and yes, he'll be placed. And, by the way, you did the right thing, bringing him here."

She smiled gratefully. Her eyes were still wet. "I'd gladly keep him, but I can't stand to think of him shut up like a criminal all day. He needs a yard or a big space where he can run around." She sniffled. "He's sort of house-trained. And he's smart, too."

"I personally know someone who'll love him. He'll have a good home."

If Charlotte didn't take a shine to Felix, Jax would find another place to live and keep the dog himself. They'd already bonded, the two of them.

Half an hour later, Jax and Nate were finished for the night. All the pets had been adopted and, although the staff looked a bit shell-shocked, everybody was happy.

He'd asked one of the techs to check on Felix's shots earlier, and he was indeed up-to-date. Jax bought a collar and a leash, and the tech added a bright red bow, just for fun.

"Here you go, little fella," Vickie had said, fastening the bow to Felix's new collar. "Such a cutie. Your girlfriend will love him."

Was Charlotte his girlfriend? He hadn't referred to her that way.

He'd said *friend*, not *girlfriend*.

And he wasn't even sure Charlotte *wanted* a dog.

He did, though. He definitely wanted a dog—*this* dog. Plus Charlotte, plus a whole passel of kids…

Still, there was no denying that Felix was a risky gift.

Maybe he should've gone with perfume or a piece of jewelry from Melody's ranch-house studio.

Once everyone else had gone, Jax took the puppy over to Nate. "If you had to call it, what would you say we have going on here, besides beagle?"

His colleague picked Felix up and ran his hands over him, then looked at his teeth. "Maybe a German pointer. Good dogs. I'd say he'll hit maybe forty to fifty pounds. A decent size, and he'll make an excellent watchdog. Not too big to handle, friendly but protective and great with kids. So you're taking this one?"

"Note the bow. He's a gift."

"So I gathered, from the tidbits I overheard. The techs think you're *awesome*, by the way, as well as cute. Personally, I don't see it."

Jax shook his head, laughing. "I'm definitely not *awesome* when it comes to picking out gifts, but I do know a thing or two about dogs. He seems like a good one. Charlotte, Mutley and Can-Can need a friend."

"Oh?"

"My new family."

"I've met Can-Can and Mutley," Nate said in his good-natured way. "And I remember Charlotte Morgan from high school. Very pretty girl. Congratulations."

Very *independent* girl.

"That's premature," Jax mumbled. Congrats were not yet in order. "I'm working on it, though." Jax retrieved Felix and wished he'd brought a carrier, but decided to hope the dog didn't act up in the car. According to his phone, it was now well past six, but then, if they hadn't stayed open late, he wouldn't have Felix.

"You'll love Charlotte," he told the dog as he loaded

him in the passenger seat. "Do not jump on her aunt, please. Just a request. You're supposed to be a happy surprise, and it would be great if you behaved. I'm giving you to her, and her to you. It's a win-win, so don't blow it."

Felix responded by hopping off the other seat onto Jax's lap, which made driving difficult, but he immediately settled down, head on his paws, so Jax let him stay put. It was only a few blocks. In the summer, he'd be able to walk to work in about five minutes.

Charlotte was going to love Felix.

He was sure of it.

Okay, it was Christmas Eve, and he might be under a spell. But the pup had those luminous, please-love-me eyes; he was one big heart with fur.

So, yes, Charlie would love the dog.

Fingers crossed…

"Work your magic," he urged Felix, stroking those silky ears with his free hand. "I'd appreciate it."

The puppy sat up and licked Jax under the chin.

A few minutes later they pulled up at Charlotte's aunt's place. As Jax eased out of the truck, the dog in one arm and a bag with heartworm medication, puppy food and treats in the other, he hoped this all went well. He hoped Mutley and Can-Can would be pleased, not to mention Charlie, her aunt and Mrs. Klozz.

Charlotte's car was in the driveway, and Jax was glad he'd taken the time to shovel the porch steps before heading for the clinic earlier.

As he approached, still lugging Felix, who was getting squirmy again, impatient to be set down, he heard holiday music playing inside. The Christmas tree shimmered and glowed in the front window. Jax paused automatically and lifted his free hand to knock at the front door, caught himself and instead turned the handle and pushed it open.

All three women had gathered in the kitchen; he heard happy voices and laughter, and the sounds reminded him of his own family's Christmas gatherings. He paused, just taking it in, struck by a sweet aching sense of nostalgia. Felix brought him around with more wiggling and a little yelp of impatience.

He put the dog on the floor, trusting that the critter wouldn't lift a leg against the nearest piece of furniture and let fly. Felix had taken care of business in the clinic parking lot, christening one of Jax's front tires with aplomb.

Jax shifted his attention to the quiet magic of that house. It already seemed like home.

Better yet, it was Christmas Eve, he had a gift to deliver and whatever Mrs. Klozz was whipping up smelled fantastic, as always.

He smiled down at Felix. "Showtime, buddy," he said. "Turn on the charm."

CHAPTER ELEVEN

CHARLOTTE FELT A warm glow of mingled anticipation and gratitude.

It was wonderful to sit around the kitchen table with Aunt Geneva again, having a cup of coffee and chatting about ordinary things. Mutley sat at Geneva's feet, gazing up at her in adoration, and Can-Can was glued to her lap.

Mrs. Klozz was bustling about, as usual, and she'd waved away Charlotte's initial suggestion that she join them.

"You two need to catch up," Millicent had said, busily pulling a pan from the oven. "Mrs. Andrews down the street lost her husband last January, and this will be her first Christmas alone. I'm hoping a brief visit and this cake will cheer her up—and, besides, she seems thinner than she should be. Don't you think so, Geneva?"

Geneva had nodded. "Why don't you invite Doris to join us tomorrow for Christmas dinner?" she asked. "Don't fret about her weight, though. She's always been on the skinny side, in my opinion. Nervous type, you know."

Charlotte had smiled into her coffee cup. *She* certainly wasn't in any immediate danger of being *on the skinny side*, she thought. Not with Millicent doing the cooking.

The next second, a deep voice said from the doorway,

"I'll deliver the cake *and* the invitation if you can take care of this little guy for a few minutes."

Charlotte swiveled in her chair and saw Jax standing there, still in his coat and scrubs, accompanied by the cutest puppy she'd ever seen.

The dog scampered straight over to Charlotte.

Mutley seemed pleasantly intrigued by the new arrival, while Can-Can hissed indignantly, hunkered down in Aunt Geneva's lap and went right back to sleep.

Charlotte, incapable of resisting, promptly picked up the eager puppy, noting his hopeful eyes and the bright red bow on his collar.

"Well," she said, laughing as the critter licked her face. "*Hello*, there, handsome."

Over the pup's head, Charlotte met Jax's eyes. He looked as hopeful as the dog, and a lot more uncertain.

Clearly, the adorable little furball was a gift—for her.

The last thing you need is a puppy, argued her sensible side.

True enough. But this guy was beyond cute, with those big brown eyes, floppy, oversize ears and assorted spots—he wasn't a purebred—and he was so busy licking her face that she gave up and let him do it. "Who would you be?"

Jax relaxed visibly. "His name's Felix," he said, still cautious. "You could change it, if you wanted."

She'd been right. *He'd actually gotten her a dog for Christmas.*

Incredible.

And, somehow, so very sweet.

Jax turned to Mrs. Klozz, who was taking in the scene with a tinsel-bright smile.

"Which house belongs to Mrs. Andrews?" he asked,

as calmly as if he hadn't just brought over a delightful but awkward gift.

Mrs. Klozz, enormously pleased, patted his cheek. "That's sweet of you, dear. Doris doesn't really know me, so you can just wish her a merry Christmas from the family and tell her we'll be having dinner tomorrow afternoon at around two, if she'd like to join us." She paused thoughtfully. "She lives in the blue house on the corner, the one with white shutters."

He departed immediately, carrying the still-warm cake pan in the box Mrs. Klozz had provided.

"Oh, he's darling," Aunt Geneva crooned the instant Jax was gone. Without disturbing Can-Can, who was snoring contentedly, she reached over to pat the puppy's head. "Mutley needs a friend, someone to keep him young. What a good idea, and what a handsome young man you have."

"You don't think giving a person a puppy is sort of, well, presumptuous?" Charlotte asked somewhat lamely, although, in fact, she was already in love with Felix.

"Presumptuous? Piffle," Aunt Geneva said. "The man is decisive, and that's something to be admired, my dear. Your young man's downright adorable—almost as cute as this puppy."

"Jax isn't my—" Charlotte began, but the objection fell away. Obviously, neither her aunt nor Millicent would believe her protestations anyway.

Besides, the puppy *was* cute.

Not necessarily cuter than Jax, but cute just the same.

For his part, Felix appeared to be even more of a mongrel than Mutley. He did have the sweetest little face, and he'd settled down in her lap, a warm weight on her thighs.

Still—a puppy?

Aunt Geneva seemed to be reading her mind. Not an unusual thing, as she recalled. "Jaxon is a veterinarian, Charlotte Jean," she said, as though that settled the matter. "You can expect a steady parade of animals through your life from now on."

"Very wise of you, Geneva," Mrs. Klozz agreed, looking thoughtful, although the oven mitts on her hands took away some of the saintly aura. "Has Charlotte mentioned her idea about turning the house into a bed-and-breakfast?"

My idea? But it wasn't. Jax had been the one to bring that up. She'd all but dismissed the whole thing out of hand.

Moreover, Charlotte knew she hadn't mentioned anything of the sort, not to Mrs. Klozz, and she was pretty sure Jax hadn't, either.

She shook her head fitfully.

And proceeded to babble. "It would be way too expensive. Jax was just throwing out suggestions. Granted, this is a big house and worth preserving and restoring, but I wouldn't know the first thing about how to run a B and B, I'm certainly not a cook like Mrs. Klozz, and the project would cost a fortune…"

Mrs. Klozz and Aunt Geneva simply watched her.

Felix, sound asleep, made a snorting noise and rearranged himself on Charlotte's lap.

Aunt Geneva, stroking Can-Can's head, broke the ensuing silence. "We could help," she murmured, musing aloud. "I have some money saved. Hoarded it like a miser, so I could leave my Charlotte a decent inheritance. Using the funds this way might make more sense, though, don't you think?"

Charlotte gaped. Aunt Geneva, it seemed, wasn't addressing her at all. She was speaking to Millicent Klozz. All of which left Charlotte feeling as though she'd lost her footing on a stream bank, toppled into the water and was now being carried swiftly away.

"Yes," Mrs. Klozz murmured. As if there weren't enough baked goods scattered across the counters, she got out a mixing bowl from one of the old cabinets. "I could provide plenty of recipes. Normally, I don't share, but in Charlotte's case I might. I'm not getting any younger."

Aunt Geneva nodded sagely.

"I'm right here," Charlotte said, the puppy on her lap. The two older women were discussing her future as if she was absent—or invisible. "Sitting in this chair. Care to include me in the conversation?"

"No," they chorused, in perfect unison, and then they laughed.

"Child," Geneva said, watching Charlotte with that benign steadiness she remembered so well. "One must take chances in this life, if one hopes to accomplish anything. Fortune favors the bold."

Charlotte had heard that speech before, variations of it, anyway, before she'd gone off to New York, but tonight it struck home in a whole new way. Cautiously, she asked, "You wouldn't mind if this was a bed-and-breakfast? It wouldn't bother you, knowing strangers were tramping in and out of your house?"

"Houses need people to give them life," Geneva said in a firm voice. "Otherwise, they get lonely. Think about it, dear. You could take care of Mutley, Can-Can and Felix, fix up this old place and provide the people who visit Mustang Creek with a truly lovely place to stay."

She was going to strangle Jax Locke, Charlotte decided. "But what about the money? Do you realize how much this could cost? The investment would be staggering."

"What if you had someone to help with the finances?" Mrs. Klozz dumped flour into the bowl, sending up a gentle cloud of white. "I have a friend who's invested in various businesses in Mustang Creek. Her name is Lettie Arbuckle. Well, I suppose now it's Lettie Calder, since she's remarried and all. She has a strong personality, mind you, but a keen eye for a business opportunity. I think she'd see the potential. She's a bit of a meddler, though. Fair warning."

She's *a bit of a meddler*, Charlotte thought in disbelief, remembering the heart-shaped chocolate chips on the cookies Mrs. Klozz had made for her and Jax.

"I know Lettie," Aunt Geneva said with enthusiasm. "Millie, what a wonderful idea."

"I'll call her tomorrow," Millicent said.

"On Christmas Day?" Charlotte asked. This whole situation was getting away from her, and if she didn't put her foot down now, who knew where it would lead? "Besides, I—"

"Why, Lettie won't mind at all," said Mrs. Klozz. "As a matter of fact, I'd be calling her anyway, to say merry Christmas."

"But—" Charlotte attempted to stem the flow.

To no avail, of course.

Geneva broke in, "Your Jaxon could help with the gardens. The flowers are almost all perennials, but the vegetables need to be tended. In the summer you'd always have fresh produce. I kept it small because it was just the two of us, but there's plenty of room for a bigger one."

"Jax *isn't* mine," Charlotte said, quite uselessly. "I—"

"She needn't spend all her time baking, either," Mrs. Klozz interjected. "The local bakeries are quite good. And there's Bad Billie's if the guests get to hankering for hamburgers and the like." She stopped long enough to add butter to whatever she was about to bake. "Not everyone likes to cook constantly, the way I do. And in the beginning, Charlotte could accept bookings only for weekends and special occasions, so she and Jaxon could have some private time together." She filled a measuring cup with sugar, emptied it into the bowl. "Naturally, pets would be allowed. Even encouraged."

Felix made a little sound in his sleep, as though agreeing.

In Charlotte's opinion, it was rather early to assume that Jax would continue living in the house, let alone want to look after the yard, take care of the pets and spend *private time* with her.

Interest danced in Geneva's eyes. Her memory might be slipping, but she was still a smart cookie in many ways, and she knew that she and her mysterious friend, Mrs. Klozz, were getting under Charlotte's skin. Can-Can raised her head, and Charlotte could've sworn the cat was amused.

"Would you two mind very much," she began, not unkindly, "if I just arranged my own future? Jax is great, but I'm not sure we have the same life vision. Besides, it isn't as if he's asked me to marry him or anything."

"He will." Mrs. Klozz took a wooden spoon and stirred vigorously.

"He will," Aunt Geneva agreed, nodding. "I know a besotted young man when I see one."

Besotted? Did anyone still use that word in real conversation? Charlotte was exasperated, tired and apparently responsible for a new puppy in addition to having two old ladies meddle in her life, with the aforementioned Lettie Arbuckle about to be thrown into the mix.

It was all too much. So she got up from her chair, still holding Felix, and announced, "I have gifts to wrap and, apparently, a dog to walk."

Mrs. Klozz turned. "What did you get Jaxon for Christmas?"

Charlotte just stood there, flummoxed. First of all, in her defense, she hadn't expected the man to show up in Mustang Creek *or* move into her house. Second, maybe the night before could be counted as a gift—but she'd enjoyed it every bit as much as he had. She looked at the clock. It was late. Way too late. All the stores were closed. Her only excuse was that her life had been taking a lot of unexpected twists and turns lately.

"Nothing," she admitted. "I didn't get him anything."

Mrs. Klozz smiled serenely. "Don't worry, dear," she said. "I've got you covered."

THE WOMAN WHO answered the door with a wan smile brightened and then hugged Jax when he handed her the box containing Mrs. Klozz's Christmas cake.

"How lovely!" Mrs. Andrews trilled, and for one awful moment, Jax thought she might actually reach up and pinch his cheek. "*Thank* you," she added. "What a wonderful surprise!"

Jax felt a rush of modesty. "I didn't really have anything to do with it," he said, feeling he should explain. "I'm just dropping it off. It's from Geneva Roberts and her niece, Charlotte Morgan. And, uh… Millicent—Mrs. Klozz. Millicent's worried about you being alone tonight."

"Millicent…?" The woman looked puzzled.

Once again, Jax had that peculiar sensation of being… adrift. Thrust into the heat of some game without a clue what the rules were. "She and Geneva and Charlie—Charlotte—thought you might be free to join us for dinner tomorrow. Two o'clock."

He was rambling.

He was also cold.

"Well," Mrs. Andrews said, still puzzled. "I'm afraid dinner is out of the question, although I appreciate the invitation. I've already made plans for tomorrow." A pause. "Sometimes I wonder if I've still got my wits about me. I've known Geneva and Charlotte for years, but I can't seem to place that other person you mentioned—"

Jax felt compelled to describe Mrs. Klozz. He wanted the neighbor's face to brighten again, wanted to hear her say, "Oh, yes, Millicent. How could I have forgotten?"

"Mrs. Klozz," he coached. "White hair, bright eyes, maybe comes up to here on a tall day." He held a hand in the middle of his chest.

"Hmm," said Mrs. Andrews, obviously at a loss. She sniffled, wiped her eyes. "My daughter's flying in from Salt Lake City in the morning. Tonight's not a perfect Christmas Eve, but this does make it better. It always helps to know someone's thinking about you. Thank you."

"Once again, I can't take the credit. I'm just the messenger. Have a wonderful evening and enjoy the visit with your daughter. I'm Jaxon Locke, and I'm boarding at Geneva's place, so if you ever need a hand, just get in touch."

"Oh, yes, you're Dr. Locke, the new veterinarian. Of

course I know where you live. Have a merry Christmas, young man, and please thank Geneva and Charlotte and—that other person for me."

He walked back to the brightly lit house, his hands in his pockets, hoping that Felix was minding his manners. "Sort of house-trained" meant accidents did happen, and he didn't want Charlotte to celebrate Christmas Eve by cleaning up after an excited puppy.

He met her on the front steps, Felix coming out first with Mutley a close second, two leashes clutched in her hand, and that little lacy hat on her head. Charlotte immediately handed him one leash. "You take Mut," she said. "I still haven't forgiven him for liking you better than me when we came home."

Jax laughed. "Charlie, where's your holiday spirit?"

She made a face at him. "At least *Felix* loves me, unlike Mutley."

The puppy sat down on Charlotte's right boot and rested his head against her leg.

Great technique, Jax thought. He needed to try it sometime. "Oh, he does, but don't write Mutley off. I was probably a novelty, that's all."

"Ha," Charlotte scoffed. "When I think of all the tennis balls I've thrown for that dog."

Jax, holding Mutley's leash, started down the porch steps. Funny, but he didn't feel quite as chilled as he had on the walk home. "Just wait until I trim old Mut's nails and give him a shot or two. You'll be golden again." He tugged Mutley toward the sidewalk. "Shall we?"

Charlotte followed him down the steps, and he was happy to see that Felix was in good spirits, trotting obediently beside her, and Mutley didn't seem to mind. Dogs could be territorial, but Mut was an easygoing sort, and at the moment, anyway, Felix wasn't a threat to him as the alpha male. Eventually, Jax knew, the older dog would put the younger one in his place; it was the natural order of things. In all the important ways, he figured they'd be totally compatible. Admiring Charlotte out of the corner of his eye, Jax wondered how he'd fare sleeping down the hall, and not *with* her.

He'd just have to cope somehow.

"Your aunt's a delightful lady," he said, partly because he meant it and partly because he wanted to steer his thoughts away from the current sleeping arrangements. "She seems healthy—maybe a little frail, but that goes with the territory. Her mind seems fine."

Charlotte nodded, and then her voice broke. "I think she *is* fine in general, but she told me about a few mishaps and slipups that frightened her, and after hearing about them, I don't want her living alone, either. I suggested that now I'm here, she could move back home. But eventually I'll have to do something, get some kind of job. Which means she'd be alone for most of the day. Oh, and thanks a lot for telling Mrs. Klozz about the bed-and-breakfast flash of brilliance you had. She told my aunt and now they're ganging up on me."

A few snowflakes had landed on her eyelashes. Jax was so fascinated by that, he almost tripped over Mutley when the dog stopped to sniff the sidewalk. "Actually, I didn't come up with that idea on my own."

Charlotte stared up at him, but she didn't seem all that surprised. "What? Then, who did?"

"Take a wild guess."

Mrs. Klozz, of course.

"Well, anyway, now she has Aunt Geneva all excited about the idea, and I'm sorry to say, it really isn't practical. Until the house is remodeled I couldn't have guests, so there wouldn't be any money coming in. The two of them had all these suggestions—Millicent knows some woman who invests in businesses, and Aunt Geneva's talking about handing over her savings. It's out of control."

Just then, Felix did a hop-skip, barking at a snowman in someone's yard, perhaps because it was wearing a red scarf. Mutley decided he ought to join in. Jax ordered, "Hey, fellas, quiet down." To Charlotte's astonishment, they both gave it a rest, Felix probably taking his cue from Mut. There was already some hero worship going on.

Jax continued, "It seemed like a good solution to me. You're the PR and business wizard, so I bow to your judgment. I was under the impression you didn't want to sell the house."

Charlotte looked away. "I don't."

And he didn't want her leaving Mustang Creek. He liked this place, and he loved Charlie. However, she'd make her own choices, and that was the way it ought to be.

He changed the subject. "Not to be selfishly occupied with my own needs, but I'm starving. The clinic was a madhouse, so I didn't even get to have one of those mint things. Oh, I'm supposed to pry the recipe out of Mrs. Klozz. Think I have a chance of getting it?"

Charlotte tapped her chin with one gloved finger and pretended to be thinking hard. "Let's see, Mrs. Klozz can't do enough for you, since you're such a fine young man. Mutley's besotted with you, and I'm ninety-nine percent certain Aunt Geneva feels the same way. Yes, I'd say you have a chance at the recipe."

"Besotted?" Jax chortled.

"Had to use it," Charlotte said. "It's the word of the evening." She stopped, looking up at him again. He felt things inside him collide and then melt from the heat of contact. "Shall we go back? As for your state of starvation, all I can say is that Mrs. Klozz has another meal ready to serve. Maybe she's forgotten that we—the rest of us—already had supper once tonight."

He smiled. "You don't mind about Felix? If you do, I'll take him. Giving someone a pet presumes that he or she is willing to invest years of care and responsibility. He was basically abandoned, and the woman who brought him in couldn't care for him, so I..."

Her eyes glimmered green in the starlight. "I've been warned that you have a soft heart. And no, I don't mind. He's precious. Plus, I suspect he'll turn out to be a challenge, but I'll cope."

This might be the time to inform her that Felix was just "sort of" house-trained. "I think some vigilance might be in order. He's still pretty young."

Charlotte shot him a dubious glance. "What does that mean?"

"Lots of walks until he gets the hang of it."

She sighed. "You know, Dr. Locke, you tend to bring turmoil into my life."

He grinned. "Merry Christmas."

CHAPTER TWELVE

THE TABLE GLEAMED with old china, inherited from her aunt's parents, so at least a century old, and Geneva never took it from the breakfront in the dining room except for Christmas and birthday celebrations. It was patterned with scenes of an English garden, cream and red, and Charlotte loved it. That china represented very special occasions, and this was certainly one. There was also the heavy old silver, as well as the antique crystal glasses, and a vase with crimson roses that Jax had ordered; they'd been delivered while he was off at the clinic. Half a dozen for Mrs. Klozz, half a dozen for her aunt and a single long-stemmed white beauty for her.

Now *that* was some serious sucking up.

She'd set the table in the dining room they rarely used and shook her head as she contemplated the thought of paying guests sitting in the formal space. Charlotte preferred to eat in the kitchen, since the room was so cozy, and it was the place where she and her aunt had always taken their meals.

Just the two of them.

Charlotte felt a whisper of nostalgia. The enormous walnut table in the dining room would comfortably seat ten people.

Looking around, she realized there were treasures everywhere. The hutch in the pantry was hand-hewn and rustic; she had no idea how old the piano in the parlor might be, but it was a Steinway, and the case was solid rosewood. The living room rug was a Bokhara and beautifully patterned, and the old grandfather clock, English, with a separate face that showed the phases of the moon.

Having grown up surrounded by these things, she'd been mostly oblivious to them, but with maturity came an appreciation of the history and beauty of each piece. Who knew what a treasure trove the attic might hold? Her aunt had mentioned now and then that there were a lot of family pieces stored up there, awaiting the inventory Aunt Geneva had never quite gotten around to doing.

Charlotte sank down on a dining room chair and stared at the painting that hung over the sideboard. It depicted horses in the snow, their manes blowing, the image skillfully done. The frame alone was probably worth thousands of dollars.

But the house needed paint, the floors refinished, the extra bathrooms had to be installed, the kitchen remodeled. The yard would need upkeep, and surely there were zoning concerns to be addressed and permits to apply for. And that didn't include expenses like insurance and a website and new bedding.

"Why that pensive look?" Jax came in and handed her a glass of wine. "This is Christmas Eve." He regarded her with an expression of gentle thoughtfulness that stirred her heart. "The table's beautiful, by the way."

He'd showered and changed since Charlotte had last seen him. His hair was still damp, and maybe in deference to the older ladies, he wore a pair of dark slacks, a white shirt and a red tie patterned with small snowflakes.

He looked great, and managed it so effortlessly that Charlotte was a little annoyed, but then, he was right. It was Christmas Eve. She took a sip of the wine—lovely and mellow, the color of burnished gold. "Thank you," she said, remembering the compliment he'd offered. "I was just…thinking."

Jax's mouth twitched. "Here's a helpful hint, never do that. Leads to nothing but trouble. Where's Felix?"

She pointed at her feet, and he peered under the table and laughed. "You have a friend."

Felix was snoozing away on her stylish boots, bought on Fifth Avenue for a small fortune. He had sophisticated taste for a mutt from Wyoming. "I was kind of hoping I had *two* friends."

"Count on it." Jax's eyes were really a remarkable blue.

"I meant Mutley." She couldn't resist a smile.

"Dang, it's true, a woman scorned holds a grudge." Jax might have said something else, but at that moment Mrs. Klozz hurried in, set down a silver platter of fresh bread, and Aunt Geneva came in at a slower pace carrying a small plate of butter. Mrs. K. fixed Jax with a stern look. "You are no longer Dr. Locke, but my personal flunky. If you want to eat, young man, you can bring in the food. Do we have a bargain?"

"Ma'am, do you even need to ask? Being a waiter was my second career choice if the veterinary gig didn't work out. I'm all yours."

"Then, come with me."

Geneva was chuckling when she took her usual chair, and Millicent and Jax disappeared into the kitchen. "I like him."

Of course you do.

Charlotte spoke sincerely. "I like him, too."

"But do you love that man?"

Charlotte considered the question. "I'm not entirely sure."

Aunt Geneva sighed heavily. "It is an unfortunate family trait that we are so emotionally stubborn. I wouldn't want you to hop on a plane to go to Las Vegas to get married or to do some other impulsive thing, but I fear you suffer from the same malady I do, which is a tendency to think about things too long and too carefully. Charlotte, my child, you know your own mind. Do you love Jaxon Locke or not?"

"Yes," Charlotte heard herself say. Interesting, she thought, that Jax had said something along those lines a few minutes earlier. She'd assumed he was joking—but maybe not.

Jax came in from the kitchen then, carrying four soup bowls on a tray, along with a tureen and a ladle, and doing a pretty good job of it, too. "First course," he said. "I'll be back to pour the water."

He was wearing one of Aunt Geneva's aprons, a faded favorite with tiny honeybees on a yellow background. Charlotte and her aunt looked at each other, and both dissolved into gales of laughter while Jax set down the bowls of soup. "What? Mrs. Klozz gave this to me and told me to put it on. I did it because she said I looked nice. Do you realize there's roast beef, mashed potatoes and gravy? I'd flap my arms and fly to the moon if she asked me to."

Aunt Geneva giggled like a young girl. "I love it."

"You two go right ahead and yuk it up," Jax said, although he couldn't quite pull off the stern act clad in a ruffled apron. "I'm willing to do whatever she says. That kitchen smells so good I'd probably walk the plank and dive into shark-infested waters for a single bite. I've already agreed to take food to about a dozen different places in town tomorrow. I think I'm under a spell."

He left, and Aunt Geneva's eyes twinkled. "So he's *the* one. What happens next?"

Well, wasn't *that* the question of the hour?

"I wish I knew."

"Charlotte," Aunt Geneva whispered. "Don't pass him by. You don't want to end up alone."

Tears brimmed in Charlotte's eyes, even as she smiled. "Are you planning on going somewhere?"

Aunt Geneva reached over and squeezed Charlotte's hand. "I won't be here forever, dear," she said. "You know that." Geneva habitually carried tissues, and now she pulled one from her pocket and thrust it in Charlotte's direction. "Give that wonderful young man a chance, sweetheart. That's all I'm asking. Take your time. Yes, think it over. Just don't think yourself into a life of loneliness."

Nothing like being called out by your elderly aunt. "It isn't as if he proposed and I'm sitting around twiddling my thumbs," Charlotte whispered.

"He moved all the way from Idaho to be near you," Aunt Geneva said. "He's living in your house, and he got you the world's cutest puppy for Christmas. Maybe I'm old-fashioned, but I'd say those are some mighty good indications that he's serious about you. Besides, I want to see you settled and happy before I die, and naturally I'd love it if the two of you turned this old place back into a family home."

"Aunt Geneva," Charlotte began, "I—"

Naturally, Jax came in at that moment with the water

he'd promised. His brows went up, so he'd noticed that she'd broken off the conversation midsentence, and he looked a little smug. He probably knew he'd been the topic of discussion. "You...what?" he asked innocently. "Don't let me interrupt."

Charlotte's first instinct was to glare at him, but that would be out of keeping with the theme of the evening. *Peace and goodwill to men. And women!*

"I would love some water, thank you," she said as sweetly as possible. "I was just saying that to Aunt Geneva."

Jax passed her the heirloom Delft pitcher. "Here you go. My work is never done, I'm afraid. I think I'm supposed to use my manly muscles to mash the potatoes. Would you mind pouring? Since you're sitting around while I work my fingers to the bone, waiting on you hand and foot?" His warm teasing smile did interesting things to various parts of her anatomy.

"I set the table," Charlotte pointed out with a grand gesture at the china and glassware.

Jax upped the ante. "*I* carved the roast beef," he said.

"Humph. Big deal. *I* wrapped the gifts." Charlotte realized she was enjoying this little exchange.

"*I* had to put on this apron and drizzle some sort of white icing on some cookie bars."

She'd been trumped. "I'd love to have a picture of you doing that," she teased. "Could you do a reenactment? I'll get my phone and record the scene for posterity."

Jax pretended to grumble, although his twinkling eyes gave him away. "You're a real comedian, Charlie. I'll have you know, Mrs. Klozz is a hard taskmaster, cleverly disguised as a sweet older lady. I need to get back in there.

Besides my potato-mashing task, I've been nominated to pipe the filling into the deviled eggs. I won't be responsible for the results." He drew in a breath. "So just pour the water, please."

Charlotte was fuzzily aware of the warmth of the house, of her aunt removing her glasses to wipe her eyes, this time from tears of laughter, of Felix making a small sound of protest as she gently dislodged him from her feet, of the soft Christmas music in the background.

Of Jaxon's *other* gift. He was here, with her and Aunt Geneva and Millicent Klozz, when he could've been in Idaho, with his own family. It would have been a simple matter of starting his new job after the first of the year, instead of arriving in Mustang Creek a few days before Christmas.

She got to her feet, pitcher in hand, and began filling glasses. As soon as Jax had gone back to the kitchen, she spoke. "I feel as though I'm standing on a precipice," she told Geneva softly. "Not sure if I should move or stay completely still."

"You never were very good at staying still, Charlotte," Aunt Geneva remarked with tender amusement.

DINNER WAS DELICIOUS, of course.

More than delicious, in fact, but as far as Jax knew, a better word had yet to be invented.

True, the deviled eggs looked as though they'd been prepared by an actual devil, instead of a well-meaning veterinarian, but he'd given the job his best shot, and a sprinkle of paprika, as suggested by Mrs. Klozz, had jazzed them up. The soup had been a holiday gift in and of itself, and by the time dessert rolled around, he'd forgiven Millicent for making him wear the bee apron and use that piping-bag contraption.

His grandmother would love these ladies and this big old house, he thought, missing his family, but content because Charlotte was sitting directly across the table from him, indulging in the chocolate confection Mrs. Klozz called Heavenly Delight. He might not be at home, but he *felt* at home.

"Melted chocolate," Mrs. Klozz had told him, while the preparations were going on in the kitchen, "some whipped cream, half a cup of coffee, a few secret ingredients and some homemade cookie crumbs on top. Easy as can be."

Now, with the four of them gathered around the dining room table, candles lit, Christmas tree visible through the wide, arched doorway, aglow with light and color, Jax was happy in a new way.

"So, Jaxon, when do you start regular hours at the clinic?" Aunt Geneva's eyes were bright, and maybe not as green as Charlotte's, but it was clear that the two of them were related.

He managed to refrain from licking his spoon before answering. "I'm on call tomorrow. Officially, I start Monday morning."

"You might have to work on Christmas Day?" Aunt Geneva queried, mildly concerned.

"That comes with the job," he replied, with a semblance of a shrug.

He'd certainly worked his share of holidays, Jax reflected. He'd never minded; it was a given, something he'd grown up with. If an animal needed care, it needed care. Didn't matter what day—or night—it was. Or what time.

"I suppose it does," Charlotte's aunt agreed, smiling at him from the other side of the table. "Come with the job, I mean. Still, I think your attitude is admirable, young man. Not everyone is capable of such selflessness."

Jax smiled back, privately dismissing the compliment. He was no saint. And he had a few very *unsaintly* fantasies regarding the lady's niece.

He stood and began gathering the plates. "Thank you," he told Geneva. Then he smiled at Mrs. Klozz. "At the risk of repeating myself," he added, "that was one terrific meal."

Mrs. Klozz looked pleased. "I'm glad you think so. Thanks, Jaxon."

"It was wonderful," Charlotte agreed, jumping up from her chair. "Let *me* handle the cleanup."

"We'll do it together," Jax said.

By then, Charlotte's aunt and Mrs. Klozz were chatting amiably about Christmases past.

"You are such a suck-up," Charlie accused in a happy whisper, as they went into the kitchen.

"If I remember correctly," Jax whispered back, "that's one of your favorite things about me."

He was rewarded with a deep blush and a painless punch in the arm.

She recovered quickly, though. "Smooth," she drawled. "Not that it's going to work with me." She reached the sink, started the water running so they could hand-wash all the dishes. Aunt Geneva's special china, never, *ever*, went into the dishwasher.

Not that the antiquated machine worked anyway.

And that was another good reason not to open a B and B. No way was she going to run an inn and serve meals to guests without a dishwasher. A high-tech, quiet one at that. Or, better yet, two of them. Another expense.

"Wash or dry?"

"I'll wash," he replied. "Since I have no idea what goes where."

"Fine." Her expression was angelic. "You know, for a man, you're pretty useful. But don't expect me to back you up if you tell anyone I said that."

Jax laughed. "Gosh, thanks," he said. "A man who wears an apron adorned with bees and some sort of flowers needs all the positive reinforcement he can get."

"I think they're peonies," Charlotte supplied, getting out the dish soap.

"What?"

"The flowers on your apron. Peonies. They bloom in the spring, smell like heaven and fade away fast. Here's the sponge."

Jax took it, after rolling up his sleeves, but the glint in his eyes was downright dangerous. "The apron story does not leave this house, Ms. Morgan."

"We'll see. I know Cameron quite well. I'm sure he'd love to hear it."

"Great," he said, with a feigned growl.

She was bluffing, and she was sure he knew it. "I'd never stoop to bringing up the bees and flowers. Or the ruffles. *Or* how you let a sweet little old lady boss you around—and liked it."

He slipped a dish into the sudsy water and went to

work. "Maybe I'm practicing for when *you're* a *sweet little old lady.* Not that you'd wait that long to boss me around."

She scooped up a handful of shimmering soap bubbles and tossed it at him, hitting the bib part of his apron. "Count on it," she said.

He grinned, taking a plate from the stack on the counter beside him and dunking it into the hot, sudsy water. "Oh, believe me, I am."

A tiny thrill raced through her bloodstream and then lodged in her heart. "How about that dessert tonight?" she asked, suddenly desperate to turn the conversation in a different direction. "If I had that recipe, I could..."

She stopped. It was fine to have a dream, but this one seemed patently unrealistic. Hadn't she already decided *against* the bed-and-breakfast idea?

"You could what?" Jax prompted, his brawny forearms immersed in the dishwater.

Charlotte heaved a heavy sigh. "I really wish you'd never put the idea in my head—the one about the B and B. I can't afford it, not without emptying my 401(k) and my savings accounts. I could mortgage the house maybe, but if things fell apart, I'd lose pretty much everything." Why was she saying all this? Worrying the same old bone, like some ancient and mostly toothless hound? She didn't know why, only that she couldn't seem to stop. "Aunt Geneva wants to chip in, but maybe she'll live for a good long time—I certainly hope so—and she might need specialized care at some point. I want to be able to help *her* for a change." She paused. "It's my turn, Jax."

He washed a glass and handed it over to be rinsed and dried. "Uh, Charlie? Taking chances is part of life. For example, I know this veterinarian guy who moved from a different state to a town where he'd never been because he had this crush on a beautiful woman. Now, that might make him sound like an idiot, but he has no regrets and remains ever hopeful that it was a wise call. So far he loves the town, is sure he'll like his new job and he gets to…ski now and then."

Maybe that old line *did* work, at least some of the time. Charlotte set the clean, dry glass aside. "I enjoy *skiing*," she retorted, tartly sweet. Then her tone softened. "Jax, why do I do this? Why do I question everything, *worry* about everything? I spent seven years in New York, worrying about schedules, deadlines, waiting at the deli down the street for twenty minutes… I'm officially putting off worrying until after Christmas."

"So you say." He scrubbed a plate and rinsed it. "I think you *want* to go with the flow, but you backslide a lot."

There was no way she could deny that.

Distracted, she lifted her eyes. And there it was, right above their heads, a sprig of mistletoe dangling from the ceiling on a narrow strand of red ribbon.

Now, how could she have missed *that*?

"She *didn't*," Charlotte murmured.

Jax was still busy at the sink but he turned. "Who didn't what?" he asked.

Charlotte pointed. "Up there."

Jax blinked. "Mrs. Klozz strikes again," he said, a slow grin spreading across his face. "She must've climbed onto a stool or something. Risked life and limb. But when?"

"She probably just floated up while she was high on Heavenly Delight," Charlotte suggested.

"If anything would make a person levitate, it would be

that stuff." Jax took the towel from Charlotte and dried his hands. "Well, if Mrs. K. went to all that trouble, I guess we ought to do our part."

"That woman is absolutely incorrigible," Charlotte said. Jax reached for her. "Absolutely," he agreed.

CHAPTER THIRTEEN

MRS. KLOZZ MIGHT be incorrigible, Jax thought, standing there in that kitchen, holding Charlotte close, but she was also a true friend.

Charlotte's tempting mouth was inches from his when he murmured, "Merry Christmas, Charlie."

He kissed her gently, trying to keep his head in deference to the season and the setting, but when she put her arms around his neck, his control slipped just a little.

Maybe a lot.

The kiss deepened, and Jax drew Charlotte even closer, so she was tight against him. "I want to feel every curve, every inch of you," he whispered when their mouths finally parted.

"Mmm," Charlie breathed. "Forget the animal-doctor gig. You should be writing romance novels." He felt her smile. "One thing's for sure—you do know how to give a girl a present."

That was when Felix, evidently feeling neglected, bombed into the kitchen, wedged himself between them and sprawled across their feet.

Charlotte laughed, a soft, breathy sound, warm against Jax's mouth. "*Besides* the dog," she added.

The second kiss was even more heated than the first. Jax, with the weight of a puppy resting on his insteps, wondered at the wisdom of taking advantage of an innocent bit of greenery when he and Charlie wouldn't have the privacy to properly finish what they'd just started.

"I thought it had gotten rather quiet in here." Mrs. Klozz chuckled in the background. "Don't let me interrupt, dearies, but Geneva would like another cup of coffee."

They broke apart, and Jax sensed Charlie's urge to dash over and retrieve the pot herself, and he caught her shoulders as she turned around, whispering in her ear, "Um, I'd appreciate it if you stood in front of me for a minute or so, if you know what I mean. And I'd be willing to bet you do. Also, if you make any sudden moves, you'll probably trip over Felix."

Mrs. Klozz grabbed the coffeepot and hustled herself out of the kitchen, pronto, but not before gracing both of them with an audacious wink.

Charlotte glanced downward, then burst into laughter.

Jax's smile was wry. "Yeah, go ahead and LOL. Just keep in mind, this is all your fault."

Her eyes were full of merriment. "Do you want me to apologize?"

"Because I really, *really* want you? No, but I'm a bit uncomfortable just now. Let me go back to washing dishes. That should take care of the problem." That or an ice-cold shower.

"If we can relocate this guy." She bent down and picked Felix up. In true puppy style, he'd nodded off, and now he looked befuddled, yawning and blinking his coffee-dark eyes. "I needed another responsibility like I needed a bad rash," she told the dog lovingly, "but you're one cute little complication."

Felix roused enough to try to lick her face, then rested his head on Charlotte's shoulder, for all the world like a tired toddler, and went back to sleep.

"It's all right, then?" There was still that seed of doubt. He'd overstepped, giving Charlotte a dog. But she seemed pleased with the gift, and of course he was glad. Felix, adorable though he was, might've been a deal-breaker.

She kissed the puppy's velvety crown. "Better than all right," she confirmed.

Suddenly choked up, Jax turned back to the sink. "Mutley doesn't seem to mind the company," he said, and then he had to clear his throat.

"Yes," Charlotte said. "And I think our Mutley has become *your* dog, by the way. He sat by your chair all during dinner."

"Maybe, but I think that means I was the person voted most likely to spill something he could snarf up." Jax drained the cooling water from the sink and turned on the faucet again, reaching for the dish soap. There were still pots and pans to wash, now that they'd finished with the china and crystal.

"No, he loves you," Charlotte insisted. "Although you *were* eating as if you were on a deadline."

"Hey, I make no apologies. Mrs. Klozz should tour the country, competing at every cooking contest there is." He waited while she set the sleeping puppy down on a hooked rug nearby and washed her hands before handing her a dripping saucepan to dry. "You seemed to be deep in appreciative mode, too, darlin'. I saw a few second helpings."

"We'll just have to walk the dogs a little more often. Visit Bex's fitness center, run the trails in spring and summer...whatever, as long as we do something physical."

He gave her a mock leer. "I have a suggestion or two," he volunteered.

"Stop it," Charlotte warned, but she was smiling.

He tried to look chagrined and probably failed. Never mind. He liked knowing that Charlotte was envisioning a future that included him. "Yep, we have to stop the insanity. How about salads at lunch from now on? No dressing."

"Now you're being ridiculous."

"I suppose so. If you think I can resist temptation, then you haven't been paying attention."

Charlie raised her eyebrows. "We appear to have a mutual flaw."

"Not the word I'd use." He passed her another pan. "I'd go with *vulnerability*."

"Oh, don't you dare be more sensitive than I am."

"Charlie, just admit it, I *am* more sentimental, softhearted and *sensitive* than you are."

She acted outraged, but he could tell she was faking it. "Jaxon Locke, that is so not true."

Recklessly, he went on, "Then, let's get a passel of dogs and adopt a few cats, too, have about six kids and the whole bunch of us can live together in this big house."

Charlotte took an audible breath. "If you just proposed to me," she said, "that was a pretty lame effort."

So much for recklessness. Jax was as careful with his response as he'd been with Aunt Geneva's prized porcelain gravy boat. "If I had proposed, what would you say?"

"I'm not sure." At least she was honest, and she hadn't turned him down flat.

Since he was already in too deep to get back to solid ground, he said, "When you figure it out, tell me and I'll try again."

CHARLOTTE WANTED TO throw a plate at him. Or throw her arms around him and kiss him crazy.

Or both.

When you figure it out, tell me and I'll try again.

Jax had an infuriatingly romantic soul, Charlotte thought, while she was…sensible.

Considering their combustible chemistry, *someone* had to be the voice of reason.

She dried a meat fork and then pointed it at him. "I'm not going to be dependent on you."

"*That's* the issue?"

Hmm. Maybe it *was* the issue.

Charlotte averted her gaze, feeling like an idiot. Then she jerked open a drawer to put the fork away. "I'm very good at self-reliance, and terrible at trusting other people to be there for me. My parents died when I was little, Jax—they were young and healthy and then they were *gone*. If it hadn't been for Aunt Geneva, there's no telling what might have happened to me. Most likely, I would've ended up in foster care, since there wasn't anybody else. She and I barely knew each other, but she took me in, loved me." She stopped, swallowed. "Geneva is the strongest, most self-reliant person I know, and look what's happening to her. It scares me."

Here she went again, worrying. She couldn't seem to help it.

"If you think we aren't *all* scared on some level, Charlotte, you'd better think again." He sounded reasonable, and firm. "My mother died, too, remember? As a kid, I spent a lot of time worrying about my dad. A few years ago, when he had his heart attack, I had to face the fact that I might lose him for real. He made it, thank God, and

I'm lucky to have a big extended family, but my epiphany came when I realized I was wasting energy worrying over something I couldn't control."

"I haven't quite gotten to that stage, I guess," she admitted. "It's good to be here at home. I just don't know how I'm going to feel when I take my aunt back to *her* new home."

Perhaps she deserved the look he gave her, a mixture of exasperation and sympathy, at least the way she read it. "The place makes her feel safe and happy, Charlie, anybody could see that. She probably has a lot of friends and plenty of activities. So take her back there when the time comes. It's what she wants after all. Visit her as often as possible, take her out to lunch once in a while, or bring her back here for a few days. But you have to get on with your own life. That's what *she* wants for you."

"Now you're being preachy." She threw her towel at him, but she did feel better.

He caught it in midair, his reflexes obviously in good shape. "Preachy? I doubt it. I have some singularly impure thoughts where you're concerned, as you know."

Felix chose that moment to wake up, rise from the hooked rug and head for the nearest corner, a move Jax seemed to recognize.

Seconds later he was crossing the kitchen. "Uh-oh, let's get this little guy outside right now. I'll take him."

"No leash?"

"No time for that." Jax scooped up the puppy and went out the back door of the kitchen at full speed, without even pausing to put on his coat.

He'd given her a puppy for Christmas. He really, truly had.

And with that puppy came emergency pee runs, as well as cuddles and dog kisses.

Just one of the hazards of being attracted to a veterinarian, she supposed, taking over the dishwashing. They were almost finished anyway.

She poured herself a cup of coffee when she was done and took it back into the dining room. Aunt Geneva and Mrs. Klozz were still chatting companionably, and she joined them. The house felt cozy and warm, the tree was lit up—everything said *Christmas*, just the way it was meant to be.

"Where's Jaxon?" her aunt asked, her gaze inquiring.

"Outside with Felix. I think we barely escaped a small accident."

"He's a darling." Mrs. Klozz sighed. "Well, the puppy is, of course, but I'm talking about Jax. He reminds me of my Nick."

Nick? As far as Charlotte could tell, this was the first reference Mrs. Klozz had made to a significant other, if indeed she'd been referring to her husband, and that was intriguing.

She might have asked about Nick, if she hadn't figured he was the *late* Nick Klozz. Charlotte didn't want to make the old lady sad, especially on Christmas Eve.

"Jax is likable enough, I guess," she said.

Considering the fact that Millicent had walked into the kitchen a little while ago and caught Jax and Charlotte in a passionate embrace, the older woman's slightly ironic chuckle was understandable.

Jax returned just then, with snowflakes in his hair and on his shoulders, Felix romping before him, skittering clumsily to a halt at her feet.

Charlotte greeted the dog, but her eyes were on Jax. "Thanks for taking him out. How about some coffee?"

"Sounds good, thanks." He settled back into his chair at the dining room table. "By the way, I think *sort of house-trained* translates into *not really house-trained*. In other words, pay attention. But he did great. He'll be a pro in no time."

That was progress anyway. Charlotte loved Mutley, but she'd never considered getting a dog of her own while she lived in the city.

Although plenty of people did it, keeping a dog in New York was a difficult proposition, or so it seemed to Charlotte, perhaps because she'd been raised in a small town.

Felix wasn't just the perfect Christmas present, she decided, but a homecoming gift, as well.

The dog trotted after her as she went back to the kitchen, plopping down to watch her pour Jax's coffee. "He walked you in the cold," she informed the dog. "Without a coat. Otherwise I wouldn't wait on him like this."

She'd bet that Mutley wasn't the only canine Jax fan in the household. Women might offer comfort and warmth, but men were *fun*, from a dog's point of view anyway.

"I heard that," Jax said. "You don't have to wait on me." He was leaning against the doorway, that engaging, lazy smile on his face. "I'm quite capable of pouring myself a cup of coffee."

"I offered."

"Charlie, will you relax? I swear I won't rush this."

"That kiss wasn't rushing it?" She handed him the cup.

"Thank you." His grin was crooked. "Well, not the first kiss. Maybe the second one."

It was impossible not to like the guy. "Have you ever had a serious relationship?" *Since we were together, I mean.*

"Once, but she lived in New York and I moved back to Idaho to help my dad run his practice. Luckily, we live in the same house now."

"Jax."

"Have *you*? Had a serious relationship, that is?"

Relationships? Yes. Serious ones? No.

She let Jax's question go unanswered.

"I figure we've been waiting for each other." Jax took a sip of coffee. "We can work out the details later."

Charlotte's laugh was weak. "But you want *six* kids eventually? Really? No pressure, obviously."

"Six is a nice round number. What's wrong with it?"

"It's *six*, that's what's wrong with it. Half a dozen small individuals in constant need of love, maintenance and protection. Six is a soccer team, isn't it? Add puppies and kittens to the mix." She pointed at Felix. "Fawns, too, I'll bet. Bunnies, tadpoles, birds with broken wings."

"Maybe. Probably. But here's what I know for sure—I love you, Charlie."

"Did…you just say you love me?"

He straightened from the doorway and moved toward her. "I believe I did."

She scooted back a half step, then forward again. He rested his hands lightly on either side of her waist and went on, which was a good thing, since Charlotte couldn't speak.

"I promised to wait, give you time, and I will. But facts are facts, Charlie. I definitely love you, and you might as well know it."

Charlotte understood what he was offering her—a life.

Love, laughter, shared responsibility, a home and a lot more besides. Nothing glamorous. There'd be laundry to do, dishes to wash, grass to mow, sack lunches to make for little people heading off to school in the mornings.

She wanted it all. She wanted that life and she wanted her own career, too, wanted to use the professional skills she'd honed. Could she—could *they*—create some kind of compromise?

Yes, she wanted it all, and yet she was terrified.

"You can stop sweet-talking me anytime now, big guy."

Jax was unrepentant. "Why? It seems to be working."

He was positively *hopeless*. Back in New York he'd still been that romantic cowboy with the sexy smile, and he should just have worn a T-shirt that read, "I was Captain of the Rodeo Team in High School." He was smart, no doubt about it, but his simple approach to life was the an-tithesis of what Charlotte had lived these past seven years, what she'd hoped and planned for her future. He seemed to know exactly what he wanted, and she envied him that.

"Can we discuss this some other time?"

He acquiesced with a small forward tilt of his head. "We can do whatever you want." He glanced upward. "Well, look at that. We're standing under the mistletoe again."

CHAPTER FOURTEEN

CHRISTMAS DAY DAWNED clear and bright. Jax rolled over in bed and accidentally dislodged Can-Can, who had evidently decided to sleep on his legs sometime during the night. The cat, disgruntled, leaped gracefully off the bed and stalked away.

"Sorry," he said. Can-Can responded with a forgiving swish of her tail before she disappeared through the partially open door.

Mutley, curled on the floor near the foot of the bed, jumped up and began wagging *his* tail with flattering enthusiasm, as if to say, "I've been waiting for you to wake up. Merry Christmas. Now can we go outside, please?"

Jax reached down to pet the dog and then got out of bed. He pulled on his clothes, finishing with a clean pair of jeans and a cable-knit sweater. If he'd had the place to himself, he would've thrown on a robe, but his usual pajama bottoms were on the tattered side and would've been inappropriate for breakfasting with two old ladies. Not to mention that the big house was drafty, especially in the mornings. The place was beautiful, with tons of character, but small eddies of cold air drifted here and there. Charlotte could be right—maybe it *would* be prohibitively expensive to get the staid Victorian in shape for guests. Still, it was built to last.

In fact, the house reminded him of Geneva, aging but lovely, and with an unmistakable serenity.

Before he'd gone up to bed, she'd patted him on the arm and said, "I agree with Millicent. You're a fine young man. Our Charlotte is lucky. Keep in mind she's stubborn, but she's also completely wonderful."

Jax sat on the bed to call his father. "Good morning and merry Christmas. How was your traditional evening with Uncle Seth?"

The elder Dr. Locke chuckled. "Merry Christmas to you, son. As for your uncle, well, he told his usual exaggerated stories, most of them outright lies. It was a good time, as always." A pause, an indrawn breath. Dear old Dad was cutting to the chase. "How goes the quest to win the fair maiden?"

"Fair maiden? Dad, have you been reading fairy tales instead of Tom Clancy and Clive Cussler?"

A chuckle sounded at the other end. "Maybe. My reading habits are eclectic. And just answer the question, why don't you?"

Jax wasn't sure what the answer was. "I'm optimistic, cautiously so. The fair maiden has a lot going on right now."

Mercifully, the conversation switched to the Mustang Creek practice, with Jax's dad asking about the clinic facilities and staff. Before the goodbyes, though, the topic swerved back to Charlotte. Jax told him about Felix, and how quickly Charlie had warmed to the little guy, taking him straight to her heart. That account won Charlotte a few points, Jax could tell.

After ending the call, he left the bedroom and went quietly down the hallway to peek through her door. Charlotte was lying on her side, and the puppy slept in the curve of her knees.

She was asleep, too.

Jax caught Mutley by the collar just as he was poised to leap straight onto the bed and liven up the party. Gently, he urged the dog back down the hall. "How about a walk?"

Mut took off, apparently in search of his leash, thumping down the stairs. Jax followed at a more leisurely pace, registering that, as usual, something smelled delicious. A pastry of some sort, he thought, and the scent of bacon drifted from the kitchen. He poked his head in the kitchen door and, as he'd predicted, Mrs. Klozz was at the stove, busy as ever, while Aunt Geneva arranged plates and silverware on the trestle table.

"Good morning, ladies," Jax said. "I'm going to take Mut out for a walk. We'll be back in a few."

"Wear your boots," the women said, speaking at the same time, and then looked at each other, chortling.

Geneva added, "And a scarf. It seems to me you'll find a package by the front door for both you and Mutley. Go ahead and open it."

Sure enough, there was a package waiting beside the door, wrapped in sparkly paper and tied with a bow. After he'd slipped on his coat, Jax opened the package and smiled. Inside were two scarves, one for him and a much smaller one for Mutley, knitted from the same bright red yarn as the lacy cap Charlie often wore. He wrapped his gift around his neck, did the same for the dog, who didn't mind it at all, which probably meant he'd worn one before, and off they went.

They weren't the only ones out. The next-door neighbor was using a snowblower to clear the sidewalk, and the way Mutley tugged at the leash told Jax they liked each other, so he stopped to say hello.

"Peterson." The older man was lean, weathered, wore a gray stocking cap and insulated coveralls, and he offered one hand to Jax as he shut off the machine with a quick flick of the other. "I've heard about you. Animal doc fella, right? You belong to Charlotte?"

He supposed that was accurate enough. "Yep," he said. "Sure am. Sure do."

Ice-blue eyes assessed Jax from beneath the stocking cap. "Old Mutley, here, he's a pretty good judge of character. If he likes you, and it seems he does, then so do I."

Jax felt a dog's recommendation was as reliable as any. And it was true that children and pets seemed to have good instincts where people were concerned.

"We have a mutual admiration society going, Mutley and I. He's a great dog."

The man gave him a level look. "Millicent asked me what I thought about that bed-and-breakfast idea you came up with. At first I wasn't sure, but now that I've considered it, I reckon if the town asked me to sign off on the plan—because of zoning and all—I'd do it. The place is practically a historical site anyhow, and it ought to be restored. Charlotte would handle it right."

Jax resisted a callow urge to shuffle one foot in the snow. "I don't know if she's really thinking about it. Not seriously."

"According to Millicent, she is."

Millicent Klozz seemed to have her plump fingers in a lot of pies, one way or another.

"We'll see," Jax said, pleasantly noncommittal.

"We all miss having Geneva around," Mr. Peterson

said. "But if there's one thing getting older teaches a person, it's that everything changes. A young family living in Geneva's house would brighten up the whole neighborhood." A smile creased the old man's weathered face. He nodded. "That's a nice scarf you've got there, Doc. Very festive. Geneva's handiwork, I'd guess. She must've decided she'd like you before you even showed up, because when she likes people, she knits stuff for them. I have quite a collection myself, as a matter of fact. There's this set of coasters, for instance. She made them because my wife used to holler at me for setting my glass on the furniture and wrecking the wood. Couple of sweaters, too, and a few pairs of socks."

Jax's head was starting to spin.

Finally, when Mr. Peterson was through talking, Mutley and Jax took their leave, heading on down the street. As they went, Jax reflected on how much he missed his family, particularly his dad and grandmother, this morning, but at the same time, he was glad to be in Mustang Creek.

He liked the place, liked the people.

Just as he was returning to the house, his phone rang, simultaneously vibrating in his pocket. He pulled it out, expecting to hear Charlotte's voice, but the caller turned out to be Nate Cameron.

"Hi," Nate said. "Where are you?"

"Standing on a sidewalk with a dog on a leash. What's up?"

Nate sighed. "We've got a problem," he said.

No surprise there.

Jax waited.

"I'm at the clinic, about to scrub up for surgery. Cocker

spaniel, hit by a car. He'll be all right, but he needs some patching up."

"Need some help?" Jax was walking fast now, gearing up.

"Yes," Nate replied, "but not with the spaniel. Tate Calder just called, and he tells me one of the mares isn't eating. She's showing signs of lethargy, a few other symptoms and in general isn't herself. I was wondering if you'd do me a major favor and go take a look."

Tate, Jax knew, was Cameron's business partner. The two of them raised horses.

"Sure," Jax said, without hesitation. Like people, animals didn't get hurt or fall sick on a convenient schedule. Moreover, Calder was married to Charlotte's friend Bex. He would've helped in any case, but this made it more personal. He pulled gently on the leash, urging Mutley to pick up the pace. "Leaving now. Text me the address."

IT WAS AN INTERESTING WAY to spend Christmas morning, Charlotte thought. When Jax had come back to the house with Mutley an hour earlier and announced that he was going out on a call, she'd made the impulsive decision to accompany him, leaving Felix and friends in Aunt Geneva's and Mrs. Klozz's care.

Charlotte had never seen Jax at work, actually treating a patient.

She'd known what he did, that went without saying, but not what he *did*.

The ailing horse was a beautiful bay with a silky mane and big brown eyes, and she was wary when Jax approached. He calmed her down easily with a soothing hand on her neck, and as Charlotte watched, he began to examine the animal, talking in a low voice.

Next to Charlotte, in the breezeway of the large stable, stood Bex, pretty and brunette, with eyes that sometimes looked green and sometimes gold. "We appreciate this."

Charlotte looped an arm around her friend's waist and gave her a brief squeeze. "No worries," she said. Their heads touched, just for a moment.

"But it's Christmas Day," Bex fretted.

"I don't think anyone told the mare," Charlotte replied, with a little smile. "And I'll bet Tate still gets up and feeds the horses and handles any problems, no matter what."

"He does. Takes care of the boys the same way." Bex's own smile trembled. "With kids, it's one catastrophe after another, around the clock."

Tate had two sons from a first marriage, Bex frequently kept her young nephew and now the Calders were expecting a baby boy. "Five males and one woman in the same house. Don't look now, Bex, but I'd say you're outnumbered."

"And that's not counting the three male puppies—now the size of Shetland ponies—that we've acquired, thanks to my new mother-in-law, the former Mrs. Arbuckle. Add the stallion we just bought, and the odds are even worse. What are we up to? Nine to one?"

Charlotte grinned. "No testosterone shortage around here," she said.

By then, Jax was examining the mare's left fetlock and frowning.

Nervous herself, Charlotte tried to distract her friend. "Jax gave me a puppy last night, if you can believe it. I've inherited Aunt Geneva's dog and cat, too, and now he's talking about wanting six kids. I may need to call you for counseling."

"It's that serious, then," Bex said, looking thoughtful. "I've also heard about the bed-and-breakfast idea. I'll bet both Mrs. A. and Tate's dad would be interested, as investors, I mean. They wanted to build a hotel right here, on the ranch, but Tate said absolutely not. Still, Mustang Creek does need more decent places to stay. I'm sure you'd be full every weekend."

There it was again. The Klozz effect.

Charlotte paused, willing to admit, if only to herself, that the B and B plan was beginning to grow on her. "Frankly, I'm torn. I don't know how to run my own business. I can manage client brands and create advertising campaigns, but that isn't the same thing."

Bex, who'd run her fitness center so well it was now a national chain, didn't blink an eye. "Of course it's the same thing," she countered. "Mel and Hadleigh and I will help out any way we can. Both Tripp and Tate know good local contractors. And you've got Dr. Do-a-lot here to lend a hand. Hire a maid or two, and get Mrs. Klozz to sign on permanently, and you'll be in business."

It couldn't be that simple.

Could it?

"It's generous of you to offer help," Charlotte began, "but you and Mel and Hadleigh all have homes and families and businesses of your own. Contractors are expensive—particularly the good ones—and—"

Bex reached out, squeezed Charlotte's hand. "One challenge at a time," she said gently.

Charlotte's inner number cruncher was in full swing.

"But it's a huge commitment, and there's no guarantee I won't fall flat on my face."

"Sounds like marriage." Bex's mouth twitched mischievously. "Anyway, my in-laws can take a financial loss if things don't work out—they'd probably welcome the tax deduction—and I'm sure they'd enjoy having a new project to argue about. Look at it that way. You'd be making two rich people very happy. It's a win-win."

"But—"

"Believe me," Bex interrupted, her eyes warm. "If Dad and Lettie don't think the idea's going to work, they'll tell you. Why not talk to them, Charlotte? That can't hurt, can it?"

The boys came tumbling into the barn just then, with the dogs in hot pursuit. Bex hadn't exaggerated; the puppies probably weighed in at around eighty pounds apiece. All three of the children, two six-year-olds and an eight-year-old, were covered in snow from head to foot.

The melee was deafening.

Jax's response took Charlotte aback. "Get the dogs and the kids out of here," he ordered tersely. "Right now. You two go back to the house with them."

Tate backed him up. "Out. Go. *Now.*"

Bex looked as perplexed as Charlotte no doubt did, but they each grabbed a child by the hand, and the dogs romped after them as they exited the barn. The older boy shot out the door ahead of them.

"What the heck was that about?" Bex asked as they followed the snowy path toward the gorgeous two-story log house Tate had built the year before. Christmas lights twinkled along the eaves, and the three boys ran ahead, apparently undaunted by their stern ejection from the barn, followed by the puppies. Charlotte figured the kids were supercharged, since this was Christmas Day. "Tate's usually so even-tempered."

Charlotte was worried, too. She'd never seen Jax like that, or heard that tone in his voice. "I'm sure they're just stressed out," she said, but it sounded lame, and she could see Bex wasn't convinced, either.

She brightened quickly, though. "It was crazy this morning," she said. "With the boys tearing open their presents. You should've seen the wrapping paper fly. Luckily, Tate cleaned up the mess before he went out to check on the horses." She looked down at her protruding tummy. "I can't bend over very well."

Charlotte merely nodded.

"Anyway," Bex said, "let's have a cup of tea."

Charlotte was all for that, but still perplexed about what had just happened. If Jax didn't have more patience than that with rambunctious children, his desire for a large family didn't make a lot of sense.

The Calders' kitchen combined country charm with modern style, and she recognized one of Melody's signature clocks on the wall, a gorgeous, custom-made silhouette of the house.

She'd love to have one with an image of her aunt's big Victorian home, she reflected, still trying to turn her thoughts from Jax's sudden bad mood. She'd commission two of them, one for the house on Maple Street and one for Aunt Geneva's new place.

Her aunt's birthday was coming up in March. Perfect.

Soon Bex and Charlotte were seated at the farmhouse-style table with mugs of tea in front of them, the noise of the boys squabbling in the background. One of the puppies decided to join the kids, so big he landed in their midst with an audible thump.

Bex said mildly, "I live in a zoo, but I've learned a lot from Tate's approach to parenthood. He only interferes if someone's well-being is in danger or permanent damage is going to be done to the furniture or anything else we value. They have to sit down when they eat, exhibit reasonable table manners, say please and thank-you if someone does something for them and bathe regularly. Otherwise, we just let them do their thing. Most arguments are resolved amicably by the parties involved. Josh is with us a lot of the time, and I'm pretty sure he's on the fast track to a career in diplomacy."

Charlotte was amused by her friend's pragmatic approach to parenting. "How do the boys feel about the baby?"

"They said it was cool when they learned we were having a boy. They want their own football team someday. A girl, apparently, would not have been *cool*. At the moment, they disdain all females except those who make them mac and cheese." Bex smiled. "I'm viewed with tolerance since I'm skilled in that department."

It was then that Tate came in, stamping the snow off his boots on the rug inside the door. He didn't take off his coat or gloves but came over to give Bex a quick kiss. "Sorry about that. I didn't mean to snap at you earlier. You won't believe what's wrong with the mare, although Jax says she should recover just fine."

Bex and Charlotte looked at him expectantly.

"Snakebite. Rattlesnake probably, because she isn't feeling very good. I know, I know—it's December, but that barn is heated, full of hay, straw and other feed for the horses, which, of course, attracts mice, a favorite snake delicacy. There's no way to completely keep out the rodents, and the snake must've figured he'd found the ideal place to spend a Wyoming winter. Until we find the culprit, no kids or dogs in the barn. Spence and Tripp are on their way over to help," he added.

A snake. Well, that explained Jax's abrupt tone, and Tate's, too. Still, Charlotte felt an immediate flash of panic. "Please tell me Jax isn't in that barn hunting down a big snake all by himself!"

Tate was calm. "We have to find it," he said, not unkindly. "Cold as it is today, the snake isn't likely to leave on its own." He stood with a hand resting lightly on Bex's shoulder, but he was looking at Charlotte. "Doc will be fine," he assured her. "I just came in to explain the situation. Jax is leading the horses out of the barn. There'll be four of us and we'll catch the snake, deal with it and that will be that." He shrugged. "It's probably been holed up there for some time, though. Not a happy thought."

Bex went pale. "I've let the boys play in that barn, Tate, and you're there every day, mucking out stalls, feeding the horses..."

"Shh." Tate reached out and touched her cheek. "The boys are fine, and so am I."

"Be careful," Bex said with emphasis. She put her hand on her rounded stomach as if offering reassurance to their unborn child.

"Will do." Tate winked at her and went back out the door.

Bex muttered, "One thing I didn't put on my gift list was a snake."

"Santa would have an interesting time putting that in

his magic bag," Charlotte said. Then, because Bex still looked a little shaken, she diverted her friend's attention. "How about showing me the nursery? I'd love to see it."

CHAPTER FIFTEEN

IT TOOK A coordinated effort, but Jax and Tate, with Spence Hogan and Tripp Galloway joining the search, finally tracked the sidewinding offender in the stable office, nestled behind a set of pressboard bookcases.

"He's no piker," Spence Hogan pointed out, and he was right. The snake was a good five feet long, and as big around as Jax's wrist. "Got the bag?"

Tripp Galloway held open an empty feedbag. "Yep, work your magic."

Hogan, the Mustang Creek chief of police, had a long implement designed specifically for capturing snakes. He kept it in his truck at all times.

The good citizens of Bliss County had paid for it with their hard-earned tax dollars because the first thing most people did if an errant reptile wandered into their homes or took up lodging in their sheds was call the police.

"Snake tongs. Ordered it online," he said matter-of-factly. "I don't want to kill anything I don't have to, so live capture is my preference. I figure snakes have their place in the natural world, even if they're ugly suckers. This guy's going to be mighty unhappy being put outside in this weather, but I know a spot that has a lot of rocks for cover, and he can sleep away the rest of the winter. He sure looks well fed."

Calder shook his head. "In a way I'll miss him. I've been patting myself on the back for not having much of a mouse problem. He's been kind of like a night watchman, making his rounds in the dark."

"He's gonna be mad, but here goes," Spence said. "If I miss, run like hell. He's kind of hard to reach from here."

Spence Hogan must've been pretty practiced because he managed to snag the rattler on the first try, and Galloway was wearing thick gloves and a heavy leather coat, so when the writhing, pissed-off creature finally went into the bag, it couldn't bite him.

All in all, the enterprise was a success, in Jax's professional opinion.

Hogan cautiously took the squirming bag in a gloved hand and said, "You're off on a little journey, pal. Once I've relocated him, I'd better get on home. Melody's roasting a turkey and there's football on TV."

"My dad and Pauline are coming over," Tripp Galloway said, "but Pauline's doing the cooking while Hadleigh keeps an eye on the baby, *if* she managed to pry the kid away from my father. It's not easy. Give him the couch, a cold beer and the baby to cradle in one arm, and he's a happy man. My son's probably watching football as we speak."

"Bex had a stroke of genius and invited Bad Billy over for Christmas dinner," Tate put in. "He's bringing the food, and the boys and the dogs love that man." He looked resigned but not at all unhappy. "I think I might be having bacon cheeseburgers for Christmas dinner, but if the crowd's content, that makes my holiday."

"And he fries up a damn fine bacon cheeseburger,"

Galloway said with a grin. "Hey, if he brings his famous brownies, you are one lucky man."

Jax was fairly sure his Christmas dinner was going to be out of this world if the meals he'd had since his arrival were any indication. He and Charlie also needed to get home. "Everyone, enjoy. I'm going to give the mare a shot of antibiotic," he told Calder. "Check on her in a little while, and if you see any change, call me. She ought to be just fine. What we don't want is an infection in a tendon sheath or something like that. She's showing some systemic reaction, but not much."

Both Charlotte and Bex Calder seemed relieved when he and Tate went inside.

Jax offered Charlotte an apologetic smile. "Took longer than I expected, but the horse should be okay. The snake's removed, and we need to be on our way. An angry diamondback is one thing, but two sweet old ladies who've been cooking all morning are not to be messed with."

Bex was laughing as he caught Charlotte's hand. "What about sweet *young* ladies?" she asked.

"If I meet one, I'll let you know." Jax grinned as he pulled Charlotte toward the door, reaching for her coat and helping her into it. "I bet both the dogs need walks, and I deliberately ate light this morning, since I was saving room."

Outside, Jax opened her door, then clasped Charlotte around the waist and lifted her into the truck. She threw him a look when he climbed in to start the vehicle. "You *are* in a hurry."

"By now, Felix has probably sprung a leak," he said. "I don't want your aunt and Mrs. Klozz cleaning up after him. I know they're both animal lovers, but house-train-ing a puppy is too much to ask." He turned onto the road leading back into town. "If you decide to kick me out, I'll take him. Puppies are a lot of work."

"If I kicked you out, Mut would be heartbroken, Mrs. Klozz might never cook for me again and Aunt Geneva would point out that I'm not getting any younger. She'd say you're a decent catch and that you have good teeth." Charlotte grinned. "For whatever reason, whenever I dated someone, my sweet aunt always commented on his teeth."

Jax said with a straight face, "Teeth can tell you a lot about a horse."

Charlie had the most musical laugh. "Seems appropriate for a vet. 'Such a fine young man, and look at those teeth. Young lady, snap him up at once.' Besides, I really think she trusts Mutley's judgment more than mine anyway."

"Well, he *is* a very smart dog."

"You're impossible."

"To resist? Now we're getting somewhere."

"It's Christmas, so I'm going to let that remark slide, cowboy. Are you sure the horse is going to be okay?"

"That was one large venomous snake," he replied, "but the main danger with snakebite is usually infection. Wash the wound, calm her down, keep an eye on her, and she should recover pretty fast. Snakes often just dry bite in self-defense, no venom involved. In this case the mare was unhappy—for good reason—but her respiration was normal. I think it actually happened hours ago and she was agitated for a while. By now, she's tired, and her leg is sore as hell."

"You love what you do." Charlotte sounded almost wistful. "I was good at my job, but I think I've been ready for a change for a while now. Parts of it were exciting, although there was a lot of pressure, too. Relaxation was not on the agenda. Even when we all went out after the office closed, it was to grab a drink at someplace crowded and noisy—and we usually talked about work."

Jax didn't comment. He wanted to say that he didn't think city life was for her, that he hadn't thought so from the moment he'd met her. The wise colleague in the high heels, Charlie's friend Kendra Nash, who'd first told him about her, had seen it, too, but most of the time people had to work things like that out for themselves.

"Not that it's perfect here," Charlotte prattled on, suddenly nervous again. "But it's, well, *familiar*, and the scenery is incomparable—the beautiful mountains, the pretty towns, friendly people…" Her voice trailed off.

Jax finished for her. "But no real excitement, no glitzy restaurants, the only theater is the occasional high school play and they roll up the sidewalks at nine o'clock. If you say *brand management*, most folks in these parts think you're talking about cattle. I grew up in the same sort of place. I guess you have to decide what kind of life you want."

Oh, yeah, and there's me, he thought, making a silent Christmas wish. *Please, Charlotte, want me.*

THE DREADED ACCIDENT hadn't happened during their absence, but Felix was very excited when they walked through the front door and—oops, a little too excited. Jax grimaced and went off to get a paper towel, and Charlotte reassured the puppy that he was still a good dog as she hung up her coat alongside the red scarf Aunt Geneva had

given Jax. He'd looked striking in it, too, the red comple-
menting his chestnut hair and sky-blue eyes.

Where Jax was concerned, she realized she was showing the Morgan stubborn streak. She'd fallen for him in
New York; she was falling twice as hard now. He was an
easygoing man, but there was real determination under
the surface he presented to the world. He knew exactly
what he was doing to her, in bed and out of it.

"Well, at least he waited long enough so I could wipe
up after him." Jax knelt down and removed the evidence,
with Felix trying to lick his face the whole time. "Apology accepted." He patted the puppy's head. "Let me wash
my hands and we can go for a walk."

Mutley ran over and barked at his leash hanging from
a hook on the coat tree. Jax amended, "We can go for a
group walk. How's that?"

"You and Mut can wear your matching scarves again."

"I love my scarf, but it does threaten my manhood
somewhat, walking a dog with a scarf that matches mine.
And guess what your aunt's doing right now? She's sitting in the kitchen at the table, drinking coffee and knitting. She's making one for Felix, almost has it done, in
fact. If I'm not already the talk of the neighborhood, I
soon will be."

Charlotte didn't bother to hide her merriment at his
chagrined expression. "Aunt Geneva just wants you to
be warm. Look on the bright side—it makes her happy.
At least the scarves aren't pink, although—hmm. A neon
pink would be very attractive on you. And since she has
a lot of time on her hands these days…"

"Charlotte Morgan, don't you dare."

She blithely waved a hand. "I make no promises. Have

a nice walk. I'm going to go set the table, since that's my designated job."

He muttered to the dogs as he went out the door, "I don't trust her."

As Jax had said, Aunt Geneva was at the table, knitting needles flashing, listening to holiday music on a small radio that somehow still worked, although it dated back several decades. It had been standing on the counter directly beneath the wall phone forever. Mrs. Klozz was nowhere in sight, and Charlotte hoped she was taking a nap. The woman deserved some rest.

As usual, everything smelled enticing. She kissed her aunt on the cheek. Can-Can was on Geneva's lap again and began to purr.

"Sorry we were gone for so long. I'll set the table."

"I think maybe the white-haired lady already did it."

Charlotte stopped in the act of leaving the room, with a sinking feeling that they were having a less than lucid moment. "Do you mean Mrs. Klozz? Millicent?"

"She's nice, isn't she?"

There was enough evasion in that answer to indicate that her beloved aunt knew who they were talking about, but didn't recall her name. At a loss as to how to handle this, Charlotte simply agreed. "Yes, she certainly is." She managed a wobbly smile. "Sit tight. I'll be right back."

Sure enough, the table was set with the holiday china, holly leaves with berries around the rim of each plate, glasses gleaming, but there were only three place settings. Charlotte walked tentatively toward the downstairs bedroom, found it tidy and quiet. There was no sign of Mrs. Klozz, awake *or* asleep.

Charlotte went upstairs and looked in every room, but as she'd half expected, Mrs. Klozz wasn't there, either.

Stepping into her own room, needing a few minutes to collect her thoughts, Charlotte instantly spotted a folded piece of paper lying on her bed. Her hands trembled as she reached for it, unfolded the single page and read the elegant, flowing script:

Dearest Charlotte,
I absolutely love the ornament! You and Jaxon are so generous. I know the two of you will be very happy together. Now that you're home to take care of Mutley and Can-Can, and to visit your aunt, I must get back home. I am sorry I didn't have a chance to say a proper farewell, but my ride will be here any moment. I left instructions for when to take out the ham, and put in the potatoes and the vegetable casserole. I also made two pies. Take one back tonight when you bring Geneva home. She dearly loves my black raspberry with a little vanilla ice cream in the evening.
Best,
Millicent Klozz

PS: Oh, yes, and tell Jaxon he'll get exactly what he asked for as his Christmas gift, since he's been a good boy. I mean, of course, a good *man*.

The good boy returned then. Charlotte heard him coming through the front door because Felix and Mutley were making a racket until he ordered them to stop, a command they obeyed with surprising alacrity.

Charlotte left her room and went downstairs, the note in hand. Jax, who was hanging up his coat and the infamous red scarf, took one look at her and stopped all motion. "What's wrong, Charlie?" he asked, his voice husky with alarm.

"She's gone," Charlotte said numbly. And instantly regretted her choice of words when she saw the expression on his handsome face.

"What?"

"Nobody's dead," Charlotte told him quickly. "It's just—well—I'm a little confused—"

Jax raked a hand through his hair, and his shoulders moved with the force of his relieved sigh.

Charlotte held out the note she'd found on her bed. "Read this."

Jax read, his brows drawing together. Then, to Charlotte's complete annoyance, he said cheerfully, "I love ham. Thought that might be what we were having but I was afraid to hope."

Charlotte was tempted to punch him in the shoulder. Or the nose.

"That's all you can say?" she demanded, in a furious whisper.

He pointed at the piece of paper. "I'm glad she corrected that boy reference, too. But I *am* good, right? I believe you said I was very good at—"

"Never mind what I said." She snatched back the paper. "What's *the matter* with you, Jax? *Mrs. Klozz has disappeared. Without even saying goodbye!*"

"From what she said in that note," Jax replied reasonably, "she hasn't *disappeared*, she's gone home. And technically, she *did* say goodbye. Read the note again and you'll see."

Charlotte began to pace. "I can't believe this," she moaned. "I can't believe *you*."

"What do you want me to do, Charlie?" Jax asked, sounding beleaguered. "Mrs. Klozz is a grown woman, sound in body and mind. If she was ready to leave, she was ready to leave."

"But where *is* home?" Charlotte had stopped pacing, partly because both Mutley and Felix were watching her with worried expressions. "There are so many things I want to ask her, and now she's *gone*."

It was obvious that Jax wanted to take Charlotte into his arms and try to console her. It was equally obvious that he didn't dare.

"Maybe your aunt knows something."

Charlotte refused to cry. "I don't think now is a good time. Aunt Geneva seems a little confused at the moment."

Finally, Jax overcame his hesitation and put his arms around her. "Everything's been kind of hectic," he soothed. "Maybe Geneva's a bit overwhelmed by it all. Once she's back home, she'll probably feel better."

"*This* is supposed to be her home."

"Things change, Charlie." It was a hard truth, Charlotte knew, but Jax's tone was tender.

His shoulder was a comforting place to rest her head for a second or two. Then she straightened. "Yes. Besides, this isn't a day to feel anything but happy. I think I need to go deal with the ham. You can be my helper. Like an elf." She rose up on tiptoe and kissed him lightly. "Thanks. Although you are rather tall for an elf." She touched the back of one hand to her right eye, then her left, hoping she hadn't smeared her mascara. "You get to read me the instructions. It doesn't sound as if I have much to do, but we don't want me to mess it up, do we?"

"You got that right." His hold lingered for a minute, and his mouth brushed her temple. "Despite sick horses, heat-seeking rattlesnakes and a desolate culinary future without Mrs. Klozz, I'm still claiming this Christmas as my all-time favorite—because of *you*, Charlie."

Now, that was sweet talk of the finest kind. Her throat tightened with emotion.

"Desolate future? I can cook," she said, with some bravado. Seven years of city living, a demanding job and being single meant that she could make a few basic meals, speed dial restaurants and whip up a decent cup of coffee with a modern machine.

Another reason to fear the idea of a B and B.

Although breakfast would be simple enough with pastries, rolls and muffins from the local bakery, fresh fruit salad, sausage, bacon, scrambled eggs—she could scramble eggs. Have a selection of coffee and let the guests choose and make their own; it was, after all, a matter of pushing a button. She could offer a variety of juices, cereal and yogurt—all easy. And maybe, down the line, if all went well, she could entertain the thought of serving dinner on Friday and Saturday nights.

There she was, thinking about it again…

And with Mrs. Klozz gone, possibly for good.

As if on cue, Charlotte's cell rang, and she fished it out of her sweater pocket. The comfortable red-and-green sweater Aunt Geneva had knitted for her several years ago to wear on Christmas Day. She didn't recognize the number, so she answered with a curious "Hello?"

The caller announced, "I am Lettie Arbuckle-Calder. Since you are answering her phone, I assume you are Charlotte Morgan. When can we meet so I can see the house?"

Charlotte was confused, and Jax, watching her face, lifted his brows, his gaze curious. "Um—er—"

Lettie Arbuckle-Calder?

Oh, yes. Bex's stepmother-in-law, one half of the world's dynamic duo.

"It's very nice of you to call, Mrs. Arbuckle-Calder. We can meet at your convenience. My address is—" Had she really just said that?

"Young woman," Lettie broke in, "I know precisely where you live. Due diligence, you realize. Even without seeing the inside, I can tell you that that house could be a real showplace with a little work. Tomorrow morning at ten o'clock would be ideal, if it works for you." At that moment, her voice took on a slightly different tone, one of almost gleeful triumph. "If my husband should call, you may tell him I am already sponsoring this project."

With that, the woman hung up.

Charlotte stared at her phone for several seconds before dropping it back in her pocket.

Jax asked cautiously, "Uh, what was that all about?"

"I think I was just run over by a bulldozer." Charlotte did feel dazed. "I'm not sure whether to blame Mrs. Klozz or Bex, but even after that brief conversation I have a feeling the bed-and-breakfast idea *you* came up with has suddenly spiraled out of my control." She looked at him accusingly. "I hadn't actually made up my mind."

Jax smiled and pointed at the note in her hand. "Yes, you had. You keep thinking about it. Now, I don't mean to be pushy or anything, but the ham? Potatoes? Vegetable casserole? Be still, my heart...or maybe it's my stomach. It would be wrong to let me faint from hunger on Christmas Day, don't you agree? If I pass out, I'm afraid my smelling salts are in my other coat."

"I'll bet a bucket of ice water would revive you," Charlotte said sweetly, but he had a point. It was time to eat, and Aunt Geneva was probably getting hungry, too. She'd always served supper promptly at five.

"You'd really do that, wouldn't you? Douse a helpless man—"

"As if you've ever been helpless," Charlotte scoffed, but she had to laugh at the image that came to mind.

It was just one of the things she loved about him. The way he made her laugh, even when she felt like crying.

Both dogs were watching her expectantly. Time for them to be fed, as well. She was in charge of a lot more than just her own life now.

She could do this. Right?

"Okay," she said, with resolution. "All elves to the kitchen."

CHAPTER SIXTEEN

DINNER, AS USUAL, surpassed even Jax's expectations, and after a few days of Mrs. Klozz's meals, his standards were pretty high. He had three helpings of the ham, and the rest of the meal was memorable, too.

When he had to refuse dessert, Charlotte smirked at him.

"I'm full," he said regretfully. "But when I get hungry again, roughly a year from now, that piece of pie has my name on it."

"From previous experience, I'd guess you'll be hungry again about an *hour* from now," Charlotte said drily, getting up to clear the table. "I don't know where you put it and, by the way, I resent you for your sharklike metabolism. There's no justice. If there were, you'd be fat."

He rose to help, but let his gaze drift over Charlotte's figure. "I wouldn't change a thing about your looks, Ms. Morgan."

Her aunt smiled sweetly. "It's good to see a young man with a hearty appetite," she remarked.

He met Charlotte's eyes just before she walked away from the table. "He certainly has one of those," she muttered.

Jax followed her into the kitchen. Much to his disappointment, someone had taken down the mistletoe. He hoped it hadn't been Charlotte.

If she'd noticed the missing license to kiss, she didn't comment on it. She opened the cupboard below the sink to get the dish soap, bending over in the process and thus giving him an excellent view of her shapely backside. "Why don't you go back in and keep Aunt Geneva company while I clean up?" she suggested.

"I have a better idea," Jax told her. "*You* keep Aunt Geneva company, since you'll need to take her home soon, and *I'll* wash the dishes."

She stopped, looking back at him over one shoulder. "You don't mind?"

"Of course not. Go," Jax said, making a shooing motion with one hand. He glanced down at Mutley and Felix, who'd trooped in after them and now sat side by side, like spectators at a tennis match. "I'll feed the dogs, too. And Can-Can, if she's willing to leave your aunt's lap long enough to eat."

Charlotte showed him where to find the pet food and went back to the dining room.

Jax made quick work of the chores, and when he was finished, he retraced his steps, both dogs at his heels, only to find the dining room empty.

Charlotte and her aunt were in the living room, seated on the couch, with Can-Can curled up between them. "Time to open gifts," Charlotte said. "I know most people do that in the morning, but this has been a crazy day and, anyway, this is our tradition."

"Okay," Jax said. "Suppose I take the dogs out for a walk while you're doing that?"

"We'll wait for you," Geneva said, with a smile.

"Right," Charlotte said, without one.

"Take this," Geneva instructed, holding up the red scarf she'd knitted for Felix.

Jax grinned and crossed the room to take the scarf. "Thanks," he said. "We're gonna be stylish, these dogs and I."

Charlotte finally busted loose with a smile. "Hurry up," she said. "I want to see what Santa left us."

Jax saluted briskly. Then he headed for the entry, where he put on his coat, donned his new scarf and, after clipping their leashes to their collars, decked Mutley and Felix out in theirs.

"We are lookin' *good*," he told the dogs on the way out. "But keep in mind, it's just for Christmas Day."

Fifteen minutes later they were back.

As a child, Charlotte had begged Aunt Geneva to change the family tradition and open gifts in the morning, pointing out that the families of all her friends did it like that. But Geneva had grown up with a father who was a physician and also ran the local drugstore. People still got sick on Christmas, he'd explained, so he kept the dispensary open until supper time himself. He went in himself, rather than asking one of the clerks to work on Christmas Day.

That was why they'd always waited until supper had been served and eaten, and that, according to Aunt Geneva, was that. As a child, Charlotte had accepted the decree grudgingly, but as an adult, she enjoyed the wait.

"We used to put real candles on the tree," Geneva reminisced, accepting the cup of eggnog Charlotte offered with a misty look in her eyes. "Can you imagine what a fire hazard that was? When I was very young, I wondered why my father kept a bucket of water handy. He'd go up into the mountains and bring a lovely fragrant Scottish pine or a Douglas fir back on a sleigh. One of my fondest memories is of going with him on those trips, all bundled up, the horses trotting through the snow, with bells jingling on the harnesses."

This year's tree was real, too, though surely it had come from a lot. No doubt Mrs. Klozz had had it delivered, and she'd probably strung the lights and hung the ornaments, too.

Charlotte and Jax exchanged glances. He said, "I enjoy sleigh rides myself. Let me continue my duties as resident elf, and I'll distribute the gifts."

JAX WAS GRATIFIED that the pale blue quilt he'd bought for Geneva was an instant hit. Charlotte's aunt hugged him, gave him a kiss on the cheek, and when she folded the quilt carefully and set it next to her on the couch, it received the real stamp of approval because Can-Can immediately curled up on it.

From her aunt, Charlotte got knitted mittens and a scarf in a green that matched her eyes, a necklace with a locket that had a picture of her as a little girl and…a vintage diamond ring in an antique lacquer box.

"It was my mother's engagement ring," Geneva said with evident nostalgia. "My parents had such a happy marriage. I know my mama—and yours—would want you to have it, and it's a pretty stone, don't you think? My father's family was well-off financially, and the ring originally belonged to his mother. Perhaps one day you'll pass it on to *your* daughter, Charlotte."

"It's beautiful." She held it up and it sparkled in the

lights from the Christmas tree. "Thank you. And knowing some of its history makes it all the more special."

Next, she opened her gift from Mrs. Klozz. It was a leather-bound book decorated with a red ribbon, and when she opened it, Charlotte's eyes widened. "It's a handwritten collection of her recipes."

Jax hadn't opened his gift from Charlotte yet; he hadn't expected to receive one. "I'm all for that. Now, let's see what you gave me."

Charlotte murmured apologetically, "I'm kind of curious myself. I didn't have time to shop. Mrs. Klozz got it for me."

The box was square, tied with another festive bow, and inside, under a layer of parchment paper, was a large cookie. Heart shaped, with white icing, and piped on it in bright red icing was one word: *Yes*.

Jax stared at it.

"What is it?" Charlotte asked, with a note of eagerness.

Jax rose from his chair and handed it to her, box and all.

"A cookie? I'm sure it's going to be delicious, but—"

"I think she meant for you to give me the *word*, not just the cookie. That word is the answer I want to an important question."

"What question?"

"Will you marry me?"

Charlotte seemed speechless, but her aunt was not. "Of course she will." Geneva stroked Can-Can's head. "Now, then," she added with a ladylike yawn, "I'd appreciate it if someone would drive me back home. It's getting quite late."

It was all of seven o'clock.

As she rose, Charlotte pinned Jax with a look that said

they'd be talking later. "I'll get your coat, Aunt Geneva," she said. "Perhaps this *nice young man* wouldn't mind carrying your things out to the car while we get you ready."

Jax nodded and went to put his coat on.

Charlotte hadn't answered his life-altering question, but he probably shouldn't have asked it in the first place. Not yet anyway.

He pondered the events of the evening while he carried Geneva's overnight bag and Christmas gifts out to Charlotte's car.

Once the women were on their way, the extra pie carefully wrapped and sent along, per Mrs. Klozz's note, Jax decided the dogs could use one more walk before turning in for the night. All three of them wore their still-damp scarves as a tribute to Christmas.

The blanket of fresh snow glistened all around and, Jax discovered, this second dose of cold, clean air helped clear his head. It would've been easy to get discouraged; he'd not only broken his own vow to go with the flow for about the hundredth time, but he'd mangled the two proposals he'd attempted so far.

As the dogs yanked at their leashes, sniffing along the snow-dusted sidewalk, he considered the possibility that he might not have been too rash but too *cautious*. All his life, Jax had believed in the power of the direct approach and, for the most part, it had served him well.

Why did he keep screwing up with Charlotte?

Probably because she *mattered* so much, more than anyone or anything in his life. Everything seemed to hinge on *getting this right*; therefore, he tended to try a little too hard.

The problem was, he didn't know any other way to operate.

After about half an hour, he and the two spiffily scarfed dogs headed back.

Charlotte was just pulling into the driveway. When she got out of the rental car, the dogs were overjoyed, straining at their leashes, leaping and barking effusively.

She smiled, ruffled their ears and met Jax's eyes, just briefly.

He had the silly and strangely poignant thought that he was wearing the red scarf and she was wearing her little red hat. All four of them matched.

If he hadn't been so damn nervous, he would have found their fashion conformity quite funny. But he *was* nervous.

"Get her settled in?" he asked, referring to Charlotte's aunt.

"Yes," she replied softly, and a little sadly. "She said she was going straight to bed, that all the excitement wore her out."

"I can identify with that," Jax observed.

Charlotte nodded, but she didn't look at him again. She locked the rental car, shifted the strap of her bag from her elbow to her shoulder and started toward the house.

Jax hesitated for a moment, then followed, the dogs prancing and wagging their tails. Inside, he bent to remove their scarves and unclip their leashes, watching as Charlotte hung up her coat and hat and kicked off her snow boots.

As soon as he freed them, Mutley and Felix bounded off toward the kitchen, hoping, no doubt, that more food had magically appeared in their bowls.

Given the arrival and then the abrupt departure of Millicent Klozz, he was starting to think anything was possible.

"Now that I don't have to drive anywhere, I'm going to have a glass of wine. Do you want some?"

So she *was* still speaking to him. "Sure, yes, that would be nice. You get the glasses and I'll open the bottle."

Charlotte selected a bottle of white wine from the refrigerator and went to a drawer to get the corkscrew. She handed both of them over, and for the first time since she'd gotten back, she really looked at him. "Fair enough," she said.

WHEN SHE HIT rocky places, Charlotte reassessed, chose a new tactic; that was her personality. Straightforward. She refused to dwell on what didn't work. Avoidance, although she'd indulged in a lot of that lately, wasn't her style. She'd been successful in her job because she was action oriented.

When Jax poured the wine into her glass and passed it to her, their fingers brushed, and in that moment, everything changed.

Charlotte knew, finally, what she was going to do with the house, with her future.

It was as if the fog had cleared, which seemed sudden, but it wasn't. She'd been considering her choices all along.

No separate bedrooms tonight, she decided.

Lights, camera, action.

Well, maybe not the camera.

She smiled at that.

She'd kept Jax on pins and needles, even though it wasn't deliberate, and that wasn't fair. On the other hand, he *had* proposed to her in front of her aunt, and *that* was unfair, too.

Pondering all these things, Charlotte leaned a hip against one of the cupboards in a seemingly casual stance and took a sip of chardonnay. "So apparently I gave you a cookie for Christmas and you gave me a puppy. Shouldn't we win an award for most eclectic couple of the year, or something like that? How can we top that next year? I'm thinking an éclair. No, I don't know how to make those, but it might be in my new recipe book. Maybe a bear claw or—"

"There's going to be a next year?" The interruption was punctuated by a smile. One of *those* smiles. "Good to hear." He drew in a breath, blew it out hard. "So how about answering my question?"

"I thought the cookie said it all."

Jax's face lit with happiness, and that was the best gift she could possibly have received—better, even, than a puppy and a diamond ring. He set aside his glass and took hers away, putting it on the counter, then pulled her close. "Believe me when I say I will never forget my first Christmas in Mustang Creek."

He kissed her in a long, slow lingering promise of all that lay ahead for both of them, and Charlotte knew she'd never forget this particular Christmas, either.

CHAPTER SEVENTEEN

IN THE LIVES of people owned by pets, privacy could be a challenge.

That night, to Jax's amused consternation, was no different.

Both dogs followed them up the stairs and jumped on the bed in Charlotte's room, ready to curl up for the evening. Can-Can arrived soon after, her fluffy tail twitching from side to side.

Jax was all for togetherness, but tonight he had his mind set on another kind of togetherness, the kind that added up to two, rather than five.

"My room," he whispered in Charlotte's ear as he eased her sweater off over her head, tossing it on the back of a chair. By then, the critters were so busy settling down for a long winter's nap, they might not even notice that they were being given the slip.

Charlotte began unbuttoning Jax's shirt. "Good idea," she whispered.

Surprisingly enough, the maneuver worked. The animals, curled in a cluster in the middle of Charlotte's bed, ignored the departing humans.

Leaving the door of his room slightly ajar, Jax kissed the sensitive spot underneath Charlotte's left ear, brushing aside her dark hair. "Mmm," he murmured, savoring the simple joy of touching this woman.

"If—" Charlotte's voice caught, and she trembled with pleasure. "If we're...um, quiet, we might get away with this."

Jax laughed quietly. "I personally guarantee this much—you are *not* going to be quiet for very long."

He felt the warm tremor of anticipation move through her body.

"You're pretty confident," she said, her eyes both mischievous and sultry as she tilted back her head to look at him.

"Yep," he said. "I'm definitely up to the job, so to speak."

Charlotte moved against him. "I do believe you are," she agreed. "And I'm willing to overlook that awful pun, too."

He grinned, bent his head to nibble at her earlobe again. She groaned.

He slid his hands up her back, unfastened her bra, tugged it down over her arms and then tossed it away.

The sensation of her bare breasts against his chest was even better than he remembered.

At that point, the next step was instinctive. He kissed her, softly at first, then with all the passion he'd been holding back since the last time they were intimate.

Charlotte's response was full-out.

When the kiss eventually ended, she stepped back, slipped out of her remaining clothes and perched, temptress-style, on the edge of Jax's bed.

She looked him over from head to foot and asked in a throaty voice, "Is there a reason you're still dressed, Dr. Locke?"

Jax grinned, shook his head and promptly remedied the situation.

Charlotte was the most beautiful woman in the world. He loved her.

And there she was, on his bed, waiting for him to make love to her.

Talk about having himself a merry little Christmas.

They lay in silence for a while, their arms around each other.

"Before we go any further," Jax said presently, his voice hoarse with everything he was feeling, "there's one thing I have to say."

She snuggled against him, warm and soft and ready. "Oh, what's that?"

He cupped her face in one hand, gently but firmly, because he wanted her full attention. "Listen closely," he said.

"I'm listening," Charlotte assured him.

"I love you, Charlotte. And it's a forever kind of love. You need to know that from the get-go."

She smiled, traced the line of his jaw with the tip of one index finger, igniting a whole new wildfire inside him. "Well, I love you, too. And I'm not willing to settle for anything *less* than forever."

Jax's throat tightened, and his eyes burned. "Good," he said. "That's good."

She moved against him. "*This* is good, too," she said.

No denying that.

CHARLOTTE WAS TRANSPORTED, swept away. Jax took his time, touching every part of her, letting his mouth linger on her breasts, kissing his way down over her belly, tasting her inner thighs, even the backs of her knees, the curves of her calves, the arch of her instep. Then he re-traced the same complicated pathways, finally urging her to part for him.

She arched her back and gasped with pleasure when he took her into his mouth and proceeded, with slow deliberation, to drive her wild, bringing her to climax with slow strokes of his tongue. Charlotte trembled on the glorious precipice and finally toppled over the edge.

He soothed her as she descended, stroking her skin, murmuring sweet nonsense.

And then he sent her soaring all over again.

He made no move to enter her until she'd finally grown still. It wasn't until the last crucial instant that he realized he'd skipped a step. Stopping wasn't easy, but he managed.

"Charlotte," he half gasped, half groaned. "I forgot— Give me a second and I'll get—"

But she wrapped her arms around him and held on tight. "No, Jax," she said, the green of her eyes deepening. "Don't stop. Please."

He studied her beautiful, earnest face. "You're sure?" he asked.

"I'm sure," she confirmed. And then she kissed him.

He entered her swiftly, deeply.

Charlotte gripped his shoulders as he began to move, her lashes dark against her flushed skin as she closed her eyes and surrendered, conquering him completely in the process.

Slowly now, Jax buried himself in her, withdrew until she clawed at his back, buried himself again.

He was lost, he knew that, but by some miracle he held

out until Charlotte's climax began. She cried out, tightening around him, and that was it.

Jax let go.

His release was intense, and when he finally spiraled back into the regular world, his heart pounded and his breath came in ragged gasps. Beyond words, he collapsed against Charlotte, murmuring into her hair.

This time, she did the soothing. She stroked his back, kissed the cleft in his chin and the hollow of his throat.

She was so soft and warm as he held her in his arms.

"If that was a dream," he said, long minutes later, "it was a great one."

Having an actual conversation took longer still. "I don't know anything about children," Charlotte said, and her tone was reflective now rather than fretful. "Any more than I know about running an inn."

Jax rested his forehead on hers. "We'll figure it out as we go along," he said.

For all her former hesitation, Charlotte seemed to want to get started on the figuring out, and a few other things, too.

"Let's get married soon," she said. "I want to be sure Aunt Geneva can enjoy the wedding."

"She'll outlive us all," he said, sensing that Charlotte needed some reassurance on that score. "But as far as I'm concerned, the sooner we make it official, the better." He kissed the tip of her nose, nibbled briefly at her lower lip. "My family will need time to make travel plans, though." A pause. "Approximately how many rooms are there in that hotel where we stayed the other night?"

Charlotte furrowed her brow, but it was a pretense of concern. "Exactly how big *is* your family?" she countered.

"Big," he said. "Our reunions are something to behold. Cast of thousands, you might say."

"And they'll all be at our wedding?"

He gave her a gentle squeeze. "Probably," he said.

"The hotel isn't nearly big enough, then."

"That's why this town needs The Inn at Mustang Creek." He grinned. "Don't worry so much," he added. "Most of them have RVs."

CHARLOTTE ALMOST OVERSLEPT the next morning.

Mutley and Felix were both early risers, and they landed on the bed—*Jax's* bed, not her own—like a pair of four-legged paratroopers.

Jax was nowhere in sight.

Charlotte wrestled with the dogs for a few minutes, laughing at their exuberant efforts to lick her face, but a glance at the digital clock on the bedside table jolted her into action.

She untangled herself from the covers, and from Felix and Mutley, jumped up and hurried into the bathroom.

She showered and dressed quickly in black woolen slacks and a blue silk blouse, and applied a little makeup.

The aroma of fresh coffee enticed her as she ran down the stairs, along with the dogs.

The meeting was scheduled for ten, and Mrs. Arbuckle-Calder wasn't the type to be kept waiting. Even without having met the woman, Charlotte knew that.

The house was sparkling clean, thanks to Mrs. Klozz, so she didn't worry too much about appearances. Better to focus on the business at hand.

She needed to make a good impression, of course, and so did the house. Still, Mrs. Arbuckle-Calder knew the place needed major renovations; that was the point of this morning's get-together after all.

Now that she was virtually committed to a future she hadn't ever really envisioned, it was time to take charge and get things moving. Face the problem and fix it; decide on a direction and follow it. Yup, that was her way.

Jax was seated at the kitchen table, as she'd expected, drinking coffee and looking good. He'd set out a cup for Charlotte, too, and it was still steaming hot.

He had a talent for timing.

"Morning." He greeted her, rising from his chair. "I just talked to my dad. By now, he's conducting an email blitz, informing the family that he's finally getting a daughter-in-law."

Charlotte crossed to Jax, kissed him on the cheek and said, "Good. I hope he's telling them to gas up those RVs of theirs."

Jax laughed and returned Charlotte's kiss, although it didn't land on her cheek. Oh, no. It was full-mouth contact, with tongue.

Charlotte groaned when it was over, at least partly because it *was* over. "Don't tempt me like that," she scolded. "We have things to do. Going back to bed is *not* an option."

Just then, Can-Can materialized in the kitchen, padding delicately over to her food dish without pausing, as she normally would have done, to wrap her furry self around someone's ankles. Charlotte, in her best black pants, would have been the logical target.

Jax kissed Charlotte's forehead. "Maybe going back to bed *now* isn't an option," he teased, "but it's going to happen sooner than you think."

Melting on the inside—thanks to Jax, she'd be tingling with anticipation all day—Charlotte wriggled away from him.

He glanced at the wall clock. "We still have fifteen minutes," he said.

Charlotte shook her head. "And I'm going to use them to set the dining room table," she told him. "It's all about ambience. I want Mrs. Arbuckle-Calder—God, I hope she'll let me call her Lettie, because her whole name is a mouthful—to see how lovely this house really is."

Jax watched her. "It's lovely, all right. Because you're in it."

"Jaxon," Charlotte said. "*Stop.* Don't you have to work or walk the dogs or something?"

"Nope," he replied lightly. "I don't start until Monday, remember? This is Saturday. And the dogs and I have already made our morning rounds."

"Fine," Charlotte responded. "Then, mind your manners, please, and quit trying to seduce me."

"Okay, I'll stop," Jax promised. "For now anyway."

She blushed.

Can-Can, finished with her breakfast, made a beeline for Charlotte.

Jax caught the cat up in his arms as she passed and quelled all feline protests by scratching her behind the ears.

Charlotte, needing to be busy, hastily collected Aunt Geneva's china and silver from their storage places and set the dining room table. Later, when the meeting was over, she'd pay a call on Aunt Geneva and break the news about her and Jax's marriage plans.

Her aunt probably wouldn't be surprised, but she'd definitely be happy.

The night before, Jax had slipped the heirloom engagement ring onto Charlotte's finger, where it sparkled like a captured star, and seeing that would please Geneva, too.

It fit perfectly, too, although Charlotte intended to have the prongs checked. Vintage ring, vintage house.

All part of the package.

"The Inn at Mustang Creek," she mused out loud, finishing with the table as Jax reentered the room, still carrying the cat. "I like it. We'll need a website and an advertising budget, and I suppose we'll have to apply for licenses and look into the zoning and all."

"Charlotte," Jax said with gentle amusement. "You're worrying again."

"So I am," she admitted. She took a deep breath, let it out slowly and admired her handiwork.

His gaze settled on her ring; he reached over, took her hand and ran his lips across her knuckles. "Are you sure you don't want a brand-new ring? One of your own?"

She met his eyes. "This *is* mine. It was given to me the day I got engaged."

"So it was."

The conversation ended there, because the door knocker sounded.

Charlotte took another deep breath and squared her shoulders. "That will be the legendary Mrs. Arbuckle-Calder, who is evidently punctual. Wish me luck."

Jax kissed her. "I'll shut the cat up in the laundry room for a while, then I'm heading out to Tate Calder's place to check on the mare. I'll be back in a couple of hours, at which time I intend to resume my campaign to get you into bed."

With that, he vanished.

Charlotte needed a few minutes to breathe, waiting for her blush to subside.

When the knocker sounded again, more insistently this time, she rushed to answer.

The woman standing on her front porch proved to be petite, well dressed and professionally coiffed. Lettie Arbuckle-Calder's manner was brisk and businesslike as they toured the house, her questions direct. To her credit, she didn't scream when she opened the laundry room door and Can-Can shot out like a bullet, bushy tailed and yowling like the proverbial banshee.

Charlotte, a businesswoman herself, liked the direct approach.

"Would you like some coffee or tea, Mrs.—"

"You *must* call me Lettie," the other woman broke in.

Thank you, Charlotte thought with relief.

"No, thank you," Lettie said.

Charlotte was momentarily taken aback, until she remembered that she'd just offered her new friend and potential business partner refreshments.

She didn't have to respond, didn't get a chance to, in fact, because Lettie was on a roll. "We'll have to have a contractor come in and help us decide where the new bathrooms should be placed," she said. "There's plenty of room."

Charlotte's heartbeat picked up a little speed. "Yes," she said, although a reply didn't really seem necessary.

"Of course," Lettie went on, "we'll need to make sure

you're left with plenty of private space. You'll need a nursery, for instance."

Charlotte stared.

Lettie laughed and waved one hand. "Don't look so surprised. You *are* wearing an engagement ring after all. It's a lovely one, too. You and young Dr. Locke will make a nice addition to the community."

"Er—thank you."

Lettie's face took on a dreamy expression. "A Christmas engagement. That's quite romantic." The next instant, she was back in business mode. "Now, then, we need to sit down and go over what all has to be done. Set up a plan."

"Right," Charlotte said, and that was about all she got to say.

"Let's see," Lettie continued, steamroller-style. "Paint, an entirely new kitchen, five new bathrooms, if not six. I suppose we'll have to wait until spring to get a feel for the landscaping. Still, a gazebo would be an attractive touch. Maybe we'll put in a small pond, too, something with a fountain."

Charlotte was a little dazed by then, but since she hadn't heard anything she disagreed with, she just nodded and went along for the ride.

The moment Lettie took her leave, Charlotte was on the phone to Bex. "I need to thank you. Your mother-in-law is…a unique personality, but we're moving forward. Thanks for sending her my way."

"I would say you're welcome, but I didn't get around to mentioning the project to Lettie." Bex sounded bemused. "What with Christmas and the mare getting bitten and everything, I never actually got the chance."

It had to be the Klozz effect again, Charlotte thought.

"Well," she said, "*someone* mentioned it. In any case, Lettie and I have an arrangement. I think the B and B is actually going to happen."

"That's great!"

Charlotte considered announcing that she and Jax were officially engaged, but in the end, she didn't. Bex was a good friend, and so were Hadleigh and Melody, and as such, they'd be actively involved in the wedding plans, as well as the wedding itself.

It was just that Charlotte wanted to tell Aunt Geneva first.

And she wanted Jax at her side when she did.

EPILOGUE

The following Christmas Eve

CHARLOTTE STARTED TO bend over, realized that wasn't going to happen and had to laugh.

She was slightly too pregnant for the gymnastics required to pick up Felix's favorite new toy and throw it to him.

Thankfully, he was understanding about it and helpfully brought it over, jumped on the bed and landed squarely on Jax's middle.

Startled awake, Charlotte's husband sat up, rubbed a hand over his face, picked up the spit-covered tennis ball and fixed the dog with a steely gaze. "I regret giving you this."

Felix wagged his tail and bounced on the bed.

"I've created a monster." Jax tossed the toy and Felix caught it easily.

"You have."

"Did you sleep okay?" It was now almost seven in the morning, Christmas Eve.

She hadn't, actually. Although she wasn't sure, she suspected she might be in the beginning stages of labor. A Christmas baby?

"Well enough," she said, fudging a little.

"Liar. You were up and down all night."

He did pay attention—even when he was sound asleep,

apparently. "I've been having a few contractions," Charlotte admitted. "I don't know if they mean anything yet."

Jax was out of bed and on his feet so quickly he almost stepped on Mutley, who was lying on the rug. "Let me help you."

"How exactly?" Charlotte inquired, touched to the center of her heart. She loved this man so much. "You can drive me to the hospital if this baby decides to put in an appearance."

Jax shoved a hand through his hair, which was already sleep rumpled. "Charlotte, this is serious. This is our *child*."

"Of course this is our child. Who else's would it be?" She sent him a twinkly smile. "And may I remind you, Dr. Locke, that you've delivered plenty of little ones in your time?"

"*You're* not a cow," he protested.

What a flatterer. "Thank you, honey," she said sweetly. "You always know just the right thing to say."

Color climbed Jax's neck, and it was impossible to not be moved by the excitement in his eyes. "I try," he said with mock humility.

Meanwhile, Charlotte's backache was getting worse.

Then an iron band seemed to be tightening around her entire midsection.

"I think something's happening. Let's go downstairs. You can grab a cup of coffee, and I'll call the doctor." Charlotte managed to get the words out without a single gasp.

"I'll carry you."

Charlotte laughed. "I'll walk, thank you very much," she said. "I appreciate the offer, though."

"I'll put on your shoes." He looked endearingly helpful.

Charlotte knew what he meant, but still, that line was too good to pass up. "You want to wear my shoes?"

Jax rolled his eyes. "Will you give me a break here? This is my first time."

"Well, I'm kind of new at it myself," Charlotte reminded him.

Jax let that one go, but he insisted on helping her into her clothes and ushering her downstairs as solicitously as if he'd been escorting Aunt Geneva along an icy sidewalk.

The decorations looked wonderful, she thought, as they made their way through the quiet house. The tree stood in the front window, packages piled high beneath it, and the refinished floors glowed with a new luster. The antique furnishings were polished and smelled pleasantly of lemon oil.

It had been a busy year.

The B and B's housekeeper, Evelyn, appeared in the kitchen doorway. "Is it time?" she asked.

"I think so," Charlotte replied. "But the dogs need—"

Evelyn, an older woman with a no-nonsense personality, swapped glances with Jax.

"Never mind about the dogs, Mrs. Locke," she interrupted, her voice kindly yet brusque. "I'll see that they're taken care of. The cat, too. You concentrate on having that baby."

Charlotte could have hugged her, but another contraction struck just then, nearly doubling her over.

"We're out of here," Jax said, taking her by the arm. "I'll call the doctor from the car."

While he was getting their coats in the entry, Charlotte slipped into the living room for a last look at the tree. Christmas Eve wasn't the worst time to have a baby, she thought with a smile.

But the smile wobbled when she spotted the ornament. Jax came up behind her then, draping her coat over her shoulders. She didn't speak or move.

She was familiar with every decoration on that tree, but this one was new. Perhaps Jax had put it there, or Evelyn, or even Aunt Geneva, when she'd visited a few days before.

The ornament was exquisite, porcelain, with a tiny image at the center.

"It's beautiful," she whispered at last. "Thank you."

Jax leaned forward to examine it. "Wasn't me," he said. "I'm going out to warm up the car. Don't even *think* about stepping outside until I come back for you."

With that, he was gone.

Charlotte rode out another contraction and continued to study the ornament.

There was a cabin with lit windows and smoke curling from the chimney, sitting snugly in a snowy clearing surrounded by tall trees. A one-horse sleigh was making its way through the woods.

Charlotte's heart skipped a beat. She'd almost missed the tiny plump figure visible through one of the windows. A woman standing in front of an old-fashioned cookstove.

Jax fairly skidded through the front door. "Okay, ready... Where's your overnight bag?"

"It's been sitting by the door for a couple of weeks."

"Right." He grabbed it. "Ready?"

She smiled, touched the ornament fondly and turned away from the tree.

"Yes," she said. "Let's go have a baby."

* * * * *

A KISS TO REMEMBER

Naima Simone

CHAPTER ONE

"Excuse me. Can I kiss you?"

Remi Donovan blinked at the tall, ridiculously gorgeous man standing at the library's circulation desk.

Impossible. He couldn't have just said what she thought he said. It was Declan Howard in front of her, after all.

"I'm sorry?"

His eyes briefly slid away before landing back on her in their lilac—yes, lilac—glory. "I know this is...unorthodox. And I wouldn't ask if it wasn't an emergency. But can I kiss you? Please?"

An emergency kiss?

Well, *okay.* She'd heard a lot of bullshit in her years—one couldn't have a high school teacher as a best friend, who regularly regaled her with students' excuses about homework and not be well versed in bullshit—but this? It definitely landed in the top ten.

But again. Declan Howard. Recent transplant to Rose Bend, Massachusetts, Declan Howard. Successful businessman Declan Howard.

Secret crush Declan Howard.

She blinked again.

Nope, the face of sharp angles, dramatic slants and masculine beauty didn't still disappear. A proud, clear brow that could rock a Mr. Rochester–worthy scowl. An arrogant blade of a nose that somehow appeared haughty *and* like it'd taken a punch and come out the winner. The slopes of his cheekbones and jaw could've received awards for their melodrama, and that mouth... Well, the less said about that sinful creation the better.

As a matter of fact...

She glanced over her shoulder just to make sure he wasn't talking to someone behind her.

When no one appeared, she turned back to him. Swallowed and forced a nonchalant shrug. He was still standing there wanting to kiss her?

"Um. Sure."

Relief flashed in his eyes. Then they grew hooded, lashes lowering, but not fast enough to hide another flicker of emotion. Something darker, more intense. Something that had her belly clenching in a hard, heavy tug...

His arm stretched across the circulation desk and a big hand curled around the nape of her neck, drawing her forward.

Oh God...

That mouth. She would be a liar if she claimed not to have stared at the wide, sensual curves that were somehow both firm and soft. Both inviting and intimidating. She'd often wondered how the contrast of that slightly thinner top lip would compare to the fuller bottom one.

Now she knew.

In complete, exacting detail.

Perfection.

Giving and demanding. Indulgent and hard. Sharp as the drop in temperature on an October night in the southern Berkshires. And as sweet as the candied apples the middle school PTA sold for their annual fall fundraiser.

His lips molded to hers, sliding, pressing… Parting. First his breath, carrying his earthy cloves-and-cinnamon scent, invaded her. Then his tongue followed, gliding over hers, greeting her before engaging in a sensual dance that teetered on the edge of erotic. And as he sucked on her tongue, then licked the sensitive roof of her mouth, she tipped closer to that edge.

A whimper escaped her, one that she would no doubt be completely mortified over later, and holy hell, he licked that up, too. And gave her a groan in return as if her pleasure tasted good to him.

She released another whimper, this one of disappointment as he withdrew from her. That whimper, too, she'd cringe over later. But now, as the library's recycled air brushed her damp, swollen lips and her lashes lifted, all she cared about was that beautiful mouth making its way back to her and—

Oh God.

She stiffened.

The library. She was in the middle of the library. During lunch hour. Right before the kindergartners from the grade school arrived for Friday Story Circle.

"Um…"

Say something.

You've got your kiss and rocked my proverbial world, now move along unless you'd like to check out a book. Can I suggest Crave *by Tracy Wolff?*

Because of course she'd noticed his preference for YA paranormal fiction. Jesus be a fence, one lip-lock with Declan Howard had rendered her befuddled. She—logical, reasonable, sometimes too plainspoken for her own good Remi—didn't do *befuddled.*

Until now.

"Thank you for that," Declan murmured. His eyes dipped to her mouth, and her breath caught in her throat.

If he tried to kiss her again, she would have to…to… *stop him*. Yes, yes. That's what she was thinking. Stop him.

Didn't matter that heat, smoky and thick, flickered inside her. She pressed her fingertips into the top of the desk, the solidity of the wood grounding her. And if she touched it, she wouldn't lift her hand to her tingling mouth.

"You're welcome. I—" She hadn't been sure what she'd been about to say, but the rest of it evaporated as Tara Merrick appeared behind Declan.

Remi knew the beautiful blonde who worked at The Bath Barn, the shop Tara's mother owned that sold bath products, lotions, perfumes and candles. This was Rose Bend, so of course everyone knew everyone. But Remi had never given the other woman cause to glare at her as she was doing now.

"Declan, I've been looking for you." Tara wrapped a proprietary hand around Declan's forearm, the sugary sweet tone belying the dark fire in her eyes.

"There was no need," Declan said, gently but firmly extricating himself from her grasp.

His purple gaze returned to Remi and, though she resented herself for it, electricity crackled over her skin. She resented it because the pleasure that had fizzed inside her chest like a shaken soda can over *Declan Howard* kissing *her* had fallen flat.

She might've sucked at calculus in college, but she didn't need to know infinitesimals to add one plus one: Declan had only kissed her for Tara's benefit. To make her jealous? To play hard to get? Remi didn't know. What she knew for certain?

It hadn't been because he so desperately needed to get his mouth on her.

It hadn't been because he wanted *her*, Remi Donovan.

And damn if that didn't just slice through her like a fierce winter wind?

"Remi, if you have a moment, I'd—"

She shook her head, cutting off Declan, not allowing her poor heart to flutter over him knowing her name. "I'm sorry but I don't. I really need to get back to work. Do either of you need to check out or return books?"

Her voice didn't waver, and thank God for the smallest of favors. Declan studied her for a long, tense moment. She forced herself to meet his gaze and not back down.

For years, she'd fought the good fight—learning to love herself and to deep-six her people-pleasing tendencies. Right now, she waged an epic inner war against the whisper-soft voice pleading with her to just *Listen to what he has to say.*

Gifting him with an opportunity to apologize for using her? No thanks. She'd had her share of Pride Smackdown XII. The pay-per-view event would air next week.

"No, all good here. Thank you, again." With a nod, he pivoted on his heel and strode toward the exit.

With one last narrow-eyed stare, Tara hurried after him.

Only after the door closed behind both of them, did Remi heave a sigh.

And as a hushed smattering of whispers broke out behind her, she closed her eyes, pinching the bridge of her nose.

Weirdest. Friday. Ever.

CHAPTER TWO

IT WAS OFFICIAL.

Declan had hit rock bottom.

How else could he describe the desperation that had him sitting in his car with an anxious stomach and a numb ass?

Damn, this was humiliating.

Yet, he didn't drive away from his parking space outside the Rose Bend Public Library, where he waited for Remi Donovan to emerge after locking up for the day. Maybe he'd missed his calling. He should've become a private investigator instead of a wealth manager. Uncovering Remi's work schedule had been ridiculously easy. All he'd had to do was sit in one of the library's reading nooks on one of the Thursday and Friday afternoons he visited Rose Bend. Soon enough, he'd overheard Remi, a coworker—a tall, lanky Black man who seemed to own an amazing number of DC shirts and Converse—and their supervisor discuss work schedules.

He shifted in the driver's seat of his Mercedes-Benz S-Class, fingers drumming restlessly on his thigh. If his colleagues in Boston could see him now, their laughter would threaten the buttons on their three-hundred-dollar shirts. After the humor passed, they'd just stare at him, bemused, and offer to escort him to the nearest high-end gentleman's club.

As if staring at another woman's body could possibly substitute for a certain five-foot-nine frame with gorgeous, natural breasts that would fill his big hands. And a wide flare of hips that never failed to draw his gaze when she strode around the library. And an ass that, by all rights, deserved its own religion.

Fine. He might be a little preoccupied with Rose Bend's beloved librarian.

The librarian whose mouth he claimed for all to see in the middle of the day for his own selfish reasons.

And try as he might—and he did try because he wasn't a prick—he could only rummage up the barest threads of remorse.

Because even though desperation had driven him to that circulation desk with the request of a kiss, desire had chosen her. The need to finally discover if that lush, ripe mouth would taste as good as it promised had won out. And at that first press of lips to lips…

His fingers fisted on his thigh, and he slowly exhaled. Lust tightened inside him… One move and he would snap. As if even now, he dined on that sweet, butterscotch-flavored breath. Licked into the giving depths of her mouth. Twined around that eager tongue. Swallowed that little, needy sound.

"Shit." He shook his head.

Reminiscing about this afternoon wasn't what he'd come here for. Wasn't why he'd set up a stakeout in front of the library. That kiss had been *cataclysmic*, but, in the end, it'd only been the impetus for a plan he needed one Remi Donovan to agree to.

That's all she could be to him—a coconspirator.

He'd learned his lesson the hard way with Tara. If he wanted to do casual friends-with-benefits relationships, he'd have to keep that in Boston, not here in Rose Bend, where the town was too small and everyone knew everyone's business.

Especially when the woman was the daughter of his mother's neighbor and friend.

Yeah, not his brightest moment.

The door to the library opened, spilling a golden slice of light onto the steps before it winked out. He opened his car door, stepping out to watch as Remi appeared, closing the large oak door and locking it.

He stared. Openly. Even though she wore a cream-colored wool coat against the night air, he could easily envision the dark green dress beneath that caressed every wicked curve. Another thing he liked about her. She didn't try to conceal or downplay the gorgeous body God had blessed her with—she worked it. And damn if that confidence wasn't sexy as hell.

Not here for her sexiness, he sternly reminded himself. *Get on with it.*

Firmly closing his car door, he rounded the hood.

Remi's head jerked up, her eyes widening as she spotted him on the curb, near the bottom of the library steps.

She didn't move down the stairs. A tight, almost-tangible tension sprang between them. It vibrated with the memory of that conflagration of a kiss. Of the need for *more* that sang in his veins.

A more he had to deny.

Christ. He tunneled his fingers through his hair. She'd been a beautiful distraction before he'd touched her, before he'd learned the butterscotch-and-sunshine taste of her. But now? Now that he knew? He was finding it difficult to focus on anything else.

He'd graduated from Boston University with a bachelor's degree in business administration and he'd gone on to acquire his dual degree, an Executive MBA in Asset Management. But at this moment, he'd become a student of Remi Donovan. And he wouldn't be satisfied until he earned a PhD.

"I'm sorry for just showing up like this," he said. "But I didn't have your phone number. And showing up during your workday again didn't seem like a good idea."

"No." She finally spoke in a husky tone more appropriate for a sultry siren in an old black-and-white film noir than a small-town librarian. "That definitely wouldn't have been a good idea. As it is, my supervisor is contemplating tacking your picture to the bulletin board with Not Allowed scrawled across the top. I'm not sure if I've successfully convinced her you didn't accost me."

He winced, only half exaggerating. "God, I hope she doesn't resort to that. The library is one of the few places I can actually find some privacy and quiet." He frowned, thinking of Tara hunting him down earlier. "Well, it used to be."

She arched a delicate eyebrow, descending a step. A spiral of gratification whistled through him at that small movement toward him.

"Last I heard, you have a very nice home at the edge of town with plenty of space and, I would imagine, privacy."

The corner of his mouth curled. "Yes, I do have a nice home with a lot of space. But I also have a mother with boundary issues and a key to said nice house, which impedes my privacy." He shook his head, holding out an arm toward his car. "Can I give you a ride home?"

She studied his hand for a moment before lifting her gaze to him. "No, thank you. I drove to work this morning. Besides, I intended to walk down to Sunnyside Grille for dinner."

"In the dark?"

Declan glanced down the street. It was a little after six and the sun had just settled beyond the horizon in a spectacular display of purple, dark blue and tangerine. If he were a sentimental man, he would remove his cell and capture the beauty of it over the small Berkshires town.

But he wasn't sentimental; he was logical, factual. A man who dealt with numbers, figures and statistics—and data that assured him a woman walking by herself after dark wasn't a good idea.

A rueful smile flirted with her pretty mouth. "This is Rose Bend, not Boston. And the diner is just a few blocks away, not a long walk at all."

"So you're telling me crime doesn't happen in this town?"

"Of course it does. We wouldn't need a police department if it didn't. And if it eases your mind…" She held up her key ring. Showing him the small canister of pepper spray dangling from it. "I'm not an idiot."

"Never thought you were," he murmured, though that coil of concern for her loosened. Silly, when he barely knew her. When today had been the first time he'd really talked to her other than a murmured greeting or nod of acknowledgment. "Would you mind if I joined you?"

She hesitated, and he caught shadows flickering in her hazel gaze. "Why?"

He blinked. "I'm sorry?"

Remi crossed her arms over her chest, but a second later lowered them to her sides. The aborted gesture struck him as curiously vulnerable—and from the trace of irritation that flashed across her face, she obviously regretted that he witnessed it.

Curiosity and protectiveness surged within him. He wanted no part of either. Both were dangerous to him. Curiosity about this woman was a slippery slope into fascination. And from there, captivation, affection. Then... *No.* Been there. Had three years of hell and the divorce papers to prove it.

And this protectiveness. It hinted at a deeper connection, a possession that wasn't possible. A connection he'd avoided in his brief attachments since his ill-fated marriage six years ago. As stunning as Remi was, he wasn't looking for a relationship, a commitment.

At least, not a *real* one.

"Why do you want to join me? And let me help you out. I appreciate the chivalrous offer, but I'm a big girl—" a humorless twist of her lips had an unconscious growl rumbling at the base of his throat "—and I can take care of myself. So what's this really about?"

He parted his lips to... What? Take her to task for that subtle self-directed dig? For cutting him off at the knees by snatching away his excuse for escorting her to the diner? Admiration danced in his chest like a flame, mating with annoyance.

"I do have something to talk about with you. Can I walk you to the diner?"

After another almost-imperceptible hesitation, she nodded. "Okay."

She turned, and he fell into step beside her. Silence reigned between them, and he used the moment to survey the picturesque town that had so completely charmed his mother three years ago that she'd moved here. Elegant, quaint shops, trees heavy with gold, red and orange leaves, lampposts and cute benches lined Main Street. A well-manicured town square, with a colonial-style building housing the Town Hall, and a white, clapboard church with a long steeple soaring toward the sky completed a picture that wouldn't have been out of place on a glossy postcard.

Walking down this sidewalk with people strolling hand in hand or as families, their chatter and laughter floating in the night air, it was easy to forget that heavily populated, traffic-choked Boston lay three hours away.

He tucked his hands in the front pockets of his pants, pushing his coat open. The night air, though cool, felt good on his skin. Inhaling, he held the breath for several seconds, then released it, slowly, deliberately.

"Remi, I apologize if my kissing you earlier today caused you any problems. Sometimes I forget how small towns can be. Especially since I'm only here every other weekend, which isn't the case for you. I'm sorry I didn't take that into account." He paused. "Has anyone…said anything to you?"

"You mean besides my supervisor, who wanted to quarter and draw you, then lectured me on professional decorum? Or do you mean Mrs. Harrison, my hair stylist's grandmother, who'd been standing in the reference section and offered me her advice on how to handle a beast like you? Her words, not mine. Or do you mean Rhonda Hammond, the kindergarten teacher there for Friday Story

Circle, who gave me a thumbs-up because she'd heard about it from a friend?"

He grimaced, nodding at a person passing by. "The grapevine is alive and well, I see."

"Thriving."

"Are you in trouble at work?" he gently asked. He'd never forgive himself if his impulsive—and yes, selfish— actions cost her job. "I know you already spoke to your supervisor, but I can, as well. I'll call first thing Monday—"

"That's not necessary." She stopped next to a bench across from the shadowed windows of a closed clothing boutique. "Declan, could you get to the reason why you showed up at the library?"

He stared down into her upturned face. Dark auburn waves framed her hazel eyes, the graceful slope of her cheekbones, the upturned nose and the wicked sinner's mouth. And that shallow, tempting dent in the center of her chin. It never failed that, whenever his gaze dropped to it, he had to resist the compulsion to dip his finger there. Or his tongue.

Madonna and Delilah. That's what she was. Saint and temptress. An irresistible lure that he had to resist.

"I need your help, Remi," he said, resenting like hell the roughened quality to his voice. Clearing his throat, he continued, "This is going to sound…odd, but… Will you be my woman?"

Her face went blank. "Excuse me?" she whispered.

His words played through his head, and he slashed a hand through the air between them. "Hold on, let me rephrase. Will you *pretend* to be my woman? *Pretend.*"

Relief and another, more complicated, murkier emotion

wavered in her expression. He peered at her. The need to delve deeper prickled at his scalp.

But that damn curiosity. That protectiveness.

He backpedaled away from her secrets like they had detonators and a steadily ticking clock attached to them.

"Maybe you should start at the beginning." She leveled an inscrutable glance on him, then turned and continued walking down the sidewalk.

Resuming his pace next to her, he huffed out a dry chuckle. "I don't know how to relay this without looking like a dick." Stuffing his hands into the pockets of his coat, he continued, "I don't think it's a secret around here that I…took Tara Merrick out a few times."

"I believe the word you're struggling to find is *date*," she drawled.

He arched an eyebrow. "And I believe *date* is too strong a word," he shot back. "I took her to the movies, dinners—a few of those were at my mom's house so they really don't count, since she and her mother are my mom's neighbors—coffee. Nothing serious."

Remi stopped in the middle of the sidewalk and whipped out her phone. Seconds later, she started tapping on the screen.

"What are you doing?" Frowning, he nudged her to the side, out of the flow of pedestrian traffic.

"I'm pulling up my online dictionary. I mean, I'm just a librarian with a whole reference desk at my disposal, but I'm pretty sure you gave me the very definition of a *date*. But I want to double-check before I call you out. I so hate being wrong."

"Smart-ass," he growled, snatching the cell from her hand and tucking it back in her coat pocket.

His cock perked up at the mere mention of her fantastic ass even as he hungered to press his thumb to the plush bottom curve of her mouth and come away smeared with her deep red lipstick.

"And for your information," he said, voice lower, heavier, unable to scrub that image of her smeared lips from his mind. "It isn't a date when I'm up-front from the beginning that I'm not looking for any kind of attachment, and I warn her not to expect anything to come out of it. We were just two people enjoying each other's company while I was in town for the weekend. Nothing more. I was very clear about that."

I always am. I always will be.

She tilted her head to the side, her long dark red waves spilling over her shoulder. "Then why bother?"

"Because..." Declan turned, strode off, and the sweet scent of butterscotch and the aroma of almonds assured him she followed. "It made my mother happy. And after years of rarely seeing her smile after my father died, giving her a reason to didn't seem like much of a sacrifice on my part."

Silence beat between them, filled by the chatter of passersby and the low hum of Rose Bend's version of Friday-night traffic.

"That kind of detracts from your dick status," she finally murmured.

He glanced at her, a smile tugging at his mouth. "Thank you... I think."

"That's why you bought a house here, too, isn't it?" She slid him a look, and the too-knowing gleam trickled down his spine like an ice cube. "Mrs. Howard moved to Rose Bend three years ago, but you didn't buy a house here until last year. You're only in town every other weekend—really you could stay with her. There was no need for you to buy a house. But you did it so she would feel like she had family here. So she had her son here."

He shrugged, not liking this feeling of... Vulnerability. Of being so easily read like one of the books at her library.

"It was nothing. Like I said earlier, I need my space. And what little privacy she allows me." He smiled, even if it was wry. "Which brings me back to why I need you." Lust struck a match against the kindling of need in his gut, flaring into flames at his choice of words. He deliberately doused them. "After our...display at the library, Tara seemed to finally back off."

"Not how I saw it," Remi muttered under her breath, but he caught it.

"True, she chased me out of there, but when I told her we were involved, and what she saw was me being dead serious about what I'd been telling her for the past two weeks—which is that there would be no more movies, no more dinners—the truth seemed to sink in. But I'm not fooling myself into believing it will stick. Not if I don't follow it up with reinforced behavior. Otherwise, she'll convince herself kissing you was a fluke, and I didn't mean it when I said she and I were over." He rubbed his hand over his jaw, his five-o'clock scruff scratching his palm. "That we were never a 'we' to begin with."

"So you want me as your beard to run her off?"

He frowned. Her bland tone didn't hint that he'd offended her. Neither did her perfunctory summation. Yet, he still got the sense he had.

"My beard?" he repeated. "No, I wouldn't put it that way—"

"What other way is there to put it?" She waved a hand, dismissing the question. "And what do I get out of this little…bargain? Well, other than the title of the latest woman you dumped when we end the charade."

Oh yes, definitely offense there. And maybe a trace of bitterness.

"Remi." He gently grasped her elbow, drawing her to a halt. "I didn't mean to insult you."

"You didn't," she argued, stepping back and removing herself from his hold. Chin hiked up, she offered him a polite smile that halted just short of her hazel eyes. "I'm sorry, but I have to turn down your proposal."

Fuck the fake girlfriend arrangement. Fuck wanting her agreement. He'd inadvertently hurt her; she didn't need to say it. The evidence drenched those eyes, drowning out the green and gold so only the brown remained, dark and shadowed.

He reached for her.

"Remi—"

"If it's okay with you, I'm going to head back to the library. I'm not hungry anymore."

She sharply pivoted on her ankle boot, but just as she started to head in the opposite direction, the door to the establishment behind them opened and two older couples and a younger one spilled out into the night.

Remi skidded to an abrupt stop, her entire body going as rigid as one of the statues that littered the Boston Public Garden. Concerned, he dragged his gaze from the small group of people to her and shifted closer. Close enough to hear her mutter…

"Shit."

CHAPTER THREE

DECLAN'S CURIOUS STARE damn near burned a hole in the side of Remi's face, but she avoided meeting that sharp lilac scrutiny. Afraid that while she stood there in the middle of the sidewalk in her own version of an O.K. Corral showdown with her parents, her younger sister, Briana, her sister's new fiancé, Darnell Maitland, and his parents, Declan might spy entirely too much.

Too much of what she didn't want him to see.

Like the hated, grimy envy that had no place alongside her happiness for her sister.

Like the uneasy mixture of love and dread for her mother.

Like the anxiety-pocked need to run, run and never stop until her lungs threatened to burst from her chest.

"Remi, honey." Her mother, voice pitched slightly higher, switched rounded eyes from her to Declan and back to her. "What a surprise."

Translation: *What's going on and what're you doing with Declan Howard?*

No. *Nononono.*

Remi smothered a groan. Why was this happening to her? Today must be cursed. First, the hottest, make-her-lady-parts-weep kiss she'd ever experienced. Then the whispers, not-so-subtle high fives and unsolicited comments and advice. Then Declan's surprising appearance after work and his, uh, unconventional proposal.

And now this.

Twenty-six years as her mother's daughter had earned Remi a W-2 and pension in all things Rochelle Donovan. And Remi recognized that particular shrewd gleam in her mother's eyes.

No way in hell could Remi have Rochelle start thinking Remi and Declan were a *thing*.

"Hi, Mom, Dad." She forced herself to move forward and brushed a kiss over her mother's cheek, then gave her big, lovable bear of a father a hug. "Hey, sis. And future in-laws." Her smile for Briana, Darnell and the Maitlands came more naturally to her lips.

After all, it wasn't Briana's fault that she was three years younger than Remi, had fallen in love and was getting married, much to the delight of their mother.

"Hi, sweetie," Sean Donovan greeted. "How's my best girl doing?"

"Hey!" Briana playfully jabbed their father in the side with an elbow. "I'm standing right here."

"Sorry, you weren't supposed to hear that. You know you're my best girl," he teased.

Remi shook her head, grinning at their father and the joke that had been running around their house as long as she'd been alive. All the Donovan girls—her, Briana and Sherri, their oldest sister—knew with 100 percent certainty that Sean loved them equally and completely.

"I was hoping you could join us for dinner tonight," Briana said, then shot her a sly smile. "But now I see why you turned down the invite. You had a better offer. I ain't mad at you," she stage-whispered.

"What?" Remi blinked, heat blasting a path up her chest and into her face. Thank God for the dark. "No, this isn't—" She waved a hand between her and Declan, silently ordering herself not to look at him. "No," she repeated. Firmly. Because that glint hadn't disappeared from either her mother's or sister's gazes. But wait. Hold up a second. "And what invitation? I didn't get..." She glanced at Rochelle.

So did Briana.

"Mom?" Briana frowned. "I asked you to tell Remi about dinner tonight. You didn't call her?"

"I'm sorry, honey. I must've forgot." She winced, lifting a shoulder in an apologetic half shrug. "You were at work anyway, Remi. And besides, you probably would've been uncomfortable as a third wheel."

Anger and hurt coalesced inside her, shimmering bright and hot.

Her mother hadn't forgotten. More like she hadn't wanted to be embarrassed by her middle daughter's perennially single status. And as Briana's gaze narrowed on Rochelle, Remi could tell her sister knew it, as well.

"But," Rochelle continued, smiling at Declan, who'd remained silent since bumping into her family, "since you're here, why don't you join us? We were heading to Mimi's Café for coffee. You, too, Declan. We'd love to have you."

Panic ripped through Remi, and she glanced at Declan. As if he'd been waiting for that moment, his eyes connected with hers, and the clash reverberated like a collision of metal against screeching metal. She *felt* him. In her chest, belly... Lower.

"Declan?" her mother asked again, breaking their

visual connection like cracked glass sprinkling to the ground.

He looked at her mother. Smiled.

"I would be delighted to join you. Thank you for inviting me."

Shit.

Again.

"WHAT THE *HELL*, REMI? I heard Declan Howard kissed you in the middle of the library today, but I thought that was just gossip! But apparently not! You've been holding out on me." Briana hip-checked Remi, her mock scowl promising retribution. "How long has this been going on?"

Remi sighed, sneaking a peek in Declan's direction. He stood with her father and Darnell near the bakery case, talking. Part of her battled the urge to save him from a possible pumping of information by her father. But the other, admittedly petty, half thrilled in leaving him served up to that grilling since he agreed to this craziness.

"Bri, we're just friends," Remi hedged. Were they even that? In the years since his mother had moved to Rose Bend, she'd barely said a handful of words to him.

"Friends who tongue wrestle?" Briana nodded. "Yes, Darnell and I are the best of friends, too."

Remi snickered, then sipped her caramel macchiato. "I have no idea how he puts up with you."

"Right?" Briana beamed. She turned, scanning the café until her gaze landed on her fiancé. And her pretty face softened with such adoration that Remi cleared her throat. As if sensing her attention on him, the handsome IT analyst with dark brown eyes and beautiful almond skin, looked up and sent his fiancée the sweetest smile.

"I'd say, 'Get a room,' but you might take that literally," Remi drawled, those conflicting emotions of envy and happiness warring in her chest again.

Briana chuckled, and Remi rolled her eyes at the lasciviousness of it. *Yech.*

"Bri, I need to borrow your sister for a minute." Rochelle appeared beside Remi, slipping an arm through hers. "You should go entertain your future mother-in-law instead of flirting with your fiancé and making the rest of us blush."

Remi bit back a groan even as she allowed herself to be led away to a corner of the café. She'd been trying to avoid her mother since arriving at Mimi's. Even a cup of her favorite hot beverage couldn't make her forget that her mother had an agenda by inviting her and Declan to join a gathering she'd intentionally excluded Remi from in the first place.

And yeah, best not dwell too long on that.

"Honey, what is that you're drinking?" Rochelle scrunched up her nose.

Dread swished in her stomach like day-old swill. "Caramel macchiato."

"That's nothing but dessert in a cup. Tea is so much better for you." She shook her head, and her disappointment dented the hard-won, forged-in-fire armor of confidence Remi had built around herself—her heart. "Now, tell me about what's going on between you and Declan."

God, if she held in all these sighs, she would end up with gastric issues.

"Mom, don't get ahead of yourself," she warned.

"You know I'm not one to listen to gossip." Remi coughed, earning a narrow-eyed look from her mother.

"But I heard about the kiss at the library. Really, Remi, a little more propriety would've been appreciated, but if the story is true…"

Remi didn't confirm or deny, just sipped her drink. But her mother obviously took her silence as confirmation, and a smile that could only be described as cat-ate-the-whole-flock-of-canaries spread across her face.

"If the story is true, then why haven't you brought him by the house for dinner? Do you know how embarrassing it is to hear that my daughter is dating one of the most eligible men in town from someone else? And here I've been so worried about—"

"Mom, please, stop. Declan and I— We're just friends," she interrupted, holding up her free hand, palm out.

Her mother's excited flow of words snapped off like the cracking of a brittle tree limb. She stared at Remi, the delight in her eyes dimming to frustration and… Sadness. It was that sadness that tore through Remi. As if her *mediocrity* actually pained her mother.

Rochelle's gaze dropped down to Remi's body, skimming her dress. Before her mother's scrutiny even lifted back to Remi's face, anxiety and unease churned in her belly. Tension invaded her body, drawing her shoulders back, pouring ice water into her veins.

She knew what was coming.

Braced herself for it.

"Maybe… Maybe if you would try to dress just a bit more appropriately for a woman of your—stature, you could possibly be more than friends. If you wore clothes that…concealed rather than drew attention to problematic areas, perhaps Declan would focus more on your lovely face and ignore everything else."

The gentle tone didn't soften the dagger-sharp thrust or make the wound bleed any less.

That it was her mother who twisted the knife and sought to slice her self-esteem to shreds only worsened the pain.

"I'm only telling you this because I love you, and I want you to be happy like your sisters. You know that, don't you, honey?" Rochelle covered Remi's cold hand, squeezed it, the hazel eyes that Remi had inherited, soft and pleading.

I don't know that! If you cared, if you really loved me like you do Briana and Sherri, then you would see how you're tearing me apart.

The words howled inside her head, shoved at her throat with angry fists. Only the genuine affection in her mother's gaze chained them inside. That and her unwillingness to hurt her mother, even though Rochelle didn't possess the same reluctance.

"If you'll excuse me," Remi murmured, setting her drink down on a nearby table. She couldn't stomach it anymore.

Couldn't stomach... A lot of things anymore.

Without waiting for her mother's reply, she strode over to the small group where Declan stood. He glanced down at her, and that violet gaze sharpened, seeming to bore past the smile she fixed on her face.

Several minutes later, before she had time to fully register being maneuvered, she found herself bundled in her coat on the sidewalk outside the café, Declan at her side.

She didn't speak as they strolled back in the direction of the library, and he didn't try to force her into conversation. The events of the entire day whirled through her mind like a movie reel, pausing on the kiss before speeding on fast-forward to him showing up at the library only to pause on her discussion with her mother.

I want you to be happy like your sisters.

Remi could pinpoint the last time her mother had been proud of her. Because it'd been the time of her last heartbreak, her last failure.

And the whole town had been there to bear witness.

For Rochelle Donovan, happiness meant a husband, marriage, children. And Remi desired that—she did. But if she didn't have them, she wasn't less of a woman, less worthy. Not having the whole fairy-tale wedding and family thing wouldn't be due to the size of her breasts, hips or ass. And she refused to decrease in size—whether in weight, personality or spirit—for someone else to love her.

She'd been willing to do that once. Never again.

And yet... Yet, for a moment, Remi had glimpsed that flicker of pride in her mother's eyes again, and her heart had swelled. It'd been so long.

She was tired of being a failure in her mother's eyes. Of being a disappointment. Was it so wrong to yearn for that light in Rochelle's gaze directed toward her, the one Briana and Sherri took for granted?

Remi knew who she was. Knew her own worth. Owned herself.

But just once...

She slammed to an abrupt halt. And turned to Declan.

To his credit, he didn't appear surprised or alarmed. He just slid his hands into his pants pockets, his coat pushed back to expose that wide chest, flat abdomen and those strong thighs. A swimmer's body—tall, long and lean. And powerful. Staring at him, she combatted the need to step close and closer still, curl against the length of him and just… Rest. She'd come to rely on herself a long time ago, but in the café, she'd uncharacteristically allowed him to take charge. And it'd been a relief. To let someone else carry the burden for a few moments—yes, it'd been a relief.

But that had been an aberration.

She just needed him for one thing.

"I've changed my mind. I'll pretend to be your girl-friend."

Declan cocked his head to the side, studied her for a long moment. "Why have you changed your mind?"

"Does it matter?"

"Yes," he murmured. "I think it does."

A flutter in her belly at his too-soft, too-damn-understanding voice. "No, it doesn't," she said. "Are *you* changing *your* mind?"

Again, he didn't immediately reply. "No, Remi, I'm not. I still need you."

Dammit, he should choose his words more carefully. A greedier woman could read more into that statement.

"Well then, I accept. But I have my own counterpro-posal." When he dipped his chin, indicating she continue, she inhaled a breath, held it, then exhaled, attempting to quell the riot of nerves rebelling behind her navel. "You have to agree to attend Briana's engagement party with me in a month. Four weeks should be more than enough time to convince Tara that we're a legitimate couple." She stuck out her hand. "Deal?"

Declan stared at her palm as if he read all her secrets in the lines and creases. Slowly, he lifted his intense gaze to hers and, without breaking that connection, engulfed her hand in his bigger, warmer one.

Then drew her closer.

And closer.

Until his woodsy cloves-and-cinnamon scent surrounded her, warmed her. Seduced her. She sank her teeth into her bottom lip. Trapping the moan that nudged at her throat and ached to slip free.

The hand not holding her hand cupped her neck, his thumb swept the skin under her jaw. She shivered.

And held her breath.

Those beautiful, carnal lips brushed over her forehead.

"Deal."

She exhaled.

These next four weeks were going to be… Killer.

CHAPTER FOUR

Declan: Hey, are you up?

Remi: It's 9:30. I'm not 80.

Declan: Is that a yes?

Remi: *sigh* Yes.

Declan: Is it ok for me to call?

Remi: Sure.

REMI STARED AT her phone screen, heart thudding in her chest, waiting on the black to light up with his name as if she were a teen and the captain of the football team had promised to call. And when the screen lit up with his name, she had to slap her traitorous heart back down with a reality check.

Fake relationship. Get it together. This isn't some chick flick starring Zendaya.

"Hello."

"Why don't I remember you being this snarky before?" he asked in lieu of greeting.

Because we've never had a real conversation past "Hi" and "Excuse me, I need to get to the creamer" at Mimi's

Café. Since saying that would reveal more than she was willing to expose, she went with, "I'm not sure I can answer that. And tell me that's not what you called to ask me."

He snorted. "No. It hit me that we didn't come up with a cover story for how we got together. If our…relationship is going to be believable, we'll have to be of one accord with that."

"Wow." Remi shook her head even though he couldn't see the gesture. "Is even saying the word *relationship* painful?"

"Oh, sweetheart, if you only knew," he drawled.

No, Remi ordered her damn heart again. You will not turn over at that endearment. *Cut the shit!*

She cleared her throat, absently picking at the thread on the couch cushion beneath her. "So do you have any ideas for how we became completely enamored of one another?"

"I'm guessing me trying to stop you from bringing disease and destruction to the earth, but we ended up falling for one another is out?"

A loud bark of laughter escaped her, and she clapped a hand over her mouth even though no one lived with her to hear it. "And what's this disease that I'm so intent on bringing to the earth? Love?"

His mock gasp echoed in her ear. "How did you know?"

She snickered. "Okay, I've read *Pestilence*, too, and Laura Thalassa is brilliant. Oh, which reminds me." She snapped her fingers. "I've been meaning to recommend *Crave* by Tracy Wolff, if you haven't read it already. I think you'll love it."

"Thank you. I'll definitely pick it up." A pause. "How do you know what books I'll love?" he murmured.

Heat surged into her face, and she closed her eyes,

lightly banging her head against the back of the couch. Dammit.

"I'm a librarian. It's my job to notice what people are reading." *Nice save*, she assured herself. She hoped. *Please God, let it be a nice save.* "Besides, when a man comes into the library and I catch him unashamedly reading YA paranormal romance, my nerd heart rejoices. And I want to feed his literary addiction."

When he chuckled, she silently breathed a deep sigh of relief. And sent up another prayer of thanksgiving. And maybe a promise to attend service on Sunday. It'd been a while.

"There's our story," Declan said. "We met at the library when you noticed what I was reading and suggested a book you thought I'd like. We struck up a conversation, I asked you out, the rest is history."

"It's like our own book nerd fairy tale."

"Book nerds are the shit."

"Hell yeah we are." Remi grinned, and once more had to order her heart to stop doing dumb things. Like swooning.

"'Night, Remi. And thank you again."

"Good night, Declan."

Remi: I've arranged our first date for Friday night after you get to Rose Bend. Hayride.

Declan: Pass.

Remi: Sorry. Bought the tickets. You wanted to be visible. What's more visible than a hayride?

Declan: Dinner. Coffee. A stroll. Standing in the damn street. All don't involve hay. Or hay.

Remi: We're doing it. Suck it up, city boy.

Declan: Why am I doing this again?

Remi: Hey! You kissed me!

Declan: Oh believe me. I can't forget.

Remi: ...

Declan: Too soon?

Remi: Bundle up. It's going to be cold.

* * *

Declan: So the hayride was fun.

Remi: ...

Declan: I can hear you saying I told you so.

Remi: Me? Nooooo.

Remi: But I did.

Declan: No one likes a know-it-all. Even beautiful ones.

Remi: You don't need to do that.

Declan: Do what?

Remi: Do the compliment thing when no one's around to hear it.

Declan: I can be truthful whether I have an audience or not, Remi.

Declan: If it makes you uncomfortable, I won't say or rather type it.

Remi: No it doesn't. Just... It's not necessary.

Declan: Are we having our first argument as a couple?

Remi: I think we are... And just for the record, I win.

Declan: Of course, dear. Yes, dear.

Remi: Such a good fake boyfriend.

* * *

Remi: Heads-up. If Tara asks, my nickname for you is baby-cakes.

Declan: WTF??

Remi: She was pushing it. Had to come up with something.

Remi: Ok, kidding. Sorta. But she did corner me today and was her usual petty self.

Remi: Why didn't you tell me you used to be married?

THE PHONE RANG seconds later, and Remi sighed before swiping her thumb across the screen. She should've expected this call, but her stomach still dropped toward her bare feet. All afternoon, since Tara had approached Remi outside Sunnyside Grille after lunch, she'd gone back and forth about whether or not she would ask Declan about his previous marriage.

Over the two weeks they'd been "together," the texts and phone calls had been constant, and when he came to Rose Bend, they'd spent every day together. As couples did. But they weren't real—no matter how her pulse tripped over itself at just the sound of his voice in her ear or the sight of his name in her messages. Or how thick, hot desire twisted inside her when his hand rested on her hip or cupped the back of her neck. A shiver rippled down her spine at just the memory of the possessive touch.

No. Not possessive. She had to remember and remind herself what this was. Fake. A sham. For the benefit of another woman who'd done what Remi could not allow herself to do.

Fall for him.

She could not be that naive or stupid.

Raising the phone to her ear, she said, "Hey."

"Remi," he replied. "What did she say to you?"

"She didn't go into details," she gently reassured him. Because from the tautness of his voice, it seemed as if he needed to be reassured. "It seemed more like she wanted me to know she had information about you that I didn't have." She hesitated but couldn't hold back the question that had been plaguing her for hours. "Why didn't you mention it, Declan?"

"It's not important."

The abrupt, almost-harsh reply echoed in the silence that fell between them, mocking his adamance.

"Your mom might not have moved to town yet during

my last relationship, so you may not have heard about it. But it was the topic of conversation three years ago, for months." She inhaled a deep breath, bile pitching in her stomach at the thought of talking about Patrick and the disastrous, public ending of their relationship. But if she wanted Declan to trust her with his story, maybe she had to take that first step.

"Patrick Grey was a resident at the hospital in the next town over but lived here. We met at the annual motorcycle rally, and I fell hard, fast. Handsome, smart, and yeah, he was going to be a doctor. Not bad, right?"

She gave a soft, self-deprecating laugh. Because, yes, bad. If only she hadn't allowed those things to blind her to his other, not-so-favorable traits.

"We were together for a year and a half. And him being a resident, we didn't have a ton of time together. But I loved and enjoyed every minute when we were. So much that when he started criticizing my dinner or breakfast choices, or offering his opinion on what I wore, I didn't see his comments as negative. Just that he was concerned with my health or wanted me to look my very best. But when he started using what he called 'reward systems'— lose five pounds and he would agree to take me to the bar around his work friends—then I couldn't deny what I'd been ignoring."

"Remi," Declan breathed. "You don't have to tell me this."

"I'd like to say that I broke up with him," she continued as if he hadn't spoken, because *yes*, she did need to get this out. She hadn't spoken about it since it happened. It was time to purge herself of this festering wound. "But I can't. One Saturday morning, I walked into Sunnyside

Grille to meet my sisters for breakfast since Patrick had to work a double shift. Or so he'd texted me. But that wasn't true. Because when I entered, there he was. Sitting in one of the booths near the door, sharing the Sunnyside Up Special with a slender, gorgeous brunette. Well, that's not true. They weren't sharing it because they were too busy kissing."

She swallowed hard, still seeing Patrick, the man she'd imagined building a life with, giving another woman what he should've only offered her. Three years had dulled that pain to a twinge.

"When he saw me, he didn't even apologize. Instead, he blamed me for sending him to another woman. He wasn't original. The usual. If I'd only taken care of myself, lost the weight, hadn't been so fat and lazy. In front of everyone in that diner. He didn't give a damn about humiliating me in front of my family, the people I'd grown up with. And I was so stunned, so hurt, I stood there and took it. Grace, the owner, came over and ordered him out. Told him to never bring his ass in there. And Cole and Wolf Dennison *escorted* him to the sidewalk." A faint smile curved her lips, and it went to show how she'd healed, because there was a time she'd never believed she could feel any humor with the memory. "But the damage had already been done. People get dumped all the time. But mine had been devastating, humiliating *and* public."

"What happened to the asshole?" he snapped.

She blinked. "Um, I don't know. I don't care. Last I heard, he found a position in a hospital out of state."

"That just means it's going to take me more time to track him down."

"What?" She laughed. "Declan, stop playing."

"Who's playing?" he growled. "And next time I'm in town, I'm treating Cole and Wolf to beers."

"That's...sweet." She smiled, and warmth radiated in her chest. "Thank you."

"You're perfect, Remi. I hope you know that. And fuck him if he was too much of a narcissistic, insecure bastard to realize it. Or I bet he did realize it. But to make himself feel better about himself, he tried to make you smaller. And I'm not talking about the size of your gorgeous ass or hips—which you fucking better not touch. I hope you know any real man would see the beautiful, sexy, brilliant woman you are and not ask you to change a damn thing. Hell, he would have to up his game to be worthy of you."

Her lips popped open. Thank God they were on the phone because she would've hated for him to glimpse the tears stinging her eyes or the heat streaming into her face. If he looked at her now, he would see her feelings for him. She didn't have to cross her bedroom to the mirror over the dresser and know that the need, the hunger, the... No, she backed away from labeling *that* emotion. But she knew those emotions would greet her in her reflection.

"Remi?" he murmured. "Sweetheart?"

Her fingers fluttered to the base of her throat, and she closed her eyes.

"I'm here. And thank you. I... Thank you."

"You're welcome, sweetheart. But I'm only speaking the truth." He sighed. "I get why you shared that with me. Thank you for trusting me. I know it wasn't easy." He paused, and several moments passed where his breath echoed in her ear. "Ava and I started dating in college. People said we were a 'golden couple,' whatever that means. I guess I can see it now. Similar goals—both financial majors, wanted to be entrepreneurs, desired a certain lifestyle, had the same ideals about the family we desired. She was beautiful, driven, ambitious, and I admired all of that about her. So after we graduated, we married."

A hard silence ricocheted down the line, deafening in its heaviness.

"I love my parents, especially my mother. But their marriage… It wasn't healthy. My father wasn't physically abusive, but emotionally, verbally? He cut her down with words, by withholding affection if she didn't have his dinner on the table on time or if she disappointed him in any small way. And my mother's identity was so entangled with his that when he died, she crumbled, didn't know who she was, how to carry on from one day to the next. That's why when she sold the house and moved here, I dropped everything and made it happen. She needed to escape anything that had to do with my father so she could *finally* discover herself apart from him. I think that was one of the things that attracted me to Ava. She had her own identity, her own goals. But I didn't count on that tearing us apart."

Questions pinged against her skull, but she remained quiet, letting him tell his story at his own pace. Yet her whole body ached with the need to wrap around him, hold him.

Protect him.

She shook her head, as if the motion could dislodge the silly idea. Declan didn't need her protection. Didn't need *her*.

"We both entered graduate school and took jobs in our fields. While my career seemed to rise fast, hers didn't go as smoothly. And listen, I'm a white man in a field that is set up for me to succeed. So I understood her frustration. I knew there were certain advantages for me that weren't there for her. But she turned bitter, and she took that bitterness out on the one person who unconditionally loved and supported her—me."

Remi almost asked him to stop because what was coming… It had turned him off relationships all these years later. So it must've scarred him.

"It started with complaining about me not having enough time for her. So no matter how tired I was from work and school, I tried to give her more attention. Then she accused me of being too needy, so I pulled back. I'd arrive at work and discover that my files were missing information, or the numbers had been transposed. Or I had to make a presentation, and the PowerPoint had disappeared from my computer. When we attended my office parties, she either flirted with my colleagues or deliberately insulted them. Or as I later found out, slept with them."

"Shit," she whispered.

"Yes, shit." He chuckled, but it didn't carry any humor. "She tried to sabotage my career before it could really begin. The betrayal…" He cleared his throat. Paused. "The betrayal when you've done nothing but love a person… It destroys something in you. Your trust. In other people. In yourself. It's not something you forget—or want to repeat."

She got it. God, did she get it.

"She didn't break you, though," she whispered.

"No," he whispered back. "She didn't."

"Declan?"

"Yes."

"I'm glad."

CHAPTER FIVE

Last Halloween, Declan attended a friend's party, dressed as a pirate, and ended up going home with a sexy as hell cat—or maybe she'd been a mouse.

The Halloween before that, he'd spent the evening at a business dinner. And had his dining partner for dessert.

This Halloween, he stuffed goody bags with candy, toys and small books for the fifty or so excited children that crowded into the Rose Bend Public Library for the Spooks 'n' Books Bash.

Being the town librarian's "boyfriend" definitely had its perks.

He smirked as he tossed a mini pack of M&M's into a plastic bag decorated with goofy ghosts, cats and witches. In the three weeks since he'd started dating Remi, he'd gone to a high school–sponsored haunted house, judged a pumpkin pie contest that she'd volunteered him for when the scheduled judge came down with food poisoning, and gone on his first ever hayride. He'd eaten his first s'more in nineteen years, tasted his first cup of homemade spiced cider ever and snacked on honest-to-God grapenut custard, hauling out and dusting off childhood memories he'd long forgotten.

Yes, these last three weeks had definitely been an experience. As different from his outings with Tara as the Patriots from the Lions. He'd had fun.

Damn.

When had his life stopped being fun?

Not that his life was bad. God, no. It would be the height of white privilege to cry about a challenging career he enjoyed, the luxurious lifestyle it afforded him, the doors to the elite business and social worlds it opened to him. And he indulged in it all.

But did he feel that pure excitement like a child on Christmas morning or a kid soaring down a steep hill on his bike at full speed? Like a teen discovering the bloom of his first crush?

No. That had been missing.

Until now.

Until Remi.

His pulse an uncomfortable throb at his neck, his wrists, he scanned the library, and like a lodestone, his gaze found her. Maybe it was the dark fire of her hair—or the brighter flame of her very essence—but she seemed to gleam like a ruby among the crowd of parents who stood in the outer ring surrounding the children who gathered for story time.

A smile flashed across her face at something, brief but so lovely, and the air in his chest snagged.

Jesus, the power of it.

Like a hard knee to the gut and a gentle brush of fingers across his jaw at the same time.

He blinked, dragging his much-too-fascinated scrutiny away from her and back to the task at hand. Goody bags. Candy. Toys.

"Is this my son over here in the back doing manual labor?" His mother appeared in front of the table, a wide smile stretched across her pretty face. Tiny lines fanned out from the corners of Janet Howard's blue eyes as she nabbed a small box of crayons and swung it back and forth in front of him. "If I didn't see it with my own eyes…"

He snorted, holding his hand out and curling his fingers, signaling for her to hand over the box. When she did, with an even-wider grin, he drawled, "Laugh it up now, woman. But just because I work behind a desk doesn't mean I don't know the meaning of labor." He arched an eyebrow. "I mean, who do you think mows that big yard I have?"

She mimicked the eyebrow gesture. "That reminds me. James Holland lost your number. But he wanted me to pass along the message that he would be glad to take care of your lawn like he does mine."

"Freaking blabbermouth," Declan muttered, dropping the crayons into the goody bag. No sense of male solidarity at all.

"Hi, Declan." Tara strolled up to them, smiling widely. "This is so cute." She turned, waving a hand in the direction of the larger area set up with game stations, the story circle and tables of books. "When Janet told me she was stopping by, I had to tag along. All this time I've lived here, and I can't believe I've never made it to this charming little event."

"It's only the second time the library has held it. Remi started it last year," he said, pride for Remi and the staff's hard work evident in his voice. He didn't even try to conceal it.

He'd only witnessed the tail end of their labor, helping set up and put up decorations, but more than one person had regaled him about all the time and effort she put into the event. And when his mother's gaze narrowed on him, he met it. There was nothing wrong with being proud of a friend's achievements.

Fuck, he was a terrible liar. Even to himself.

His mother and Tara glanced at one another, then Janet hooked an arm through Tara's, clearly telegraphing where her allegiance lay. "Well, that's nice. I just remembered you mentioning you were spending Halloween here, so I thought we'd come over and see if we can convince you to join us for coffee afterward."

We.

He didn't bother looking at Tara, but kept his attention focused on his mother. "I'm sorry. Remi and I already have plans after this wraps up." Technically, they didn't, and he hated fibbing to his mother, but if he had to take Remi to Sunnyside Grille for a late dinner to make the lie true, he would. "But thanks for supporting the event."

His mother's smile tightened around the edges, and she turned to Tara. "Honey, would you mind giving me a moment with Declan?"

"Not at all," Tara said. He ignored her and the smug note in her voice.

If she expected him to bow to his mother's coercion on her behalf, then neither woman really knew him.

"Son—"

"Mom, I love you, and I would never intentionally disrespect you." He interrupted her before she could get on a roll. He flattened his palms on the table and leaned forward, lowering his voice, not desiring an audience for this long-overdue conversation that he would've preferred to have in private. "But that—" he dipped his head in the direction Tara had disappeared "—is not going to happen. There has never *been* any chance of it happening. Something I made very clear to Tara even if she decided not to hear me. I only took her out those few times because it made you happy to see me with her. Or with someone."

He stretched an arm out, clasped his mother's hand in his, squeezed. "I love you, Mom. You're the most important person in the world to me. And I would hate to see our relationship damaged in any way by you choosing this hill to die on. Tara's not for me."

"And this new woman is? A woman you haven't brought around and introduced to me, I might add?"

True. And he'd purposefully avoided doing so. His and Remi's relationship was fake; having her meet his mother smacked too much of "real." It crossed a boundary into territory he hadn't been prepared to enter. But Janet arriving here tonight might snatch that choice out of his hands.

Especially since Remi was headed their way.

He straightened, his gaze shifting from his mother and over her shoulder to the sexy, stunning woman walking toward them. How could she make a simple long-sleeved, V-necked shirt, a dark pair of high-waisted skinny jeans and ankle boots so hot?

Lust rippled through him, and he clenched his teeth against the primal pounding of it in his veins... In his cock.

Goddamn.

Kittens batting balls of yarn. Dad's old baseball mitt that smelled like Bengay and sweat. Grandma Eileen's dentures in a glass on the bathroom sink.

Thinking of anything that would prevent him from springing an erection in front of his mother and all these kids. But most of all his mother.

"Oh." His mother hummed. "That's the way of it."

Declan didn't tear his gaze from Remi. Couldn't. But if by some small miracle he could, yeah, he still wouldn't. Disquiet scurried beneath the throb of need. And he didn't want to glimpse the acknowledgment of that disquiet in his mother's eyes.

"Hey." Remi smiled, glancing down at the table packed with goody bags. "Thank you, Declan. So much. First you saved me with the pie contest and now with this. When my volunteer called out, I thought I was going to have a bunch of screaming kids on my hands." She laughed and turned to his mother. "We've met before, Mrs. Howard, but it's nice to see you again. Thank you for coming tonight."

"Nice to see you, too, Ms. Donovan. Or is it okay to call you Remi, since rumor has it you're dating my son?"

The pointed and faintly accusatory tone wasn't lost on Declan, and apparently not on Remi either, since pink tinged the elegant slant of her cheekbones. But to her credit, she didn't back down.

"Rumors in a small town?" Her lips curled into a rueful twist. "If only we could monetize it, we could single-handedly support our economy. And yes—" she nodded "—I would be honored if you would call me Remi."

Declan smothered a bark of laughter. *Nice side step.* "Remi, my mother's not new to a library. When I was a kid, she used to take me there often and let me pick out any book I wanted, then let me participate in the scavenger hunts or watch afternoon movies. And she even volunteered at our school library sometimes. Or maybe she just wanted to keep an eye on me," he teased.

His mother snorted. "Both."

"Mrs. Howard, I don't know if you'd consider it, but the library can always use volunteers," Remi said.

"Volunteer? Me?" She scoffed, but Declan glimpsed the interest flicker in her eyes, even though her features remained guarded. "What could I possibly do?"

"Whatever you enjoy." Remi half turned, sweeping a hand toward the room. "If you like clerical duties such as helping us entering patron info into our computer system or returning books to the shelves or manning the help desk, that would be wonderful. Or since we are an interactive library, if you love working with the children, you can read to them, help with tutoring, assist us with our events or even man one of those scavenger hunts Declan mentioned."

Declan stared at her. Excitement shone in her hazel eyes, the gold like chips of sunlight, and enthusiasm lit her face so brightly, he blinked at its gleam.

She was beautiful. No—such a paltry, lazy word to describe the purity and loveliness of a spirit enhanced by a stunning face and body.

He'd met gorgeous women, dated them—fucked them.

But they all faded into an obscure corner of his past the longer he looked at Remi. His heart thudded against his sternum, a rhythm that drowned out the chatter of adults, the happy squeals of children. His world narrowed to her, to the fine angle of her cheekbones, the sweet sin of her mouth, the alluring dent in her chin. To the lush, sensual curves of her body.

Panic ripped through him, and out of pure survival, his mind scrambled back from a treacherous edge his damn heart should've known better than to go anywhere near.

"Declan?" Fingers touched the back of his hand, and just from the delicious burn, he didn't need to glance down and identify its owner. But he did anyway, because *not* looking at Remi Donovan wasn't even an option for him. A small frown creased her brow. "Everything okay?"

"Yes, fine." He flipped her hand over, rubbing his thumb over her palm, catching the small shiver that trembled up her arm. And because that vulnerability still sat on him, he repeated the caress. "I was just thinking how lucky this place is to have someone as loyal, hardworking and beautiful as you."

Her eyes widened, an emotion so tangled, so convoluted flashing in them that he couldn't begin to decipher it. He'd surprised her. Good. Though they were engaged in this arrangement, there was something freeing about being able to touch her, to murmur compliments and neatly, *safely* categorize them under "for the charade."

Like now.

"Thank you," she murmured, giving him one last lingering look before shifting her attention back to his mother. "Do you want to get a cup of hot chocolate, and we can talk more about volunteering?"

"Yes." His mother nodded, and warmth slipped into her expression and voice. "I would like that very much."

"Wonderful. Let's go before the kids beat us to it." She laughed, leading Janet away.

"Is that her plan, then?"

Declan clenched his jaw. Hard. Until the muscles along his jaw ached in protest. Instead of replying to Tara, he walked away from the table, knowing she would follow. Pausing next to a volunteer, he asked her if she would mind watching the goody bags for a moment, and then he continued to a quieter side of the room.

Before he could speak, Tara crossed her arms over her

chest, her lips forming a sulky pout that he hoped to God she didn't think was attractive.

"Is that her new plan? To ingratiate herself with your mother?"

"No," Declan said, arching an eyebrow. "That's your strategy. Hers is simply being her. Interested in other people and their needs. Being *nice*. That's who Remi is."

"Please." Tara sneered. "It's an act. No one is that nice. Not without a motive."

"You don't say," he drawled.

Red stained her cheeks, and she huffed out a breath, her chin hiking up.

"That's not what I meant," she said through gritted teeth. "And you know it."

Declan sighed, pinching the bridge of his nose. Briefly closing his eyes, he dropped his arm and met Tara's dark brown eyes, glinting with tears.

"Don't." He didn't bother blunting the sharp edge of his tone.

Maybe if he suspected the tears were authentic, he would've. But he'd witnessed this ploy before; she'd tried to use it on him with no luck, and she regularly employed those tears with his mother with much more success.

"I'm going to say this once again. And this will be the last time, Tara. I've been patient and have tried not to hurt your feelings, but you don't seem to understand kindness. Or you see it as something to take advantage of. There. Is. No. Us. There never was. There never will be. Hear me. Accept it. Move on. And if you genuinely like my mother and enjoy spending time with her, then fine. But if you're doing it only to get to me, then leave her alone, too. I won't allow you to use her, and more importantly, I won't let you hurt her."

"Where was this concern for a woman's feelings when you led me on?" she scoffed. Tears no longer moistened her eyes, but anger glittered there, and it pulled her mouth taut, turning her beauty as sharp and hard as a diamond. "You shouldn't have slept with me if you *claim* we didn't have anything."

He nodded. "You're right. I shouldn't have allowed my dick to do my thinking. But I've never lied to you, Tara. I was always up-front that we wouldn't have a relationship—that I didn't want that with you. With anyone. I convinced myself that you accepted that, when obviously you had other intentions the entire time. That's on you, not me."

Tara shook her head. "That's not true," she said, quietly, sounding a little lost.

And for a moment, he softened. Thrusting his fingers through his hair, he said, "Tara, I didn't want to hurt you. It's the one thing I actively tried to avoid. And I'm sorry if I did."

"It's just…" Tara turned from him, tightening her arms around herself, her lips rolling in on each other, thinning. When she faced him again, her shoulders lifted, and she fluttered a hand between them. "I know there is affection between us."

"Tara."

"Y'know, whatever you're doing with Remi Donovan isn't fooling me or anyone in this town."

And that quickly, any sympathy for her evaporated. He stiffened, studying her, the frustration pinching her skin tight and adding a jerkiness to her usually fluid movements.

"I don't really give a damn what other people think, including you."

He ignored the voice that pointed out that he'd proposed the bargain with Remi in the first place because of Tara.

"Obviously. Because the thought of you wanting *her*, being with *her*, of all people, is laughable. She's boring, fa—"

"Shut the hell up," he growled. "Say one more word, Tara, and I'll forget that I was raised not to disrespect women."

"Excuse me."

Declan jerked his head up and to the side just as Tara whipped around.

Fuck.

Remi stood there, perfectly composed and calm. And if not for her eyes… His gut twisted, and he fisted his fingers, the blunt tips biting into his palms. The brown nearly swallowed the bright green and gold. If not for that darkness, he would assume she hadn't overheard Tara's ugly words.

Would assume those words hadn't landed direct, agonizing blows.

"Remi." He moved forward, Tara forgotten, his one goal to get to her. To somehow ease that hurt, make it disappear.

But she shifted backward. Away from him. And damn if a spike of pain didn't jab into his chest.

"We're about to give out the goody bags. When you're free, we could use your help passing them out." Dipping her chin, she pivoted and left, shoulders straight and without a glance back at them.

"Tara." His mother stepped forward, and for the first

time, Declan noticed her. "I'm going to catch a ride home with a friend. I've known you for three years now, and you've never been anything but kind to me. But hearing you speak so horribly about someone a couple of minutes ago?" Janet shook her head. "It makes me wonder who you are when I'm not around. And if that is a person I want to know."

Janet reached for Declan, squeezed his hand and glanced in the direction Remi had disappeared.

"She's special, and you'd be a fool to let her get away." Brushing a kiss over his cheek, she left.

"She didn't mean..." Tara whispered, her voice catching.

Declan glanced over his shoulder at the other woman, spotting the moisture in her eyes, and for the first time, he believed her tears were real. But they failed to move him.

"She did. You just looked the consequences of your spite and pettiness in the face. I hope you remember them."

He walked away, leaving her alone. Like she deserved.

CHAPTER SIX

WHO KNEW A person could be completely numb inside and still smile, laugh and behave as if humiliation and pain hadn't pummeled her with meaty, bruising fists until she'd become a block of ice?

Seemed every day Remi discovered something new.

Returning to the Halloween event after overhearing Tara and Declan's conversation, then pretending nothing had occurred, had been one of the most difficult things she'd ever done. She'd been grateful for the coldness that had seeped into her veins, her chest.

But the library had emptied of parents, children, staff and volunteers forty-five minutes earlier, and now she sat in the passenger seat of Declan's car as he drove through the quiet streets. She couldn't escape the slow thawing around her heart. Couldn't escape her relentless thoughts. Couldn't escape *her*.

You wanting her, being with her, of all people, is laughable. She's boring, fa—

Remi squeezed her eyes shut, blocking out the scenery passing by her passenger window. Too bad she couldn't block out the memory of Tara's words. The other woman hadn't needed to finish the sentence for Remi to discern how it ended.

Fat.

Boring and fat.

Oh God how that hurt.

The mental door to that vault she tried so hard to keep shut creaked open and more memories crept out. Memories of her mother's and Patrick's voices.

A minute on the lips, a lifetime on the hips, Remi.

I just want you to be healthy, Remi.

Are you sure that choice of dress is wise? It's not very forgiving, is it?

The judgments, backhanded compliments and criticisms framed as concern poured into her mind. It'd taken Remi years, but she'd come to love and accept herself. But there were moments like tonight—like the other night with her mother in the café—when her hard-won confidence took enough of a hit that she wavered.

When she had to remind herself she wasn't lovable *despite* her weight or size.

She was lovable *because* of them.

Smothering a sigh, she silently urged the car to go faster. She longed to get home, drag on her favorite Wonder Woman pajamas, pop open a bottle of wine, put on *Pride and Prejudice*—the version with Keira Knightley and Matthew Macfadyen otherwise known as *the best version*—and lick her wounds.

Tomorrow. Tomorrow she would be okay, but God, she needed tonight.

"Remi, we need to talk about tonight."

The thaw inside her sped up, the red-tinged hurt throbbing. *Home. Just get me home.* It'd been years since she'd last cried in front of someone, and she didn't intend to break that record tonight. Not with him.

"I didn't get a chance to thank you for helping out with

setting up and then stepping in when my volunteer didn't show. I really appreciate it. We all did," she said, switching the subject from what she suspected he really wanted to talk about.

"You're welcome. And the deflection isn't going to work," he murmured, voice gentle but firm. Too firm. "Since she would probably never apologize, I'm going to say 'I'm sorry' for Tara. What she sa—"

"Forget it. I have."

"Remi," he tried again.

"Let. It. Go."

Silence permeated the car, weighing down her shoulders, pressing on her chest. She desperately counted the minutes until she arrived home. Rose Bend wasn't that large a town, but right now it felt like the size of Boston.

Finally, he pulled up outside her house. Any other time, she would've taken a moment to admire the cute, quaint cottage that she'd saved for and bought on her own not far from the beautiful Kinsale Inn. But now, the sight of the yellow-and-white home only inspired relief. She reached for the door handle.

"Remi." Declan's hand clasped her wrist. "Wait."

She paused but didn't glance over her shoulder to look at him, instead perched on the passenger seat ready to flee.

"Please don't leave like this. Talk to me, sweetheart."

She trembled at the "sweetheart," her eyes briefly closing.

Whatever you're doing with Remi Donovan isn't fooling me or anyone in this town.

She wasn't his sweetheart, and everyone knew it. Hell, even her own mother found it hard to believe. Because a man like him couldn't desire, couldn't... *Love* a woman

A KISS TO REMEMBER

like her. A beautiful, charismatic, brilliant, sexy as hell man couldn't want a successful, independent, educated woman just because she happened to wear a size sixteen.

At least, that's what they believed.

Her? Well, before tonight, the last three weeks had offered her hope that Declan was attracted to her. Her mind had warned her that the heated glances, the fleeting caresses to her cheek, the holding of her hand, the jokes and laughter they shared, the phone calls and texts they exchanged—they were all part of the charade. But her heart failed to get the message. Her stupid heart took each gesture as proof that he felt *something* for her.

And she understood now why she grasped that hope so desperately.

Because in these three weeks, each caress, each glance, each compliment had worked toward transforming her longtime crush for him into love.

Yes, she so, so foolishly had fallen in love with Declan Howard.

Her head bowed, forehead pressing against the cold window.

She'd fallen for the most emotionally unavailable man in Rose Bend.

"Talk to you?" she said, leaning back in the seat and turning to him. "What is there to *talk* about? I told you I'm *fine*."

"Actually, you didn't. You just ordered me to let it go. But too many people in your life have done that, and I refuse to be another one who ignores your pain."

She stared at him, forcing her fingers to remain flat on her thighs and not to ball into fists. "Do you want me to admit that what Tara said hurt? Okay, yes. It hurt like hell. Do I want your apology on her behalf? No. I don't want it or need it. It's insulting to both of us. That should sum it up, right? Are we done here? Good."

"Hell no, we're not done. We're friends, dammit."

Oh God, didn't *that* just punch a hole in her chest?

"There. Satisfied? Now, good night."

She reached for the door handle again.

"If you get out of this car, I will follow you to that front door, Remi," he rumbled.

She threw her hands up in the air, loosing a harsh laugh that abraded her throat. "What more do you want from me? A pound of flesh? According to your ex-girlfriend, I can afford to sacrifice a few—"

His arm shot out, and his hand hooked behind her neck, hauling her forward. His mouth crushed down on hers, swallowing the words from her lips. Her moan surged up her throat, offering itself like a sacrifice to him. She was helpless at the erotic onslaught, opening herself wider and wider to this wild thing that masqueraded as a kiss. He took from her over and over, slanting his mouth, diving deep, sucking harder as if starved, as if desperate.

As if afraid she would disappear if he didn't gorge himself in this moment.

Or maybe she was projecting.

Declan lifted his other hand to her chin, swept his hand over the shallow cleft there. Once and twice. Such a simple, small caress, but it echoed in a soft flutter between her legs, and she clenched her thighs against the sweet, erotic sensation.

God, touch me there... Kiss me there.

The plea bounced inside her head, words she longed to

utter aloud. She'd never believed that opportunity would be hers.

Did you want it to be?

The low, insidious whisper slid through her lust-hazed mind. And no matter how hard she pressed her lips to Declan's, how hard she thrust her tongue against his, she couldn't evict the question from her thoughts. Did she? If she took this step with him, there was no coming back. And for her, it wouldn't be just sex. Not with him. Her heart was already involved. Giving him her body, too, would cement an epic fall that would make Icarus's look like a mere stumble.

"Invite me inside."

Declan issued the hoarse plea-wrapped-in-a-demand, and it reverberated loudly in the confines of his car. She stared at him, emotionally on a precipice. One step off could mean joy for her… Or utter heartbreak.

Was she brave enough to find out which?

He brushed his thumb under the curve of her bottom lip, the hand at her nape a gentle weight. But he waited, allowing her to make this decision, even though desire darkened his eyes to indigo and his mouth bore the damp, swollen mark of their raw kiss.

"Come inside."

Inside my house. Inside my body. My heart. My soul.

She issued the invitation, knowing he would only take her up on two of those. And even as he exited the car, rounded the hood and opened her door, she accepted it.

Moments later, she led him into her home, and as soon as they crossed the threshold, Declan closed the door behind them, twisting the lock. All without removing his hooded gaze from her.

Need dug its dark claws into her, and her thighs trembled with the force of it. How was it possible to *want* this much? To feel like if he didn't put his hands on her, his mouth on her, his cock *inside* her, she would crawl out of her skin? Lose her mind?

"Touch me."

Two words. They were all she could push past her constricted throat. They were all that were necessary.

He stalked forward, shrugging out of his coat, peeling his sweater and dark T-shirt over his head, dropping all the clothing to the floor. Her breath expelled from her lungs on a hard, long *whoosh*.

Jesus Christ.

Clothed, he was beautiful.

Bared, with golden skin stretched across taut, flexing muscle, he was magnificent.

She couldn't move, her gaze greedily bingeing on the wide breadth of his shoulders, the wall of his chest, the corded strength of his arms. That ridged ladder of abs with the dark silky line of hair that disappeared beneath the waistband of his pants.

A waistband his hands had dropped to.

"Wait." She popped her palms up in the universal sign of Stop.

"Let me," she whispered. "I want it." She clasped her hands together as if holding her passion for him between them. "I want you."

"I'm yours." He beckoned her closer, and as imperious as it seemed... Damn, it was hot, too. "Come get me."

Oh God, if only that were true, she mused, crossing the few steps toward him. If only he was really hers. To keep. She shook her head. No place for those thoughts here. Stay in the now.

"What're you telling yourself no about?" he murmured, tugging her closer, tunneling his fingers through her hair, his nails scraping over her scalp. Her lashes fluttered closed, and she turned into his big palm, sinking her teeth into the heel, giving him back a little of the pleasure/pain he'd doled out to her. A hiss escaped him, and when he fisted the strands of her hair, pulling, she nipped harder. "This is going to be over before it begins, sweetheart," he warned, dipping his head to take her mouth in a brief but thorough conquering. "Now what're you telling yourself no about?"

No way in hell could she answer that loaded question. So she didn't.

Instead, she tackled his belt and the closure on his pants. Desperation climbed high inside her, neck and neck with lust. She wanted to drown herself in pleasure. In need. In him. Forget about what awaited her tomorrow. Forget the uncertainty.

For the first time, she was taking for herself and damn the consequences.

But he covered her hands with one of his, halting her frantic actions. The other cupped her cheek, tilting her head back.

"So many times I've wondered what goes on behind these lovely hazel eyes. What secrets you're keeping. And it's those moments, I consider switching careers and becoming an archeologist whose main job is unearthing those treasures." He danced his fingertips over her cheekbone, the arch of her nose, the top bow of her lip. "You wouldn't give up those secrets easily, but they would be worth the work. *You* are worth the work."

Her chest squeezed so tight, she locked her teeth around a cry. No one had ever spoken to her like that. She closed her eyes and bowed her head on the pretense of pressing a kiss to the base of his throat. Anything to avoid having him see the love she knew was in her gaze.

Declan gripped the sides of her shirt, balling it in his fists until it untucked from her jeans and bared her stomach. She lifted her arms, stamping down the nerves in her stomach. That dark hot need in his eyes couldn't be faked. He wanted her; he liked her body just as she did. Still… When the top cleared her head and the heat in that indigo gaze flared, the lingering remnants of doubt dissolved like mist.

"Fuck, sweetheart." Lust stamped his features, pulling his skin taut over his cheekbones, his lips appearing fuller, more carnal. "Let me…"

"Please," she damn near whined.

He lifted his hands toward her, but at the last minute, lowered his arms.

"Bedroom," he ground out.

Wordlessly, she turned and led him down the hall and into her shadowed bedroom. Moonlight streamed through the large windows, providing more than enough illumination. But Declan must not have thought so because he crossed to the lamp on her bedside table and switched it on, bathing the room in a warm, golden glow. Then he crossed back to her in that sensual, almost-feline glide of his, and lust wrenched low in her belly, high in her sex. She couldn't contain her whimper. Didn't even try.

When he reached her, Declan slowly lowered to his

knees, his pose worshipful, reverent. As were the hands that removed her boots and jeans. As were the lips that pressed a kiss to her hip just above the line of her black panties.

As were the words that ordered her back on the bed, heels to the edge of the mattress.

She shuddered, excitement and vulnerability dueling inside her as she lay exposed to him, evidence of her overwhelming desire for him evident in her soaked flesh, in the damp panel of her underwear.

Teeth nipped at her sensitive inner thigh, and she jerked at the sensation and the taut anticipation of his mouth giving her what she so desperately hungered for.

"Shh," he soothed, brushing a caress over the tender area. "Tell me I can have you, Remi." He grazed his fingertips over her folds, and she gasped at the featherlight touch, arching into it. Her hands fisted the covers at her hips, needing something to anchor her.

"Have me, Declan." She bit her lip, trapping anything else that would've spilled forth without her permission. "Please have me."

Without further prodding, he stripped her panties off and dived into her.

He tongued a path up her folds, swirling and licking. Sucking. No part of her remained a mystery to him. She dived her hands into his hair, clutching the strands and holding on as he lapped at her, his ravenous growl vibrating over her flesh and through her sex.

Two thick fingers pressed against her entrance then inside her, stretching her, filling her. She cried out, grinding against his hand, his mouth. Pleasure struck her, bolt after bolt streaking through her. And as his lips latched on to her clit, and his tongue flicked and circled the pulsing nub, she curled into him, breathless, *aching*.

Declan rubbed a place high inside her, and she exploded, came so hard black crept into the edges of her vision. She tumbled back to the bed, her breath a harsh rasp in her lungs, her bones liquefied. Dimly, she was aware of Declan standing at the foot of the bed and the whisper of clothes sliding over skin.

The mattress dipped, and she focused on the gorgeous sexual beast crouched above her. While she silently watched, he tore open a silver packet, removed a condom and sheathed himself. And *oh God...*

Renewed lust fluttered, then flowed inside her in a molten rush. A cock shouldn't be lovely, but then again, this was Declan. It didn't seem possible that anything about him could be less than perfect. Including his dick. And long, thick, with a flared, plum-shaped head, he was indeed *perfect*. And mouthwatering. Before her mind could send the message to her body, she was reaching for him...

"No, sweetheart." He caught her wrist, bending down to crush an openmouthed kiss to the palm. "I want to make it inside you. Sit up."

He didn't wait for her to comply but tugged on the hand he held. Quickly, he divested her of her bra and dipped his head, sucking a beaded nipple into his mouth. Cradling her, he lifted her breasts, his thumbs circling the tip he hadn't treated himself to yet. Yet.

She clawed at his shoulders, tipping her head back, those pulls of his mouth echoing in her sex. Where she needed him. Now.

"Declan," she whispered. Pleaded.

"Take me in, Remi." He took her hand, wrapped it around him. "You take me."

She did.

Raising her hips, she guided him to her, notched him at her entrance. And cupping his firm ass, welcomed him inside her.

Their twin groans saturated the air.

She'd thought his fingers had filled her. No, they'd just prepared her for this... Possession. This branding.

Never had she felt so *whole*.

Slipping his arms under her shoulders, he gathered her close, and she did the same to him. Clinging to him. He held himself still, allowing her to become accustomed to the size and width of him. And yes, she needed those few moments. But as a fine shiver rippled through his body, she nuzzled the strong line of his jaw, nipping it.

"Move," she urged, flexing her hips against him. "Your turn to take me."

Tangling his fingers in her hair, he tilted her head back and claimed her mouth just as he claimed her body.

Over and over, he tunneled deep, burying his cock inside her, marking her as his. She undulated and arched beneath him, giving even as she accepted. The slap of skin on skin, the musk of sex, the damp release of sex greeting sex punctuated the room, creating music for their bodies' erotic dance. Each thrust, each grind, each growled word of praise shoved her closer to the edge, and she flitted close, then scampered back, not wanting this to end. Needing to be in this moment, in this space with him forever, but the pleasure—the mind-bending, body-aching pleasure—wouldn't permit that.

He reached between them, rubbed a thumb over the

rigid bundle of nerves cresting the top of her sex. The scream building inside her was more than a voice; it was physical. And when he pistoned into her once, twice, three times, her body gave it sound.

She flew apart.

Her body. Her mind. Her soul.

Pieces of her scattered, and she doubted she could possibly be whole again.

As he stiffened above her, his hoarse growl of pleasure rumbling against her chest and in her ear, she gave in to the darkness closing in on her.

I love you. I love you.

And as she let go, she whispered the words in her head that she could never permit herself to say aloud.

I LOVE YOU.

Remi's whisper echoed in Declan's mind, crashing against his skull like waves against the shore.

I love you.

She probably hadn't meant to let the admission slip out; she'd been halfway asleep as she uttered those three words that carved fear into his chest.

Maybe she didn't mean them. People said things like that in the heat of passion all the time, and they regretted it later. Let sex—especially such cataclysmic, hot as hell sex—get mixed up and muddled with emotion, and they were temporarily confused. Yes, that was it. Remi didn't—

That wasn't Remi. She might not have meant to say she loved him—might not have intended to let him know—but she'd meant it.

Or else Remi believed she did.

He propped his elbows on his thighs and dropped his head into his hands.

I love you.

A howl churned in his gut, surging up his throat, but at the last second, he trapped it behind clenched teeth. Pain, fear and anger—yes, anger—eddied inside him in a grimy cesspool. He wanted to lash out. To yell that he didn't ask for her love. That love wasn't part of their deal.

He wanted to curl his body behind hers and beg her to take it back, to please take it back. Before *love* crushed them both and he lost the woman he'd come to depend on, to admire, to desire, to need... God, he'd come to need her. Her texts, her calls, her smiles, her...

Everything.

Love would ruin who they were to each other.

Just as it'd diminished his mother, so she'd had to rediscover who she was as a person.

Just as it'd morphed into something ugly and destroyed his marriage.

People used that particular affection as a reason to hurt and damage one another every day, and he wanted no part of it.

Not even from Remi. Especially not from Remi. Because to witness how it would extinguish the light from those beautiful hazel eyes... How it would steal the radiance that shone from her like a beacon piercing darkness...

"I'm surprised you're still here."

Declan slowly straightened, glancing over his shoulder. Remi, with the cover tucked under her arms, sat up, her expression shuttered. Grief careened through him. It'd been weeks since he'd seen that look on her face. Since she'd closed him out.

"Remi..." he murmured, turning to her.

She shook her head. "At first, I thought it was a bad dream, but when I woke up and saw you fully dressed and sitting on the side of the bed as if you couldn't wait to bolt out of here, I knew it wasn't a dream. More of a nightmare."

"Remi, I don't want to hurt you."

She huffed out a low, dry chuckle. "This isn't about hurting me, but just the opposite—you're the one who doesn't want to be hurt."

He couldn't deny that. Hell, if he were brutally honest, he'd been running scared since he'd signed his divorce papers. But he'd been doing it so long, he didn't know how to stop. Didn't know if he had the courage to stop.

Even for her. And if anyone deserved someone to be brave on her behalf, it was Remi.

"You don't want to take the risk of falling in love and being hurt again, of being betrayed. And your greatest fear, Declan? You're afraid of loving someone so much, so deeply, that you lose yourself. That you become your mother. And there's nothing I could say... Not that I would never betray you, never do anything that would demean you rather than support you. Not that I might very well hurt you, but I would hope my love would pave the way for forgiveness, that you would see it wouldn't be intentional. True love only makes you stronger, better. You could never lose yourself in it. Because it would never allow you to become lost."

She spread her hands wide on her crossed legs, staring down at them before lifting her gaze to him. Tears didn't glisten in her eyes, but he almost wished they did. He'd rather have the tears than the bottomless, hard resolve he saw.

"But there wouldn't be any point in trying to make you believe that, because your heart is closed by fear. I'm scared, too, Declan. Scared to trust, to take a leap of faith on love when it's only disappointed me in the past. But I'm willing to take a risk on you. On us." She shook her head. "What I'm not willing to do is fake it any longer or settle."

Her shoulders straightened, and the deep breath she drew in resounded in the room. That, too, held the ring of finality.

"I love you, Declan. And you need to leave."

"Remi, I'm sorry."

"I know you are. And that makes you refusing to fight for yourself, for who we could be, sadder. Now, if you have any feelings for me, any respect at all, please go."

Stay, dammit. Don't you fucking go.

But he stood, exited the bedroom and her house as she requested.

Like the coward he was.

He drove through the dark quiet streets of Rose Bend, images of the evening bombarding him. Of them laughing and working together at the library. Of their kiss in the car. Making love in her bedroom. Of her eyes, dark with pain and pride, ordering him out.

A while later, he pulled his car to a stop and switched it off. But he didn't sit, parked outside his home.

Opening his car door, he numbly climbed out, rounded the vehicle and climbed the steps to the blue-and-white Victorian with the dark blue shutters. Even before he knocked, the front door swung open and his mother stood in the doorway.

"Declan? What on earth? What's wrong?" she asked, tying her robe belt.

"Mom," he rasped. "I messed up."

CHAPTER SEVEN

"I LOVE YOUR MOTHER," Briana growled, sailing up to Remi with a smile that appeared more like a feral baring of teeth, "but she is seriously working my last living nerve."

Remi hid her grin behind her glass of wine, sending up a prayer, not for the first time, that she'd found a safe corner out of the path of Hurricane Rochelle. The whole week before the engagement party, their mother had been driving all of them nuts with the preparations. And today, with guests crowded into their home, enjoying the hors d'oeuvres and sipping a variety of beverages and celebrating the happy couple, Rochelle hadn't calmed down yet. After being ordered twice to circle the room with the appetizers, then told she wasn't doing it right, then being barred from the kitchen, Remi had been trying to fly under the radar.

"You know she's in her element. Even if she's acting a little batty. She just wants everything to be perfect for you." Remi slipped an arm around Briana's shoulders, hugging her close. "Besides, you have to give it to her. The place looks ah-mazing. The food is great. The guests are enjoying themselves. And you're engaged to a truly great guy."

"Yeah, you're right," Briana grumbled, then chuckled. As if she couldn't help herself, her sister sought out her fiancé, locating him next to the living room fireplace, surrounded by several of his friends. "He's wonderful. And I can't wait to marry him."

"There you go. Just keep that in mind. And avoid Mom, like I'm doing."

Briana laughed, wrapping an arm around Remi's waist and squeezing. But then she sobered, wincing. "God, Remi, I'm so sorry. I wasn't thinking. Are you okay being here with all—" she twirled her hand in the direction of the party "—this? You know I wouldn't have minded if you begged off. I would've understood."

"*I* would've minded, though. And I'm fine. No way I would've missed my sister's engagement party. But thank you."

God, she loved her sister. Both of them. After Declan left her house a week ago, she'd called her sisters. Sherri and Briana had come right over and stayed with her for most of the weekend, holding her while she cried, bingeing Netflix and snacks with her when she didn't. And they'd been running interference with their mother, whose disappointment at her and Declan breaking up had seared her.

But it didn't make her change her mind or call him. She'd made the right decision for herself.

"What are we doing over here in the corner?" Sherri shoved a sun-dried tomato and basil roll-up in her mouth, following it with a healthy sip of champagne. Her older sister, barely five feet and willow thin, could eat her weight in hors d'oeuvres, run roughshod over her adorable three-year-old twins and rule her husband, who worshipped the ground she walked on. "Talking about people? Ditching Doug so he can't leave me with the kids? Avoiding Mom?"

"C," Remi said, taking her sister's glass and sipping.

"Oh, me, too." Sherri scrunched her nose. "And you

know I was just kidding about the kids, right?" When Remi and Briana gave her the blandest of bland looks, she sighed. "*Fine.* Sue me. Doug so owes me for...for sticking his penis in me."

"Wow." Briana slipped the champagne away from their sister with a snicker. "We're going to lay off these until the toast, 'kay?"

"What? No, I—" The doorbell rang, and she clapped her hands, nearly bouncing on the balls of her feet. "That should be the babysitter. She was running late so she offered to pick the twins up from here. Sooo..." She snatched her glass back and took a healthy sip.

"You'd think she didn't get out much," Remi drawled, laughing, but as her mother led the newest guest into the living room, the humor died on her lips. *"Oh God."*

Declan.

Her breath stalled in her lungs, increasing the deafening thud of her heart in her ears, her head. Adrenaline rushed through her, temporarily making her dizzy, and she pressed her palm against the wall, steadying herself.

What was he doing here?

"What is he doing here?" Sherri whispered, echoing the question in Remi's head. "I thought you said he wasn't coming."

Remi had confessed everything to her sisters—the true reason behind The Kiss, the fake relationship, Declan's agreement to be her beard at the engagement party.

"I didn't think he was, either." She couldn't remove her eyes from him. No matter how much her pride begged her to stop making a fool of herself in front of all these people.

She'd been here before, except this scene had taken place in a diner, not at an engagement party. But her ro-

mance woes being center stage for the townspeople of
Rose Bend again? No. Thank. You.

She straightened, pushing off the wall, and maybe he
sensed her movement, because his gaze scanned the room
before unerringly landing on her. It was like crashing into
a star—hot, consuming and so close to flaming out.

She froze.

Inside, she longed to flee. Away.

Or straight to him.

"Sweet baby Jesus, Remi, that man is in love with you,"
Briana breathed.

Remi tore her gaze from Declan and frowned at her
younger sister.

"What? What're you talking about, Bri?"

"C'mon, Remi—the man showed up at an engagement
party. No man shows up at an engagement party all alone,
voluntarily, unless, A, he's the groom or one of the parties
involved is family, B, he's being blackmailed, or C, he has
an agenda. You, big sis, are his agenda. That man is so in
love with you." She leaned forward, jabbing a fingertip in
her arm. "But I swear to God, if he proposes to you at my
engagement party, I'm tackling him to the ground like J.
J. Watt. And then I'll show up at your wedding and an-
nounce I'm pregnant. And expecting quadruplets."

Remi stared at her sister, caught between laughing hys-
terically and being horrified. Because she suspected Briana meant it.

"Remi, can you help me in the kitchen for a moment?"
Their mother appeared in front of their trio, smiling
brightly, but Remi spied the taut edges.

"Sure."

She followed her mom, pausing to smile at a few guests,

putting on a good front, but her belly twisted into knots. Strain rode her shoulders, so by the time they entered the spotless kitchen, where more food platters covered the butcher-block island, her body was rigid with the strain.

"Declan showing up is certainly a surprise," her mother said, leaning back against the edge of the island.

Jumping right into it, are we?

Remi smothered a sigh, wishing she'd stolen Sherri's champagne.

"It is."

Rochelle threw her hands up, huffing out a breath. "Remi, he's here. That means something."

"It could mean a lot of things. The main thing being not wanting to be rude by not showing up." Although, she wondered, too. As of the night she'd kicked him out of her bed, her house, he didn't have an obligation to her anymore. "Mom, don't get your hopes up." She was preaching to the choir. "He's a nice guy, and that's all there is to it. We're done."

"Honey." She shook her head. "Why can't you just put in a little effort? You had a man who actually took an interest in you, and what happened? What did you do?"

Hurt slapped at her, and her head jerked back. "What did *I do*?" she whispered. "Why do you assume it's my fault?"

"Oh stop," Rochelle snapped, slicing a hand through the air. "I'm not assigning blame. I'm just saying I wish you would try harder—"

"And do what?" A calm settled over her. Almost as if she stepped out of her body and gave herself permission to speak, to no longer hold back on every hurt, every wound that she'd paved over with excuses, disregard or laughter. "Talk less, laugh softer. Wear baggier clothes. Lose fifteen pounds. Try harder for Declan or any other man? Or try harder for you, Mom?"

"Remi?" She frowned. "Whatever are you talking about?"

"Maybe at this point you've become so used to criticizing me that you don't notice. And I don't know which is worse—doing it on purpose or being so accustomed to taking my inventory that it has become habit. The problem is, with you, I always come up short. I've never been enough."

"Remi, honey," she whispered, tears glistening in her eyes. "That's not true."

"It is. I don't doubt you love me, Mom. But you have a lousy way of showing it. And if you don't change it, I won't be coming around as much. I can't accept that toxicity in my life anymore. I won't."

She crossed the space separating them, cupped her mother's arms and kissed her cheek.

"I love you, and I love myself. I need you to accept that."

Tears pricked her own eyes and her pulse pounded like a snare drum. She turned and exited the kitchen, moisture blinding her.

"Hey, I got you."

She didn't hesitate. Didn't question. She wrapped her arms around Declan, burying her face against his hard, welcoming chest. And when his arms closed around her, she sighed, relaxed into him. Feeling home.

"Come on, sweetheart," he murmured.

She didn't really pay attention to where he led her, but then the cold air brushed over her face. The backyard. Inhaling a deep breath, she pulled her hand free of his and paced several feet away. His earthy cloves-and-cinnamon scent clung to her nose, and she longed to roll in it, bathe in it. She had to move away, because yes, in a moment of weakness, she'd leaned on him, but she couldn't depend on that. Couldn't depend on him.

"What are you doing here, Declan?"

He studied her for several long moments, his lilac gaze piercing. "You did good, Remi. And I'm damn humbled by you."

She blinked. And blinked again. Stupid tears. Not now. Not in front of him.

"What?"

"I overheard what you said to your mom. That was incredibly brave, and I want to live up to you. Be worthy of that courage." He paused. "I should've never left your house last week. I should've told you no, I wasn't leaving, that I would fight for me, for you. For us."

If she could move, she would've stumbled backward. Or run to him.

But fear, doubt—hope—kept her frozen.

"You called me out, and I was afraid. *Was*, Remi. I knew as soon as I drove away that I made the hugest mistake of my life. Over the last month you have become my friend, my confidante, my lover, my delight, my…freedom. You've helped me free myself from my past simply by being you. By showing me bravery, hope and faith. I want to take that leap with you, Remi. And I'm sorry that I hurt you, that I might've been one more person to make you doubt how beautiful, special and precious you are. If you can trust me with your heart again, I promise never to break it."

He reached into the inside pocket of his suit jacket and withdrew a folded sheet of paper and extended it to her.

As if her arm moved through water, she reached for that paper, accepted it. Her breath whistled in and out of her parted lips, and she tried to tamp down the hope that seemed determined to rise within her, but it welled too big, too huge.

She unfolded the sheet and scanned it. Once. Twice. After the third time she lifted her gaze to him. That hope she'd tried to stifle soared, and she didn't try to control it. Not when love surged with it.

"You're moving here full-time?" she rasped, the paper trembling in her hand.

"Yes." He moved closer to her, paused, but then eliminated the space between them. His hand rose, hovering next to her cheek, but he didn't touch her. "I'm leasing the building next to Cole Dennison's law firm. Of course, I'll still need to go back to Boston for some meetings, but I can run my business from anywhere. And I choose for it to be here. With you. Because I love you."

She cupped her hand over his, turned her face into it and pressed a kiss to the palm. Then rose on her toes and pressed another to his lips. On a groan, he took her mouth like a man deprived of water, of breath. And she was his oxygen.

God, she knew the feeling.

"Does this mean you're giving me your love again?" he asked, resting his forehead against hers.

She cradled his face between her palms, brushing her thumbs over his cheekbones. Smiling, she brushed a soft kiss to his mouth.

"You never lost it."

* * * * *

Get 4 FREE REWARDS!

We'll send you 2 FREE Books **plus** 2 FREE Mystery Gifts.

FREE Value Over **$20**

Both the **Romance** and **Suspense** collections feature compelling novels written by many of today's bestselling authors.

YES! Please send me 2 FREE novels from the Essential Romance or Essential Suspense Collection and my 2 FREE gifts (gifts are worth about $10 retail). After receiving them, if I don't wish to receive any more books, I can return the shipping statement marked "cancel." If I don't cancel, I will receive 4 brand-new novels every month and be billed just $7.24 each in the U.S. or $7.49 each in Canada. That's a savings of up to 28% off the cover price. It's quite a bargain! Shipping and handling is just 50¢ per book in the U.S. and $1.25 per book in Canada.* I understand that accepting the 2 free books and gifts places me under no obligation to buy anything. I can always return a shipment and cancel at any time. The free books and gifts are mine to keep no matter what I decide.

Choose one: ☐ **Essential Romance**
(194/394 MDN GQ6M)

☐ **Essential Suspense**
(191/391 MDN GQ6M)

Name (please print)

Address   Apt. #

City   State/Province   Zip/Postal Code

Email: Please check this box ☐ if you would like to receive newsletters and promotional emails from Harlequin Enterprises ULC and its affiliates. You can unsubscribe anytime.

Mail to the **Harlequin Reader Service:**
IN U.S.A.: P.O. Box 1341, Buffalo, NY 14240-8531
IN CANADA: P.O. Box 603, Fort Erie, Ontario L2A 5X3

Want to try 2 free books from another series! Call 1-800-873-8635 or visit www.ReaderService.com.

*Terms and prices subject to change without notice. Prices do not include sales taxes, which will be charged (if applicable) based on your state or country of residence. Canadian residents will be charged applicable taxes. Offer not valid in Quebec. This offer is limited to one order per household. Books received may not be as shown. Not valid for current subscribers to the Essential Romance or Essential Suspense Collection. All orders subject to approval. Credit or debit balances in a customer's account(s) may be offset by any other outstanding balance owed by or to the customer. Please allow 4 to 6 weeks for delivery. Offer available while quantities last.

Your Privacy—Your information is being collected by Harlequin Enterprises ULC, operating as Harlequin Reader Service. For a complete summary of the information we collect, how we use this information and to whom it is disclosed, please visit our privacy notice located at corporate.harlequin.com/privacy-notice. From time to time we may also exchange your personal information with reputable third parties. If you wish to opt out of this sharing of your personal information, please visit readerservice.com/consumerschoice or call 1-800-873-8635. **Notice to California Residents**—Under California law, you have specific rights to control and access your data. For more information on these rights and how to exercise them, visit corporate.harlequin.com/california-privacy.

STRS21MAXR2